NOT YOUR GIRL

KNOX COUNTY
BOOK 2

RACHAEL OGLE

For my own grandfather(in-law), Clifford, who might not be a
moonshiner, but is every bit as fiesty as Pap.
For nearly twenty years, you've loved me like your own blood
and have never failed to offer me sage advice or be my hype man.
Love you, Pa.

AUTHOR'S NOTE

Dear Reader,

Although *Not Your Girl*—like every other true romance book—has a happy ending, you will find Josie reluctant to grab hold of hers. For some reason, I like messy love and emotional scars and this story is no different. Topics discussed in the following pages include **death of a sibling** (off-page, historical), **death of a grandparent** (off-page, historical), **death of a child** (not belonging to either MC and historical), **genetic issues** and its impact on one's **fertility**.

My goal is to always be transparent when detailing my content warnings since mental and emotional health is precious and should be protected at all costs.

XOXO, Rach

CHAPTER ONE

JOSIE

My well-earned vodka cranberry is halfway to my mouth and I'm trying to focus on what my date, Troy, is saying about NFTs or something when I'm struck from behind by something very solid and large. The force of the blow causes the contents of my glass to go flying, landing solidly on Troy's shirt, causing him to yelp as the cold liquid splashes all over him. "Watch it," I toss over my shoulder, but with the noise of the bar, it'll be a wonder if whoever ran into me will be able to hear it. I turn my attention back to Troy.

"My bad," a deep, masculine voice pipes up. "Let me get you a towel." A man steps between my date and me and signals to the bartender.

"Hey, dude, we're on a date here," Troy says.

The interrupter, a white guy who looks to be in his mid-thirties with a ruddy complexion, is now standing about six inches away from me and is tall. *Really* tall. He's also currently giving me a warm smile, revealing straight white teeth. "Sorry. I'll replace your drink, too."

"I said we're on a date; I'll take care of her drink," my date objects, annoyance evident in his tone as he mops his shirt with a towel.

Something flashes in the man's eyes, but as we've not even been introduced, I have no clue what the emotion is. He ignores Troy and instead turns his body toward mine. "Is this your first date with him?" he asks, gesturing toward my date.

I frown. "I'm not sure that's any of your business. Especially seeing as how you spilled a drink I was very much looking forward to enjoying."

"Trust me; you don't want that one. Not unless you want to run the risk of not being able to remember the rest of your night. Your 'date' put something in your drink when you checked your phone a minute ago."

My mouth falls open and I stand from my stool, peeking around him to look at Troy. "Did you put something in my drink?"

"N-No, of course not," he stammers, his cheeks flaming.

The guy holds up his phone and waves it back and forth. "Pretty sure a video would say otherwise."

All the color drains from Troy's face and he stands and begins to back away from the bar. My mouth instantly goes dry with the knowledge that this stranger may have saved my life. Indignant rage floods me and I lunge at Troy just as he begins to turn, but the stranger grabs me around the waist and stops me from pummeling him and Troy is out the door in about three seconds.

"What the hell?" I kick and elbow, trying to get the stranger to release me, but he's a lot bigger and taller than I am and simply sets me back on my stool. "Why did you let him leave?"

"Because the bartender's already been notified and they're going to send the security camera footage to the cops. I'm assuming you have his name and number?"

"I guess. At least, the name on his dating profile."

He signals to the bartender again and takes the stool Troy vacated. "Can I buy you a replacement drink?"

"I'm good, thanks. Pretty sure I'm going to go."

"Are you sure? You said you were very much looking forward to your drink."

"Yeah, before I knew it was possibly drugged."

"What if I promised not to drug your drink?"

I snort a laugh. "Wow. The bar is literally on the floor these days, isn't it?"

He flashes me that great smile again. "So, is that a yes?" He extends his hand. "I'm Ford, by the way."

I glance down at the large hand he's offered and debate walking away, but he did possibly save my life, right? "Josie," I say, shaking his hand. I let my eyes travel up his forearm to muscular biceps rivaling my personal trainer brother's even under the flannel he wears. Taking my gaze farther north, my eyes sweep over defined shoulders and traps and a thick neck up to a square, chiseled jaw covered in dark red stubble.

He's undeniably handsome, with full lips and thick, dark brows over blue eyes, complete with long, lush lashes any woman would envy. His deep red hair is shot through with shades of copper and gold and is short on the sides and longer and a bit wavy on top. The only thing out of place on his face is a crooked nose, but even that looks good on him.

Ford's hand is calloused but warm, and his grip is firm enough to get your attention but not hard enough to make you think he's trying to prove a point. Releasing my hand, he nods. "Josie. Well, it's nice to meet you, Josie."

"You as well, Ford."

The bartender finally makes her way over and I reorder my drink and Ford orders a beer. When our drinks are delivered, I also give her the information about my date for the cops.

Keeping my hand on top of my glass when I'm not looking directly at it, I turn my attention back to Ford. "I didn't thank you earlier; I appreciate what you did."

He jerks his chin down at my covered glass. "Can't be too careful these days. I just happened to be at the right place at the right time. No thanks needed."

"Apparently, I wasn't careful enough," I admit. "So, Ford, what brings you in tonight? Or do you regularly troll bars looking for helpless damsels?"

Ford gives me a lopsided grin. "Something tells me you're not all that helpless. I'm guessing if I hadn't held you back, that guy would've left here short a set of balls."

I can't help but laugh. "You're probably not wrong. You still didn't answer my question."

"I didn't, did I? I'm in town for a job interview."

I give him a thoughtful frown. "And what field would that job be in?"

He considers my question for a beat before saying, "Management."

I narrow my eyes. "Vague. So, are you only in town for today?"

He lifts a brow. "Why? You wanting a second date already?"

A bark of shocked laughter falls from my mouth. "Wow, cocky much? That would require a first date."

"What do you call this?" he asks, gesturing between our bodies.

"Not a date."

"Why not?"

"Because you don't live here. And I don't sleep with tourists."

His eyes widen in amusement. "Now who's getting cocky?

And I don't live here *yet*. I'll have you know that I nailed my job interview, so your argument is invalid since I'll be moving to town. I won't be a tourist."

"How about, if you actually move to town, we can see about a date. And where will you be moving from, may I ask?"

"San Jose."

"You're a long way from home. What makes you want to move to Knoxville, Tennessee?"

"I never said San Jose was home. You just asked where I'd be moving from. Home is wherever my kid is. Currently, that's Knoxville. Thus the move." I drop my gaze to his left hand and he holds it up and shows me his empty ring finger. "Not married. My ex-wife is getting married. Her new husband's family is here. She doesn't have any family, so they moved."

I nod. "I see."

"Do you have kids?"

I sip my drink. "I have a dog."

"And what do you do, Josie?"

"Lots of things," I offer. I don't want to admit how much I'm enjoying this back-and-forth with this handsome giant of a man, but I am—a lot. Much more than I was enjoying Troy's inane blabbering about his career in finance. Ford's also not hard to look at in the least and if he were local, I definitely might consider agreeing with him about this being a date.

He narrows his eyes and parrots my earlier answer. "Vague."

"No sense in telling you my whole life story if this isn't a date."

"I thought since I was moving to town, we could call this a date," he says with a sly smile.

"That wasn't what we agreed."

He considers. "Okay. How about you go ahead and give me

your number? That way, when I do get moved to town, you can take me out."

"I can take you out, huh?" I ask, amused.

He shrugs. "I figure you know all the best places, so yeah." He pulls out his phone, taps on the screen, and extends it in my direction.

I can't say I'd be disappointed if Ford's name appeared on my screen. He's good-looking, funny, and most likely can be trusted with a drink. He's a dad, but I'd probably never meet his kid. What the hell, right?

I take his phone, type my name and number in, and pass it back to him. He smiles and taps on the screen for a moment and my phone vibrates in my back pocket and I lift a brow. "Making sure I didn't give you a fake number?"

"Can't be too careful." He checks his watch before pulling out his wallet and tossing some cash onto the bar. "Sorry, I'm going to have to cut our date short; I have a previous engagement."

"Not a date, remember?"

"I bought your drink; I have your name and number. Sounds like a date to me."

"Again, the bar is literally on the floor," I say with a laugh.

He grins and stands and I take in the rest of his form. Again, I'm struck by how tall he is. He's got to be at least six-four. He's dressed in worn jeans and a flannel over a tee shirt that does nothing to hide how solid he is. The man is built like some sort of Viking lumberjack and apparently, Vikings and lumberjacks happen to be exactly my type. Because, *damn*.

"See you later, Josie."

"We'll see, Ford," I reply coyly.

He taps on the bar and gives me a wink before turning to leave. I must say, the view from the back is just as nice as the one from the front; solid, thick calves and thighs leading up to a gloriously sculpted ass. Once he's stepped out the door, I pull my phone out and check the screen. Along with his name, Ford texted me emojis of a superhero and a cocktail and I can't help but smile.

CHAPTER TWO

FORD

Although I didn't intend to meet anyone when I stopped at the bar, I can't say I'm mad about how things played out. I'd only dropped in to celebrate how well the interview had gone with the team before heading to Piper and Conrad's to see Emerson.

I was two drinks in when I saw the brunette in the shredded black jeans, an off-the-shoulder, olive-colored sweater, and brown boots sit at the bar with the blonde douchebag.

It was her tattoo that drew my eye first. Even in the dim light of the crowded bar, I could see it was huge, probably at least a half-sleeve, starting at her right shoulder with colorful splashes of varying shades of pink that only stood to highlight her fair skin. And from my vantage point at the end of the bar behind her, I couldn't even see her face.

But after their drinks arrived, she took a sip and set it back down. She pulled her phone out and the guy nodded and she focused her attention on the screen for a moment. It was then that he put some kind of liquid into her cocktail and my stomach dropped.

All I could picture was some fucker doing that to Emerson once she starts dating and I sprang into action and notified the bartender before making sure Josie didn't consume any of the drink. I might be big, but I'm also quick. I would've done it for anyone—not only for a woman—but seeing how beautiful she was when I stepped between her and the douchebag didn't hurt.

Big brown eyes, a heart-shaped face, perfectly full lips, and freckles. Fuck, I'm a sucker for freckles. And then, when she stood to deck the would-be date rapist, I couldn't help but notice the great ass and tits. I'm only a man, after all.

I truly didn't expect to leave with her number; I thought for sure she'd bail—at least until I saw her check me out. And now, I'm one number richer and in an exceptionally good mood when I pull into Piper's driveway.

I could begrudge the fact that my ex-wife moved across the country with our kid to get married, but in all actuality, my days in San Jose were already numbered. At my age, another injury would've most likely taken me out of the game permanently anyway, so at least this way, I can say I left on my own terms.

Knocking on the door, I check my watch, glad to see I'm only a few minutes later than I told Emerson I'd be here. Conrad answers the door with his usual wide grin and ushers me into the house. "Ford, welcome. Glad you found the place okay."

My ex's fiancé is around six feet and slim with warm, medium-brown skin, short curly hair, and light brown eyes behind black plastic-framed glasses.

I shake his hand and give him a warm smile. "Good to see you, Conrad." I gesture around the living room. "Looks like you guys are mostly unpacked. It's looking good. How's the new office?"

He shrugs. "Still work. How did the interview go?"

"Yeah, how did it go, Daddy?" Emerson asks, walking around the corner into the living room. Her smile is hopeful as she comes to give me a hug.

I pull her into my chest and drop a kiss on the top of her blonde head before releasing her. "It went great. The owners seemed to really go for the ideas I had for the team." I look around. "Piper's not home?"

Emerson shakes her head. "Yoga class."

"Gotcha. Well, I should know something in the next couple of days. My agent said there's a possibility of interviewing with the Nashville team if Knoxville doesn't work out, so I'd still be relatively close, but I'm hopeful about how this went."

Conrad nods. "I'm sure Nashville would be better money, though, right? It's a lot bigger organization than Knoxville."

"Yeah, but with the travel and postseason, I might as well still be in San Jose." I squeeze Emerson's shoulder. "Money's never been why I love hockey; the closer I can be to Emmy, the better." I smile down at my daughter. "You ready to go eat?"

She nods. "Yeah. Let me grab my phone." She hustles off toward the hall.

Conrad turns his gaze on me. "So, have you started looking for a place yet?"

"I've got some feelers out. Didn't want to get too far ahead of myself, but I've got a couple of places I'm going to see tomorrow before I have to fly back to San Jose to tie up loose ends with the team there."

"You think being off the ice this season will be weird?"

"Definitely. I've been on it since I was four. But it's time." I tap my temple. "Gotta keep what brain I've got left, you know?"

He grins. "Yeah. Well, hopefully, Knoxville pans out. I know Emerson and Piper have missed having you around." He seems to remember something. "Oh, yeah. You're coming to my bachelor party, right?"

"You send me the dates and I'll make sure I get it on my calendar." Some might think it's strange to be invited to your ex-wife's future husband's bachelor party, but I guess it's safe to say our family isn't exactly conventional. Conrad's a great guy and I set Piper up with him, so I couldn't be happier that they're getting married. He's good to my kid; she loves him, and I couldn't ask for more than that.

"Ready, Daddy," Emerson trills as she returns to the living room. I examine her face as she comes closer. She looks to have put some makeup on and I'm not sure how I'm supposed to feel about that. It's not lost on me that she's fifteen, but to me, it still seems too young.

"Great. Let's go. Conrad, want to join us?"

He waves off my offer. "Thanks, but I've got some work to catch up on. Y'all have fun."

"Can I drive?" Emerson asks, her tone hopeful.

I hold out the keys. "Let's do it." She snatches them from my hand with a squeal of delight and runs out the front door.

"Y'all be careful."

It's a bit surreal to get into a car with my daughter and have her be the one behind the wheel. I remain quiet as she adjusts the mirrors and driver's seat and settles in. Knowing she'll be sixteen in only a few months, this part of things is much less nerve-racking than it was six months ago. She needs minimal correction anymore and I'm just there for moral support for the most part.

After we get onto the road, she asks, "So, do you think you'll like Knoxville?"

I shrug. "I've only been in town a day, but so far, so good. How has it been for you?"

"Good. Made a couple of friends at school. Swim team tryouts are in a few weeks, so we'll see how that goes."

"What about boys?"

She blushes. "Daddy."

"What? You're in high school. There aren't cute boys?"

"Well, yeah, but I'm a sophomore. Nobody notices me."

"Good. You should focus on your studies anyway."

She rolls her eyes and pulls out onto the highway. "I make straight A's."

"Because you're not boy crazy. Let's keep it that way, huh?" Changing the subject, I ask, "Excited about the wedding?"

"I guess. It's just a big party, right?"

"Knowing your mom, it will be."

"Are you bringing a date?"

"Not sure. Maybe I'll wait and see the pickings at the wedding. Maybe there will be a pretty bridesmaid who will dance with me."

Emerson snorts. "You do know I'm the only bridesmaid, right?"

I give her a wide grin. "Exactly. Save your old man a dance?"

"Can you still dance with all those old joints?"

Clutching my chest, I feign injury. "Ouch. That's below the belt. I'm not old."

"I think you should bring a date. You need to find a girl-friend. Especially now that you won't be traveling so much, you have time to date. If you get this job, you'll be in town a lot more, right?"

"Yeah, from my understanding."

"Okay, then you need to find a girlfriend. Or, better yet, a wife."

"Damn, kid. A wife? Why would I want one of those? I've done that before."

"Yeah, because of me. Wasn't that great?"

I nod. "Yeah, you're the best thing I've ever done, Emmy; you know that. But that doesn't mean I need a wife."

"Well, even if you move here, I won't be around forever. I'll move off to college and you'll be all alone. Mom and Conrad have each other. I want you to be happy, Daddy. And you really aren't getting any younger."

"You sound like your mother."

"Well, she's pretty smart. But for real, don't you want someone to spend your life with?"

"Maybe. I'm okay, though. Even if I never get married again, I'll be all right. I have you. I have Uncle Luke. I'm not lonely, honey."

"If you say so. But if you want me to try to set you up with one of my friends' moms, I can put in a good word."

I huff a laugh. "No. I'm capable of finding my own dates, thank you very much. For your information, I got a woman's number at a bar after my interview." Emerson's mouth drops open and she looks at me. The car starts to drift and I gesture to the road. "Eyes on the road, Emmy."

She corrects the vehicle and scoffs. "Way to bury the lede, Daddy. What's her name? What's she like? Are you going to see her again?"

I shake my head and smile. "I'm not giving you anything. I don't even know her last name, but I feel like you'd have her dissected on social media in about thirty seconds and I only got her number."

"Okay, well, what did she look like?"

"Beautiful. Huge tattoo on her shoulder and arm."

"Young?"

I shrug. "Early to mid-thirties, maybe."

"Are you going to ask her out?" Emerson asks, hopeful.

"If I get the job, I might."

"Well, now I hope even more that you get the job so you can ask her out."

———

Later, after I've dropped Emerson back at Piper's and made it to my hotel room, I take a quick shower and fall onto the bed dressed only in my boxers. I make it a point not to check my phone when I'm with Emerson since I expect the same level of courtesy from her, and I've not looked at it since I left the bar.

I originally intended to verify the information about the house I plan to see tomorrow. Instead, my eye snags on a reply from a certain tattooed brunette and I'm pleasantly surprised.

> Josie: I'm not sure if the emojis are meant to be cute and memorable or just plain dirty. There are SO many names that could be made with a superhero and cocktail emoji.

But she doesn't leave it at that. There are several other texts, all with varying degrees of perverted intent.

> Josie: Super Cocktail Man?

> Josie: Cocktail Super-Man?

> Josie: Super Cock Man?

> Josie: Or, would it be just plain "Super Cock"?

Seeing that the last text was sent about an hour ago, I wonder if Josie kept drinking and maybe decided to tipsy text the guy who saved her from possible harm. And since I don't have anything better to do, I crack open a mini bottle of whiskey from the in-room bar and shoot off a text of my own.

> Ford: Actually, Freckles, I was going for the Vodka Avenger. I've never felt the need to convey the superiority of my cock in any form. Emoji or otherwise. It usually speaks for itself.

Might the vulgarity of my text be a turn-off for her and possibly get me blocked? Definitely. Although, something tells me Josie's not a wilting flower or some kind of a prude and this won't be the thing that does it.

Downing the liquor, I drop my phone onto my chest and reach for the TV remote, flipping through channels until I come to an old episode of *Iron Chef*. Ten minutes later, though, my phone vibrates and I pick it up to examine the screen.

> Josie: Freckles, huh? Well, if we're giving nicknames based on appearance, I'd probably have to call you Erik the Red.

> Ford: Well, my mom is of Norwegian descent, so I very well could be a Viking. It wouldn't be the first time it's been implied, either. You're going to have to be a lot more original than that.

> Josie: Yeah, because "Freckles" is groundbreaking. Pot meet kettle.

> Ford: It's only day one. Give me time. I'm sure if I got to know you, I could come up with all kinds of nicknames for you.

> Josie: Day one would imply there will be numbers after that.

Ford: That's because there will be.

Josie: We'll see, Viking. Goodnight.

CHAPTER THREE

JOSIE

"Earth to Josie." Ada waves her hand in front of my face to get my attention. Unfortunately, all I've been able to think about for the past twelve hours is a certain tall, stocky redhead.

"Sorry, what were you saying?"

My sister-in-law and best friend rolls her eyes. "I was asking if Silas showed you the pictures we took the last time we went to the farm. What's with you? You've been spacey the whole time we've been here," she says as she mops up the last of her syrup with a bite of pancake.

"Yeah. He showed them to me when I was at the gym yesterday."

She tilts her head in confusion, her gray eyes narrowing. "Are you okay?" A thought occurs to her. "How did your date go last night? Did you meet up with the guy from that app or whatever?"

I nod. "It went. Down in flames in spectacular fashion."

She blinks in surprise. "What happened?"

I sigh and give her the play-by-play and her mouth falls

open in shock. "You know your brother will try to track that guy down and murder him, right?"

I dismiss her question with a wave. "The cops already took care of him. They called me this morning."

"So, the guy who stepped in, cute?"

I nod. "Too cute. Too tall. Too built. Too perfect."

Ada shakes her head and sips her coffee. "No such thing as too tall. Or built, for that matter. Besides, you like bigger guys. What's the problem?"

"He doesn't live here. And I enjoyed texting him too much. He called me Freckles."

She grins. "That's adorable."

I roll my eyes. "You know I hate cheesy nicknames. 'Freckles' is definitely cheesy and generic."

"Well, give him time. From what you said about his texts, he's smooth, right? He'll probably be able to come up with something that pushes all the right buttons," she says, wiggling her eyebrows.

"Plus, he has a kid."

"Yeah, so; you love kids."

I level her with a gaze. "I love *your* kid. Bea is the exception. If she wasn't so cute, it might be different."

Ada chuckles. "You only think she's cute because she looks just like you in the face. I swear, those Campbell genes are strong."

"At least she got your eye and hair colors. Marvel of genetics with that one. She's such a split mix of Andrews and Campbell. Maybe the next one will look like you."

"I'm too tired for another one just yet. I just got Bea potty trained. I'm not exactly looking to jump right back into diapers just yet."

"I can understand that. But have y'all talked about having any more?"

"Yeah, of course. If I were younger, Silas would probably have me talked into five more. But honestly, I think two will be plenty. If we wait another year to start trying, and if I got pregnant right off the bat, I'd still be thirty-five when the baby came. I know lots of people do it later than that, but I want to enjoy being young enough to chase them around. Most days, I already have aches and pains when I crawl out of bed."

I sip my coffee. "That could have something to do with the person you sleep with."

She laughs. "Probably. Your brother is definitely not the easiest of bed partners. It's like trying to snuggle next to an alligator that's gone into a death roll."

"You're one to talk; you're a spider monkey. I never could escape your clutches during our sleepovers."

"True." The server stops to pick up our empty plates and drop off the check and Ada snatches it before I have a chance. "So, what's on your agenda—work-wise?"

I mentally check my calendar, ticking off tasks on my fingers as I speak. "Pap has a doctor's appointment. I'm house-sitting for Hensley for a few weeks while she's in Fiji. A few other errands I need to run for other clients. I've got a catering gig later in the month."

She nods. I know she struggles not to suggest I return to a "real" job. So do Silas and our parents. Possibly the only ones who don't give me shit for my current vagabond lifestyle are Pap and Jess. But if anyone respects someone wanting to carve their own path, it's my grandfather.

"All right. And Hensley is paying you?"

I roll my eyes. "Yes. We have a contract and everything. It's through a house helper app. I make good money house-sitting, dog walking, and running errands for people. It's almost like being a personal assistant without the nine-to-five." I pat her hand. "I know you and Si worry about me. I'm fine. I'm happy.

Simply because I no longer subscribe to a 'conventional' way of life doesn't mean my life is lacking. If anything, getting out of the rat race has made me appreciate my life even more."

Ada gives me a warm smile. "I know. And I will never fault someone for making their living how they choose. I'm an artist, so I get not wanting to conform. But you're doing okay? For money?"

I sigh. "Y'all don't need to worry about me; I'm good. I still have quite a bit in savings, and Hensley has me lined up to house-sit for all her country club friends for the next year. Sometimes having friends in high places has its perks."

I can tell she wants to say more, but thankfully, she changes the subject. "You're still okay to keep Bea the weekend Silas and I go to New York over New Year's, right?"

I nod. "Of course. I've already put it on my calendar. Is Si excited?"

"Are you kidding? He's planning a whole itinerary. I think all the planning Cole did rubbed off on him."

It's always amazed me how easily she and Silas can talk about Cole. And if I didn't know them—their history—it might seem strange. But I do know the history. And seeing the way both Cole and Silas have loved Ada would make the most cynical person believe in love. Well, except maybe me.

Not that I don't believe in love itself. I've watched my parents and grandparents love each other selflessly. I've watched Ada—who grew up with parents who treated her like an afterthought and not one of the most amazing and talented people I know—experience great love not once, but twice with my brothers. I'm just not sure I believe in it for myself.

And maybe it's because I'm not a romantic anymore. Not in a long, long time. I don't enjoy gushy rom-com movies or the thought of someone buying me flowers and candy. That's not to say that I don't enjoy dating or sex because I very much enjoy sex. But I've yet to meet a man with whom I enjoy it more than a few times. The moment they begin showing interest in anything resembling a future, they stop doing it for me. It seems like Cole and Silas are the only ones in our family who inherited the "true love" gene.

I nod, letting my thoughts return to our conversation. "Well, Bea and I will be sure to binge all the *Rocky* movies and *The Godfather*."

Ada rolls her eyes. "Whatever. You know she'll have you watching some animated musical with talking animals." She starts gathering her things. "I have to go. I've got a video call with an author about a book cover design."

"Sure, I'll walk you out."

As we say our goodbyes and I slide behind the wheel of my car, I slump in my seat. I love Ada very much like the sister she is to me. I love Silas and our parents. And knowing how settled and *fine* everyone is these days, I can understand their concern for my ability to earn a living. But having to justify why I no longer feel the need to punch a clock every day is getting really old.

Starting the engine on my cherry red Mini Cooper, I crank up The Clash's "Should I Stay or Should I Go" as it spills from the speakers. I point the car toward home, drum my fingers on the wheel, and sing at the top of my lungs.

Pulling into the garage ten minutes later, I'm mildly disappointed to see that Jess isn't home. I haven't seen him in nearly a week and I miss my roommate and best guy friend. As I step out of the car, I shoot him a text.

> Josie: Just getting home. Feel like we haven't hung out in forever. Will you be around any tonight or do you have to work?

I unlock the door and as usual, nails click against the hardwood floors as Gouda, my yellow labradoodle, comes barreling toward me. I squat down to greet her and she sniffs my entire body to ensure I've not cheated on her. "I promise, there's no one else for me, pretty girl."

She immediately drops to her belly and rolls, exposing her tummy for a good rub. Indulging her, I give her a long scratch before leading her through the kitchen toward the backyard.

While I wait for her to do her business, I check my phone and see I have two texts—one from Jess and one from Ford. Unable to stop the smile from spreading, I thumb to Ford's message.

> Ford: You better be ready to take me out on the town, Freckles. As of this morning, I'm no longer a tourist. I got the job.

I roll my eyes at the nickname but am secretly glad he remembers me. I remind myself that he could be texting ten other women and nicknames are how he tells us all apart so he doesn't accidentally call anyone the wrong name. The joy dies almost immediately and I decide to leave him on "read" for a bit so I don't appear too eager and navigate back to Jess's response.

> Jess: I'm yours for the night. Want me to pick up supper? Pizza?

> Josie: Pizza is perfect. Beer?

He sends me a thumbs-up emoji and I usher Gouda back into the house once she's finished doing her business and I take a moment to clean up the evidence of said business.

"So, did that guy really drug your drink?" Jess asks, pulling a slice of sausage and bacon pizza onto his plate.

"Apparently," I reply around a mouthful of food.

"Okay, so the guy. Are you going to go out with him? You know, when he finally gets moved to town?"

I shrug, sipping my beer. "We'll see. He said he was in 'management.' Do I really want to associate with a corporate type? I left all that behind. Just thinking about what we might talk about makes me want to break out in hives. I swear, if I hear another person talk about spreadsheets or projections or PNLs, I will lose my shit."

"But you liked him, right? Did he strike you as the stuffy suit type?"

I shake my head. "Not really. He was wearing a flannel and jeans and had a three-day beard."

"And you thought he was hot?"

"My vagina sure did."

He laughs and rolls his eyes. "Yeah, that hussy knows what she likes."

"What can I say? I have discerning tastes."

"Well, if nothing else, he might be a good time. I know you like 'em big and tall. Does he really look like a viking?"

I nod. "Imagine Joe Manganiello with dark red hair, but much taller and stockier." I add as an afterthought, "And a crooked nose. But it totally works for him."

"So, just imperfect enough to make him relatable. Damn. Could give us mere mortals a complex. He could toss you around like a rag doll."

I wiggle my eyebrows and give him a slow smile. "I know."

"Okay, so why haven't you texted him back yet?"

I shrug. "He has a kid."

"Did he say something about needing a mommy for said kid?"

"No, he's divorced. His ex and her husband live here. That's why he's moving."

He nods, considering. "All right, so maybe he's like you and he's not looking for commitment. Maybe he's just one of those guys who doesn't hide the fact that he has a kid, but he's not expecting you'll ever meet them."

"Maybe. It's just that every other single dad I've gone out with *is* looking for a stepmother for their kids or someone to give them more kids. That's not me. I'm never going to be a mom."

"So just have fun. No one is saying you have to marry him on the first date. Why are you being squirrelly? Is it the management thing? You're afraid to get roped back into that lifestyle?"

"I don't know," I admit.

"Well, only one way to find out." He slides my phone closer to me on the table. "Take the man up on his offer. He's obviously interested if he's texting you updates about his employment status."

I sigh and roll my eyes. "Fine."

CHAPTER FOUR

FORD

As I exit the plane in San Jose, I power my phone back on. It dings for a solid thirty seconds as messages pour in. Knowing it will take more time than I have between the walk from the tarmac to my 4Runner in short-term parking, I shove it back in my pocket.

It's not until almost an hour later that I can finally pull it out and look at it. I ignore the texts from my agent, Fiona, since she probably only wants to get the scoop on everything about the job. I reply to a text from Emerson to let her know I landed safe and to give her my official moving date.

Seeing a voicemail from the realtor about the house I'd viewed, I listen to it, pumping my fist in the air when I learn the seller has agreed to my offer on the house I saw. Granted, I'd been looking at homes online and had been in contact with the realtor for several weeks, so doing the walkthrough was really just a formality. I'd pretty much decided it was the right house before I'd ever stepped foot in it.

I give her a quick call back to schedule the next steps and can't keep the smile off my face as I unpack my suitcase and toss my dirty clothes in the hamper. Afterward, I shower to wash off the travel before heading down to the kitchen to grab a beer from the fridge and plop onto the sofa to finish going through my messages.

> Luke: Text me when you get back in town.

> Fiona: Call me. ASAP.

Everything with Fiona is "ASAP," but in this instance, there may actually be something she needs to discuss with me since I accepted the position today. As I call her, I roll my shoulders and twist the cap off the beer bottle. Putting the phone on speaker, I toss it onto the coffee table. She answers on the second ring. "Well, Mr. Brickman, nice of you to return my call."

"Fiona," I reply with a yawn.

"I was going over the contracts for the new position. Want to tell me why this salary isn't what you and I discussed?"

"Because they can't afford it."

"Who are you to say what they can and can't afford? If they want you, they'll make it work."

I sigh. "Fiona, you know I wasn't the only one in the running for this job. I need them more than they need me. I've done my homework about their past performance and future projections. I'm not a dumbass and you know it."

"Nashville wants you; we can go there," she offers.

"Nashville is three hours from my kid. I'm not living that far away from her. And yeah, Nashville might be more prestigious, but I don't give a shit. You know—you've always known —Emerson is my number one priority. I was only going to take Nashville if Knoxville passed. And you also know I've never done this for the money. You'll still get your fifteen percent. Don't act like you don't have five other clients who want you chomping at the bit to get them the most money possible.

"I've already signed. Your argument is moot at this point. Now, congratulate me on my new head coaching position. Maybe if you're nice, I'll invite you for a cookout at the new house once it warms up."

"Tell me again why I keep you around?"

"Because you think I'm cute and I took a chance on you after you broke my heart in high school. And because I have such a sterling reputation and charming personality, I handed you all your other clients on a silver platter."

"Nice to see you're still as cocky as ever. And for the fiftieth time, I did not break your heart. I came out of the closet after we made out at a party when we were sixteen. Really, I should thank you for making me realize I truly did like girls. Because if you didn't do it for me, no guy would ever do it for me." After a beat, she asks, "So, are you going to be content in a market this small? I know you've already signed and it's a little late to ask, but I don't want you to regret it. Taking off the agent hat here."

"Yeah. You know me, I'm adaptable. I'll be fine. Emerson is happy, so I'm happy. Piper and Conrad are settled; hopefully, it's the final move I'll ever have to make. And Knoxville might be a smaller market, but the city's not that small. There's a ton to do and I'm looking forward to getting to know the town." The idea of *doing* a certain freckled brunette comes to mind when I think of things I'm most looking forward to in Knoxville as soon as I get moved.

"Okay. Well, I guess if you're happy, I'm happy. How's Luke taking the news?"

"I haven't spoken with him. He's probably going to want to kick my ass. If he murders me, say nice things at my funeral?"

Fiona huffs a laugh down the line. "Will do. Have you already listed your house?"

"Not yet. I have a meeting with the front office in the morning to handle the PR end of my retirement, but I've got some numbers for realtors already."

"Well, Val and I were talking and you know she's always loved your house. When she found out you were probably moving, she immediately started in on me about it. Before your realtor lists it, have them give me a call?"

I nod, pleased. "You've got it. It's awfully big for just the two of you, though, isn't it?"

She's quiet for a minute and then clears her throat. "Hopefully, it won't be just the two of us much longer. We've decided to become foster parents."

"Fee, that's awesome. Well then, you will need the space. Congrats."

"Thanks. We're excited. All right, I'll let you go; I know you're probably beat after the quick trip and back. We'll talk more before you're officially in Knoxville."

"Sounds good." Downing the rest of my beer, I shoot off a reply to Luke.

> Ford: I'm back. Wanna come hang? I'll order pizza.

His response comes through five minutes later.

> Luke: Be there in twenty.

Sure enough, twenty minutes later, Luke pulls his Tesla into the driveway and jogs up the sidewalk. He enters without knocking and when he finds me in the kitchen, he takes the beer I'm about to open out of my hand and leans against the counter. I roll my eyes and get another one from the fridge.

"So, you're just going to skip town and not even tell me, your best friend? That's some bullshit, man."

I twist the cap off my bottle and examine Luke's dark brown face. Under the anger and indignation that he's been left out, there's hurt and something twists uncomfortably in my chest. His golden-brown eyes search mine and I shrug. "Sorry. I didn't want to say anything until everything was said and done. I knew you'd get pissed and I didn't want to have this fight until there was a reason to."

His jaw clenches and he downs half his beer in one long gulp before setting it on the counter. "You know, it would've been one thing if you'd even given me a heads up. But I had to learn from my goddaughter? What the fuck, Ford? Thirty years of friendship and you can't even give me a fucking courtesy text to say you're moving? I know I've been a little preoccupied lately, but I'm not that out of it."

I sigh. "I know, but yeah, you have been preoccupied. Your wife is having triplets. It's a lot. I didn't want to add to your stress. And your goddaughter is just excited I'll be in the same city as her again."

He drags his hand down his face. "I know. And I know that's important to you, but Knoxville? Really? What, Mayberry wasn't hiring?"

I shake my head and laugh. "You say it's like it's this hick town. It's not. Is it San Jose? No. But it's also not some no-stop-light village in the middle of bumfuck nowhere. And I've already had this fight with Fiona today; I don't have the energy to have it with you, too. It's done. I've already put in an offer on a house and everything."

"And you really think you'll be okay with not being at the net anymore?"

I shrug. "Physically, yeah. Mentally? Only time will tell. You could always come with me, you know. They told me I could pretty much write my own ticket in terms of staff."

He snorts a laugh. "Layla would have my balls if I took her

away from her mother this close to the babies coming. Besides, I'm not quite ready to hang up my skates just yet. I think I have a few good seasons still left in me."

"Yeah, you probably do. You haven't taken as many pucks to the face as I have."

He laughs. "True." He starts to say something else, but the doorbell rings, and I hustle to grab the pizzas. After we sit on the couch with a rerun of *Psych* playing, he asks, "So, since you're finally going to have free time, are you going to find some pretty thing to settle down with?"

"Emmy put you up to talking about relationships with me?"

He shrugs. "She might've mentioned she's worried about you being lonely." I open my mouth and he points the lip of his bottle at me. "And I don't count, especially not if we're not even going to be in the same state anymore. It's not like you're still hung up on Piper. You set her up with Conrad, for fuck's sake. What's your deal?"

I chew my bite and swallow, giving myself a minute to stall. "Since the divorce, the only women interested in me have been puck bunnies. They don't want me; they want the notoriety of being with a star player."

"Well, you're not going to be a star player anymore. Do people in Knoxville even know anything about hockey?"

"I'm sure they do."

"But it won't be like it is here or how it was in college. Tennessee's not exactly a hotbed of hockey action. I'm sure Nashville gets a lot of attention, but Knoxville? Nah. I bet you'll be pretty anonymous there."

"That would be something. But I tried marriage. I don't think I'm up for it again."

Luke heaves an exasperated sigh. "You were nineteen. You and Piper were babies who had a baby. You two should've just stayed friends and co-parented Emerson. I know you all tried to do the right thing and be a family, but admit it, you and Piper have always been better friends than 'more.' You're both happier with how things are now, right? I mean, she's marrying Conrad."

"I'm stoked for her. Conrad's great, and I'm glad being married to me didn't put Piper off wanting to do it again. Emerson's happy. At this point in my life, I feel like that's all I can hope for."

"Ford, you're not sixty; you're thirty-five. You have plenty of time to find some great woman who won't give a fuck that you had the most saves in the division three seasons in a row."

He runs his hand over his smooth scalp. "Am I happy you're moving twenty-five hundred miles away? Fuck no. You and I have been in the same city since we were four years old. You're my brother, man. But I get why you're going. I'm sure part of me always knew that when Piper and Conrad got serious, she could move and you'd follow to be with Emmy. I'd do the same for my babies and they're not even here yet.

"Just promise me you won't start saying 'y'all' and dipping Skoal. You might be moving to the country, but I swear, if I come to visit and you're drinking bootleg moonshine, I'll lose my shit."

"I'll do my best," I say with a grin. I nudge him with my elbow after a minute. "I'm going to miss you, too, man." And, God, how I'll miss him.

While Luke was visiting, my phone buzzed and I saw Josie's name pop up on the screen, but I didn't want to read her text while he was here. Lying in bed later, I finally give myself permission to open it.

> Josie: Congrats on the job, Viking. Holler
> when you get moved.

After my conversation with Luke about puck bunnies and my wanting to finally be anonymous, I can't help but wonder if Josie is a hockey fan. I didn't see any hint of recognition in her gaze as she looked at me, but maybe she hid it? Who knows? I'm definitely interested in seeing her again, but the thought of waiting until I'm in town again to talk to her doesn't sit right. And although she might not respond or want to talk until I get into town, I still send her a reply.

> Ford: So, I'm not allowed to reach out until
> I'm officially moved?

Knowing it's nearly midnight in Knoxville, I don't expect her to reply, but I'm pleasantly surprised when the dots start bouncing a moment later.

> Josie: Nope. I don't do long-distance
> relationships.

> Ford: So many rules, Freckles. You don't
> sleep with tourists. You don't do long-
> distance. What do you do?

> Josie: I guess you'll just have to wait and see
> until we're in the same state again. And do
> you give nicknames to all the women you
> pick up so you won't have to remember real
> names?

> Ford: No, Josie. I don't normally give anyone
> nicknames—only the ones I save from
> douchebags.

Josie: So, you do remember my name. Nice. Save a lot of women from bad dates, do you?

> Ford: Not typically. Right place at the right time sometimes. As a girl dad, I've become much more suspicious of my own species. See something, say something, you know?

Josie: I appreciate it. It saved my brother the hassle of having to murder the asshole. You know, if I had survived the date.

> Ford: Glad I was there to step in. Now, this brother of yours. Older? Younger? Someone I need to impress to be in your good graces?

Josie: [eye roll emoji] What is this, 1957? I don't need anyone's permission or approval, thanks. It's me you have to impress.

Josie: In fact, impress me right now. One-word answers only to the following questions. Be aware that your answers will be HEAVILY judged.

I can't help but smile. I like this easy exchange with Josie. Granted, I've known her for about five minutes, but she hasn't asked me any questions about hockey, so my guess is she doesn't know who I am.

> Ford: Am I allowed to ask for clarification? Am I allowed to ask questions of my own?

Josie: No and no. You're trying to impress me, remember? First question: Favorite food?

> Ford: Pickles

Josie: Cake or pie?

Ford: Pie

Josie: Beach or mountains?

Ford: Mountains

Josie: Book or Movie?

Ford: Book, duh.

Josie: One word, remember? Text or talk?

Ford: In person. Preferably over drinks with a beautiful woman.

Josie: You think being smooth will earn you brownie points?

Ford: You tell me.

Josie: I think you'll have to find out when you get to town.

Ford: Does that mean you'll take me out when I get to town?

Josie: Provided I'm not already occupied.

The thought of Josie going out with someone else sends a spike of jealousy through me. I've always been a possessive man. Guess I still am. Even for things—people—who aren't mine. Not yet, anyway.

Ford: Don't be occupied, Josie.

Josie: Don't tell me what to do, Ford.

Ford: Why? You afraid you might like it?

CHAPTER FIVE

JOSIE

Ford: Why? You afraid you might like it?

My pulse tics up reading Ford's last text. I don't respond and leave him on "read." Yes, I think I'd very much like Ford to tell me what to do. Probably too much. Enough to overlook the fact that he's probably a corporate goon? Debatable. Enough to ignore the fact that he has a kid? Maybe.

Granted, I love my niece. She's the light of my life. The idea of anyone else's toddler putting their sticky, grimy hands all over my face gives me all the ick. Finding out about the HCM gene I carry and watching it kill my brother was enough to push me squarely into the "child-free by choice" camp. I now have the tied tubes to prove it. And nine days out of ten, I'm good with my decision. Some days, though, I wonder.

I'm content being someone's aunt. Aunts get to have all the fun without any of the responsibility. The idea of being anyone's mother — biological or step — isn't something I'm sure I'm comfortable with. Not anymore. Do I understand that might relegate me to a life of perpetual singleness? Yep. Is that something I can live with? Also yep.

Although knowing I'll probably get bored with Ford way before the point I meet his ankle biter, I can have fun with him, right? We'll see. Does that mean I won't have fun until he gets to town? Hell no. A girl has needs, after all.

Other than some sporadic back-and-forth texting between Ford and me, I've not spoken with the viking who's occupied my thoughts more than I'd like to admit over the past few weeks. And try as I might, I haven't been able to find anyone else to help me take him off my mind.

I know from our brief-ish communications that he's officially moved as of this week and is settling into his new house. And despite the thrill that shot through me knowing this, I decided to play coy when he'd texted me this morning.

> Ford: I believe you owe me a date, Freckles.
> Take me out tonight.

> Josie: Sorry, I have plans.

My "plans" consist of playing third wheel to Silas and Ada for our weekly night out while Mom and Dad are on Bea duty. Ford doesn't need to know how mundane they are, right?

> Ford: I know you do. With me.

Something about the way Ford is a bit bossy scratches some itch in me. As a woman who's decided to live a mostly flippant existence as of late, part of me still craves some structure, some control. Or, more accurately, control from someone else.

Leaving the nine-to-five corporate life meant no one was in control of me anymore. Maybe I'm missing some of that control?

> Josie: If I have plans with you, what do they consist of? Because they're going to have to be good to get me to change the ones I already have.

> Ford: It's a Thursday; what kind of big plans can you have on a Thursday? You know, besides what you're going to do with me.

> Josie: Well, I can't say since you won't tell me what you THINK I'll be doing with you. Make me an offer I can't refuse.

> Ford: Your plans consist of having drinks with me while you answer all of my rapid-fire questions about you. On our last date, you wouldn't tell me your life story. I expect to hear it tonight.

> Josie: Need I remind you that wasn't a date? But sure, I'll have drinks with you. I'll send you the place. See you at 8.

> Ford: Make it 7, Freckles.

I should find his bossiness annoying, but I don't. His next text has me smiling, though.

> Ford: Unless you really can't do that early. I'd rather see you at 8 than not at all. But if I can spend more time with you, I'll take it.

> Josie: 7 it is. See you then, Viking.

Sending him the address for the bar, I call Silas to fill him in on my change of plans. "Hey, Jos. What's up? We're still on for tonight, right?"

"Yeah, of course. I kinda also have a date, though."

I can hear the smile in his voice. "A date? Who's the guy? Need me to be in big brother mode?"

I snort a laugh. "Not necessary. Pretty sure he could take you. It's that guy from a few weeks back who kept me from getting drugged on that other date."

"Nice. So what, are we turning this into a double date?"

"No, I'm still meeting y'all at six as planned. He's coming at seven. I'll meet him at the bar. Y'all don't need me to be the third wheel all night and I'm weirdly excited about meeting up with Ford."

"What do you know about this guy?" Silas asks, protective big brother hat securely in place.

"He's built like a viking and his texting game is strong. He's in management somewhere—I didn't ask—and he's new to town. He has a daughter. I also didn't ask about her and don't plan to. He's hot; I'm horny. What more do you need to know?"

"Shit, Josie, I just ate. I don't want to hear about your need to get laid."

I roll my eyes. "Listen, just because you and Cole decided to be these virtuous, chaste princes doesn't mean I have to do the same thing. While you all were pining over Ada, I've lived my life. I'm so happy you've got your happily ever after, but I'm allowed to have fun. If that includes a lot of really hot guys, so be it."

"It's your life, sis. I swear, one of these days, you're going to eat your words. That person is out there and he'll be the one to make you want your own happily ever after. Don't knock it till you try it."

"Well, I'll tell you this. It sure as hell won't be some titan of industry, corporate type who wears suits and ties all day long and has a bunch of minions to do his bidding. I don't care how hot he is. Ford might be a lot of fun, but I want nothing to do with a suit."

"If you say so. Like I said, I hope some guy knocks you on your ass someday—figuratively. Maybe it'll be this Ford guy."

Silas, Ada, and I are enjoying our drinks at our favorite bar as I watch the door for Ford. "You know, your sister is awfully antsy for someone who says they're indifferent about this guy."

My brother grins at his wife. "It does seem so, doesn't it, Wednesday?" He presses a kiss to her temple and a pang of jealousy for what they have shoots through me, but I push it down.

"You can both shove it. Like I said, he's hot and I'm horny. That's the only reason I'm antsy."

Silas chokes on his beer and I laugh. Movement at the door catches my eye and I watch as Ford enters, a ball cap pulled down low on his forehead. The only reason I know it's him is because he's wearing the same flannel as the day we met. Jesus, I forgot just how big he is. Big and gorgeous and walking toward the bar, waiting for me.

Ada nudges me. "Is that him?" I nod without taking my eyes off Ford. "Good lord, you weren't kidding. He's a giant."

Silas huffs a laugh. "I could take him."

"Ass, my love, you think you could take anyone. I'm pretty sure that guy's got about five inches and fifty pounds on you. I'm guessing your sister could take him, though. The way she's practically drooling tells me she plans on doing exactly that."

I down the rest of my vodka cranberry and swipe on some fresh lip gloss. "Here goes nothing."

Silas grabs my arm and I give him my full attention. "We'll

stay for a little while; make sure you're okay. Send up a flare if you need me."

"I'll be fine, Si. Y'all enjoy the rest of your date. And instead of worrying about my personal life, why don't you take your wife home and spend some alone time with her?" I ask and wiggle my eyebrows and Ada blushes. "I'm good." I slide out of the booth and blow out a breath as I make my way over to the bar.

As he's positioned at the end of the bar against a far wall, he sees me approaching without difficulty. He stands as I get closer and I'm thankful the wedged ankle boots I'm wearing give me a couple of extra inches because otherwise, I'd have to tilt my head back even farther to meet his eyes.

Ford gives me a warm smile and pulls my stool out for me. "Have you been here a while? Did you come from the other side of the bar?"

I nod and turn to gesture to where Ada and Silas are seated. "My brother and sister-in-law. We come out once a week. I told you I already had plans."

Silas jerks his chin down in acknowledgment, but keeps his expression neutral, while Ada gives us a big smile as Ford offers up a small wave. "So, do I need to be worried about your brother coming to give me one of those speeches?"

I chuckle and shake my head as I turn back to him. "No. I think he's just mad because you're a lot bigger than he is."

Ford laughs. "Well, I'm a lot bigger than a lot of people. Your brother's not small, though."

"No. Silas is a personal trainer, so he's plenty strong, but I think he always wishes he were bigger."

"Personal trainer? He any good?"

"Why, you in the market for a new trainer?"

"Well, I did just move to town, so maybe."

"You wouldn't be trying to earn brownie points with me by sucking up to my brother, would you?"

He shakes his head. "No. I'll earn your affection on my own merits, thanks."

The bartender stops by after Ford signals to him and we each order. I stick with my vodka cranberry and he gets a beer. After our drinks arrive, I gesture to his hat. "Trying to be incognito or something? I might not recognize you if you weren't wearing the same flannel as the day we met."

He grins. "Something like that. And I'm glad to see I made an impression."

"Hard not to notice you."

"You, too, Freckles." He tilts his chin down, motioning to my tattoo. "Can I ask what it represents, or is it only because you liked it? That's what first caught my eye the day we met."

I glance down at my right shoulder, currently bare due to the off-the-shoulder sweater I'm wearing. It's a different color than the one I was wearing that day, but I may or may not have this exact sweater in several different colors. I nod. "Yeah, you can ask. My brother had this same tattoo on his chest. His had white flowers instead of pink and he had the Latin name below it, but it's a tribute of sorts."

He examines the dogwood tree spanning my entire shoulder and upper arm and looks over at Silas before returning his gaze to me. "Not that brother," I explain. "We had another brother who passed away about five years ago, Silas's twin."

Concern flickers in his gaze. "I'm sorry to hear that."

I sip my drink and nod. "Thanks. Ada, my sister-in-law, drew Cole's original one and this one."

"Is she a tattoo artist?"

I shake my head. "No, but she's an artist. She mainly does this amazing fan art for different fantasy book series and she's recently begun branching out to book covers. She only does tattoo designs for family. Silas has a heron on the inside of his left bicep."

He frowns in consideration. "A heron? What's the significance of that?"

I'm not sure whether to be impressed or annoyed by the fact that he's asking about my family and not grilling me. I choose to be impressed. "How much time you got? It's a kinda long, complicated story."

He shrugs. "I'm pretty sure I can keep up. And I've got all night, Freckles."

I roll my eyes. "Okay, *Viking*. I'll tell you. So, to tell you how the tattoo came to be, I have to go back farther."

"Sure. All the best stories start with 'once upon a time,' right?"

I huff a laugh. "Right. And I guess this one is no different." I sip my drink and settle in. "Ada and I have been friends since we were ten. She's got these amazing gray eyes and I've always been fascinated with them. She also didn't come from the best home, but you don't know things like that when you're little. All I knew was that she was this sweet girl with pretty eyes.

"I invited her over for a sleepover for my birthday and from that day on, she was pretty much family. My parents always made sure she had plenty to eat and clean clothes when she was at our house and she spent most weekends and summers with us because her dad was a piece of shit and didn't care what she did. Most of the time, he never knew where she was and didn't even bother to check on her.

"Anyway, my brothers, Cole and Silas, tortured Ada relentlessly. Pulled her hair, teased her, the works. She and Silas have always butted heads and were able to give as good as they got. Her relationship with Cole was always more peaceful and sweet.

"Well, in our first year of high school, Ada returned from

visiting her mom in Texas for the summer, and Cole and Silas noticed how beautiful she was. Cole called dibs."

Ford holds up his hand, pausing my story. "Wait, Cole? Not Silas?"

I nod. "Just wait; I'm getting there. So, as I was saying, Cole called dibs and they started dating. They were together for fifteen years—all through high school and college and up until Cole died."

He blinks and opens his mouth, but I continue. "Cole had something called hypertrophic cardiomyopathy. It's a heart condition that caused the muscles of his heart to thicken and made it have to work harder. When he was thirty-one, it gave out. We knew he had it—well, everyone except Ada. He made us promise not to tell her. But knowing he had it and could pass it on to kids, he never wanted to have kids or get married in case he ended up needing a transplant. He didn't want Ada to be saddled with a ton of medical debt.

"But the whole time Cole and Ada were together, Silas was in love with her. Cole knew. I knew. Our grandfather knew. Ada didn't know, of course. It wasn't weird or anything—well, maybe it was—but it's just how it was. They didn't talk about her or anything while they were together, and honestly, Ada barely tolerated Silas because he was always an asshole to her."

"Why, because of the jealousy?"

"That was probably part of it. Plus, he felt like she was Cole's, so he didn't have a right to feel anything about her, so why try, right? Then, a month after Cole died, a package gets delivered to Silas. It has all these letters and tasks he wants Silas to help Ada complete. It was sort of like a bucket list, but not. It was random, everyday stuff."

"Like what?"

I think back and count off on my fingers. "Goat yoga, crashing a wedding, UFC fight in Vegas—and that's where they

got the tattoos— going to a rage room. Different stuff. But everywhere they went, they were supposed to scatter some of his
ashes. Cole planned everything as a way to bring Ada closure
and, ultimately, help her and Silas fall in love."

His brow furrows. "So, let me get this straight. Both of your
brothers fell in love with the same girl. Cole called dibs and
Silas, what, backed off?" When I nod, he continues. "And then,
before Cole died, he put together all these tasks for them to
complete in the hopes that his girl would fall in love with his
twin brother?"

"I mean, that's a really simplified version of events, but
yeah."

"Okay, so where does the tattoo fit in? You said Vegas?"

I nod. "Well, when they went to do the goat yoga, they
stayed at this cabin on a river. It belongs to a friend of our
grandfather's and Silas often went there. He likes the quiet and
it's kind of like his happy place. He took Ada there and they
took a boat out on the river and he showed her the nesting
grounds for some herons."

I can't help but smile. "Silas says that it was the first trip
they went on when they completed those tasks that she started
acting like herself again. She started drawing again on that trip.
It was a few months after Cole died.

"So, the following month, they went to Vegas and Ada
talked Silas into getting a tattoo. If you know Silas, it's this huge
thing because he's terrified of needles. And not only did she
convince him to get a tattoo, but she also convinced him to get a
blind tattoo."

"A blind tattoo?"

"They picked out tattoos for each other and neither knew
what they would get until it was finished."

"So, she has one, too?"

I nod. "Yeah. But she'd sketched a picture of a heron since

they'd gone to see the herons on the river and that's what his tattoo is."

"And what about her tattoo?"

My smile widens. "It's a silhouette of Wednesday Addams." He frowns in confusion and I explain. "When Ada first came over to our house, my mom put her hair in these braided pigtails. And because her hair is almost black and she's so fair, she really did look like Wednesday Addams. So, Silas has called her Wednesday since we were kids. So, her tattoo is his nickname for her."

CHAPTER SIX

FORD

"So, it's not weird for your family?" I can't help but ask as I listen to Josie tell this outlandish story about her brothers and sister-in-law.

Josie shrugs. "I'm sure to people who never knew Cole or saw him and Ada together versus how she is with Silas, it is. And I know Silas felt guilty for several months about the whole thing, regardless of Cole giving his blessing to everything. But he felt like he didn't deserve to be happy since Cole was gone."

"But he is now?"

She smiles. "Yeah. And Ada is, too. They're sickeningly perfect and have the cutest little girl on the planet who looks so much like both of them that it's unreal. I mean, they still give each other massive amounts of shit, but I think it's their love language at this point."

I nod as I chuckle and take a pull of my beer. "I like that. And what's yours?"

Shaking her head, she sips her drink. "Nope. That's not a first-date question. That's a trap."

"A trap?" I ask with a surprised laugh and signal to the bartender for another drink.

She nods. "Well, duh. If I tell you my love language, you'll use it against me and I'll think you're this insightful and sensitive guy when really, it's only my own brain manipulating me into thinking you're perfect."

"Touché. But for the record, I would never use anything you tell me against you. I mean, I shared with you that my favorite food is pickles. That's not something I tell just anyone, you know."

Her brows lift in amusement. "Well, don't I feel special? Why are pickles your favorite food? It's such a weird favorite. I expected you to say pizza or burgers or something normal."

I shrug. "What can I say; dill pickles are kinda like the perfect food." I count off the reasons on my fingers. "For starters, they taste like pickles. The juice is actually better to replace electrolytes than Gatorade. And you can't beat that satisfying crunch. What's your favorite food?"

"Avocado toast."

I nod, considering. "Spoken like a true millennial."

"Hey, at least my favorite food is versatile. It can be breakfast, lunch, or dinner. It can be dressed up or down. What are pickles except pickles?" She scrunches up her nose.

"Don't tell me you're a pickle hater."

"Can't stand 'em."

"Well, that's good. You can give me all your pickles. You know, they always say, in each relationship, there's one person who hates pickles and one who loves them. We're off to a great start, wouldn't you say?"

She snorts a laugh. "That would imply this is a relationship."

"Isn't it?"

"Um, I think this is our first date," she says with narrowed eyes.

I shake my head. "It's our second date. And we've been texting since we met. That sounds like a relationship to me."

"Not if we've also been texting other people during that time."

"Have you?" I ask.

"If I had, would that make you jealous, Ford?"

"More than I'd like to admit." The corners of her lips twitch as she tries to conceal her smile. "Have you, Freckles?"

"Yeah."

I clench my jaw. Despite only knowing what I currently do about her, I don't like the thought of her telling the same stuff to other men that she has me. "Well, you can go ahead and ditch those other numbers."

"And why would I want to do that?" Her full lips purse in smug amusement and I suddenly want to see how those lips taste.

"Because you're going to be too busy with me."

She laughs. "Wow, does that macho possessiveness actually work?"

"On the right woman, it does."

Her nostrils flare and she lifts her drink to her lips. "And you assume I'm the *right* woman, Viking? You don't know anything about me."

I let my eyes trail down her face to her chest, where the barest hint of cleavage peeks out of her sweater, down to her thick thighs encased in skinny jeans, and on down to the wedged ankle boots she wears and back up to her warm, brown eyes.

"I know, whatever job you do, it's on your own terms. You don't seem like the type who likes to take orders." I smirk. "Outside the bedroom, anyway." A pleasant blush creeps into her cheeks and I let my smile widen. I take her hand in mine and turn it over, uncurl her fist, and drag my fingertips along her palm and down her fingers. "You have elegant hands, but they're calloused. You're not afraid to get them dirty or work hard." I flip them over to reveal her short, uniform, unpolished nails. "You also aren't overly obsessed with your looks."

I run my hand up her wrist and stop at the bottom of the sleeve of her sweater. "This is the same sweater you wore the day we met, just in a different color. You find something you like and stick with it." Her mouth falls open and I know I'm correct in my observation. I continue trailing my hand up her arm to her tattoo. "You were close with your brother; if you have any other tattoos, they also have significance."

Tapping the back of her phone where it lies on the bar, I add, "You also respect the company you're with. Your phone has buzzed no less than four times while you've been sitting here with me and you haven't even glanced at it, so I must at least be better at keeping your interest than the guy who spiked your drink the other day. But judging by how shallow you've kept our texts over the past few weeks, you're not interested in anything long-term.

"You haven't asked about my job or my kid or anything a woman who's looking for 'forever' does." She opens her mouth to protest and I press on. "That's not negative or positive; it just *is*. I'm simply telling you what I've observed, so don't read anything into it." She closes her mouth again, but the blush returns.

"You also find me as incredibly attractive as I do you. And even if you're only interested in a 'for now' kind of thing, I'm okay with that." I drop my hand from the bar to her knee and wrap my fingers around the outside of her thigh, keeping my eyes on hers. "But I don't share."

Again her nostrils flare, and if I'm not mistaken, her chest seems to be rising and falling more swiftly than it was a moment ago and I want to smile, but I don't. Instead, I rub my thumb back and forth over her thigh. "You still think I don't know you, Josie?"

I sip my beer and she leans in and pushes up the brim of my hat and even though I don't react, I'm sincerely hoping she doesn't take it off. I'm under no illusions I'm a known entity here or anything—this is SEC football country, after all—but the announcement was made today on the local news stations, along with the press conference I did. So, I still might get recognized and I'd rather focus my attention on Josie than have to field questions or sign autographs.

It turns out, she only raises it enough to see my eyes better. "That was pretty good, actually. And I'll be honest; what you do doesn't matter to me. Also, if I'm honest, I've never had anyone keep my interest long enough for me to ever get to the 'meeting the kids' stage, so I don't need to know about her either."

"Is that a challenge?"

She laughs. "No. Just stating a fact. And I'm not looking for forever, just so you know. Pretty sure that's not in the cards for me."

"Still not a challenge?"

Her expression grows more serious. "No." She downs the remainder of her drink. "But you're right. I do find you as incredibly attractive as you find me." She leans in and plants her hands on my knees. "And my roommate isn't home, so if you're interested in 'not sharing' tonight, you can follow me home. Provided you can prove you're not a thief, rapist, or serial killer."

I snap my fingers and give her a pained smile. "Damn, I was so close. Two out of three's not bad, right?" She snorts a shocked laugh and I pull out my wallet, complete with my new Tennessee driver's license. "Send this to your brother or sister-in-law or your roommate. Whoever. That way, they'll know who went home with you." I know full well that whomever she sends it to may recognize my name or they may even look me up online, but I'd rather chance getting this extra time with her than not, so it's a gamble I'm willing to take.

She nods, picks up her phone, snaps a photo of my ID, and taps furiously on the screen for a solid thirty seconds before tucking it into her purse. "All right."

Fishing some cash out of my wallet and tossing it onto the bar before shoving it back into my pocket, I nod. "All right," I echo. She stands and I do, too, and we make our way out of the bar.

Josie gestures to a red Mini Cooper as we near the parked cars. "This is me."

"Nice."

"The gas mileage definitely is." She pushes up on her toes and presses a kiss to my cheek, a whiff of cranberries and vanilla hitting my nose. "See you soon." She drops back to her heels and begins to turn away. I grab her hand and she stops and looks up at me, expectant.

I tug her back to me and run the back of the fingers of my free hand along her jaw before sliding it to the back of her neck to hold her in place. She doesn't pull away and I let my eyes wander over her face so there's no question of my intention. "That was not a proper goodbye kiss, Freckles." I bend until my lips meet hers and that cranberry and vanilla scent is even stronger than before.

Dropping her hand to wrap my arm around her waist and pull her closer, she comes willingly and seems to almost melt into me, her hands coming up to grip my hips. Tilting her head back farther so I can deepen the kiss, her lips part in welcome, the taste of tart cranberries greeting me when I sweep my tongue against hers.

And for several seconds, I simply enjoy the feel of her pressed against me; the taste and smell of her making for a full sensory experience. When she lets out a soft moan, the sound goes straight to my cock and I'm forced to pull away, lest I try to figure out a way to fuck her in my 4Runner and end up getting fired for having sex in public. The payoff would be getting Josie naked in about five seconds, but it would probably make for the shortest head coaching career in the history of hockey. Also, I'm not built for car sex and I'll be damned if the first time I get this woman under me, I'm worried about getting a cramp.

Josie's chest heaves. "That's because it wasn't a goodbye kiss. And neither was that. Shit."

I huff a laugh. "Good to know."

"My house is ten minutes away."

"Thank fuck."

She laughs and unlocks her car and slides behind the wheel. "See you there." I'm quick to follow suit, climb into my SUV, and make sure not to lose her on the drive to her house.

Two miles from the bar, she turns onto a quiet street full of homes beginning to decorate for the holidays. I guess it doesn't matter where you go; some people can't wait to get into the Christmas spirit, even before Thanksgiving. Another mile or so later, Josie switches on her blinker, turning into a driveway of a small colonial-style home as a garage door opens.

I pull in behind her, and after parking and shutting off my engine, I climb down. She motions for me to follow her through the garage and I step into the large space just before she hits a button on the wall to lower the door.

Following her lead, I trail her into the house and after we leave our shoes by the door, she stops once we get to the kitchen. "Gouda," she calls.

"Gouda?" I ask, curious.

"My dog."

"Oh, right. Do I need to worry about being viewed as an intruder?"

Josie laughs. "No. She may lick you to death, but she's good."

I hear the nails clicking on the floor before I see a large yellow, curly ball of fur coming straight for us. She turns in a circle quickly in front of her mistress, who squats to give her affectionate pats and a belly rub. It takes her a moment to notice me, but when she does, she sniffs my offered hand and barks, tail wagging excitedly.

Bending to offer my own scratches, Gouda rolls onto her back, exposing her belly. "She's beautiful. How old is she?"

"Three. Some asshole bought her from a breeder, kept her locked in a kennel twenty hours a day, and then was surprised when she became aggressive and destructive. He took her to be put down. I've fostered animals before, so the vet called me to see if I'd foster her and train her until a permanent home could be found for her. I failed at fostering, obviously," she says with a smile.

"You train dogs?"

"Not really, but I think a lot of dogs are like people. You find out what motivates them and figure out how they best communicate and they're pretty easy to get along with. She's smart as a tack and knows a lot of basic tricks. She was house-broken in a week and is great with kids. She has a lot of issues with kennels, for obvious reasons, so that's the only time she's anything less than a joy." Josie stands and walks to a sliding glass door and lets the dog outside.

"She'll need a few minutes. Do you want a drink? Water, whiskey, beer?"

"Water's fine, thanks." I lean against a counter and look

around a kitchen that appears to have been renovated in the last few years. "This is a great kitchen."

She nods. "Jess is a bit of a foodie, so he sprang for the higher-end appliances when he remodeled."

"Your roommate is a man?" I try to keep my tone even, but my mind immediately goes to a roommates-with-benefits situation.

"Yeah," she says, her expression and tone telling me she knows exactly what I was thinking. "Is that a problem? Like I told you, he's not home tonight."

"No. But would it be an issue for you if he were?"

Again, that amused smile pulls at the corners of her mouth and she hands me a bottle of water she retrieves from the fridge. After a beat, she shakes her head. "No. Jess and I aren't *those* kinds of roommates." I nod, taking a drink of my water. "We've slept together, but it was in high school. We're just friends now. Like I told you, no one keeps my interest," she replies honestly.

"Does he still have feelings for you?"

She snorts a laugh. "No. We dated for a few months and decided to lose our virginities. Things fizzled pretty quickly after that. He had a new girlfriend a week later and it didn't bother me. A couple of years ago, he was looking for a room-mate and posted something on social media. I messaged him and the rest is history. He's a great guy. He has a serious girl-friend who travels a lot for work. She's here when she's in town, even though she technically has her own place. I'm not sure why they don't just make things official, but who am I to give anyone relationship advice?"

I am relieved I probably won't have any jealous run-ins with the roommate. *You're getting ahead of yourself, Ford. You might only get this one night.* I find myself vowing to make sure that's not the case.

Gouda barks at the door, and Josie lets her into the house.

She flips a lock on the door before walking over to me. "We're good now." Taking a step back, her eyes drag down my body. "How tall *are* you?"

I huff a laugh. "Six-six, two-seventy." I take a step forward and she slowly backs toward a hallway. "I do my bench press burnouts at two-ninety. I squat four hundred. I deadlift five hundred. I max out my hip thrusts at seven-fifty. I can run an eight-minute mile and work out six days a week." She stops at a bedroom door. "Any other stats you need to know?"

Shaking her head, she bites her lip coyly. "So, I take it your stamina is pretty good?"

I almost laugh, but I don't. It's a fair question to an average man. I am not average. Until a month ago, I was a professional athlete. "My stamina is excellent."

She reaches behind her and twists the doorknob, grabbing the front of my shirt and tugging me into the room with her. Hitting a wall switch, a lamp next to the bed switches on. She grabs the back of my neck and pulls my mouth down to hers for a searing kiss and I push the door closed with my foot as I enter the room more fully.

Running my hands down her back and over her hips, I grab two handfuls of her glorious ass and lift her. She wraps her legs around my waist and I carry her over to the bed and turn to sit on the edge. Josie straddles me and I kiss my way down her cheek and jaw, neck, and bare shoulder.

She rips my hat off and tosses it to the floor before running her hands through my hair and letting out a soft gasp when my teeth nip at a sensitive spot under her ear. When her hands run up my chest and under my flannel, I allow her to push it off my shoulders and I make quick work of discarding it on the floor on top of my hat before tugging Josie's sweater over her head, revealing a black lace bra.

"Fuck, you're beautiful."

She blushes with the compliment and yanks up the hem of my tee shirt. I pull it over my head and she inhales a quick breath as her eyes travel down my arms and torso. "You're one to talk," she says, her voice filled with awe as she drags her fingertips down my chest and abs.

I wrap my arms around her waist and roll us on the bed until she's below me, her knees bracketing my hips. I bend to brush kisses across her chest and down over the swell of her luscious tits. When I skim my tongue under the lace trim of her bra, she lets out a soft moan, her hips grinding against my already hard cock currently straining behind the zipper of my jeans.

I raise my face to look into her eyes. "Have you thought about what this might be like since we met?" She blushes but doesn't answer and I run my hand up her waist and over her breast to settle on her jaw. "Have you wondered if my cock was super, Josie?" I slide my hand down the side of her neck and let my fingers wrap gently around the column of her throat and Josie inhales sharply. "Have you?" She doesn't take her eyes off mine and gives me a subtle nod. I slightly increase the pressure on my hold and excitement flashes in her eyes. "Okay?" I ask and she nods again, this time with more enthusiasm. "Do you have a safe word?"

Her eyes widen in surprise. "No. Do I need one?"

I lower my mouth to the valley of her breasts and trail kisses down her sternum. "You tell me. Have you ever needed one before?"

"No."

"Ah. I see." I kiss my way back up her chest and raise my face to look at her again. "Maybe the reason no man has been able to keep your attention is because they haven't been enough for you." Her nostrils flare and I ask, "Are you kinky?"

She chuckles. "I haven't ever thought about it." While I

keep my hand on her throat, I let my other hand roam freely over her tits, waist, hips, ass, and thighs.

"So you don't have any kinks that you know of?"

She bites her lip. "I mean, doesn't everyone?"

"Yes, I'm sure they do."

"I'm guessing you have a list?"

I press a kiss to her lips, an amused smile on my face. "Yeah, actually."

Her brow ticks up. "What's on it?"

"Do you want me to tell you, or do you want to find out?"

"I suppose that depends on how extreme it is." She runs her hands up my arms. "Do you like to tie women up? Beat them? Humiliate them?"

I shake my head. "No. I'm not really into degradation. And while I like a little spanking, I'm not a sadist. And shibari is an art form; I'm not really that patient."

Her brow furrows. "*Shibari*? What's that?"

"Intricate rope bondage. It's beautiful, but not really my thing. Some people get off on it, though. I like to be touched, so the idea of having my partner's hands bound doesn't exactly appeal to me."

"You know a lot about kink, do you?"

It's my turn for my brow to lift. "I know what I like."

Her hand comes to rest on the one I have wrapped around her throat. "And this? You like this?"

"This," I reply, giving a gentle squeeze, "is about trust. I wouldn't actually play like that during sex. Not until I've built up substantial trust with my partner. I wouldn't do more than what I'm doing now during foreplay. I'm not really even constricting bloodflow. Some people don't like it at all. For some, it's a hard limit."

"Do you have hard limits?"

I nod. "Everyone does. My list of 'nos' is much longer than

my list of 'yeses.'" I press a kiss to her lips. "I also have no issues with vanilla if that's what you're into."

She huffs a laugh. "Pretty sure this is the longest discussion I've ever had before sex."

"Communication is key." I release her throat and grip her chin. "And like I said, maybe your issue with having someone keep your interest is because they didn't know what you needed."

CHAPTER SEVEN

JOSIE

"And like I said, maybe your issue with having someone keep your interest is because they didn't know what you needed."

Well, this night has not turned out anything like I'd planned. And simply based on my text exchange with Ford and his assertiveness, I suspected he might have a dominant streak. But this is more than I expected. And, God, is it hot.

"Maybe. Why don't you see if you can keep me occupied," I challenge.

His brow tics up and he bends, drawing one taut nipple into his mouth through the fabric of my bra, making me gasp. I run my hands up his inked, muscled arms and over his shoulders to thread into his hair and grasp the strands.

During our conversation, the hand he didn't have wrapped around my throat was lightly skimming over the rest of my body. Not enough to be considered groping, but enough to make my skin hum with awareness. I'm more turned on than I've been in my entire life and we haven't really even done anything. I'm not even naked yet.

Ford continues to work my nipple through the lace, and the

texture of the fabric combined with the wet heat of his mouth is nearly too much, but I also don't want him to stop. So, I simply close my eyes and give in to the sensations as scorching need settles low in my belly. I roll my hips, feeling the very prominent evidence of his desire straining against his jeans' zipper. He lets out a soft groan and pins my hips in place with his own and I scoff. "That's not fair."

Raising his head to look at me, my nipple tightens even harder when his heat departs, replaced by the ambient chill of the room. "Neither is you doing that." He reaches between us and rubs my pussy through the denim of my jeans, and a slow smile pulls at the corners of his mouth when I inhale sharply. "I'm going to take care of you; don't worry. But you also don't get to rush me. You keep grinding on me and you'll make a liar out of me about my stamina. This isn't going to be some quick fuck, Josie." He presses his finger harder and I let out a soft moan when he hits my clit. "I hope you don't have early plans in the morning because I plan on taking up most of your night."

His words make my skin prickle and my brain begins to work up fantastical scenarios of what a whole night of sex with Ford might be like. And fuck, do I want to find out if he can deliver on what he's saying.

He bends to press a kiss to my lips before pulling back. "Does that sound like something you might like?"

I huff a laugh. "I think I'm amenable to what you're offering."

He grins. "Good." He brings his hands up and plants them on either side of my head while still keeping my hips pinned. "I do have a few more things I'd like to discuss."

I frown. "Right now?"

He nods. "Like I said, communication is key."

"Are you this *communicative* with all your dates?" I ask with a smirk.

He runs a knuckle along my jaw. "Only the ones I don't plan on it being a one-time thing with."

"Oh, so you think this isn't going to be a one-time thing?"

"No," he replies matter-of-factly.

"You sound awfully confident."

"Freckles, I didn't get to where I am in life without being able to back up what I say. This won't be a one-time thing. Whenever I leave here, it will be with you already wanting me again."

I try to remember if I've ever been with anyone who's this sure of himself; I know I haven't. I don't know why I find it as sexy as I do, but it's definitely doing something for me.

"All right, what other things do you want to discuss?" Try as I might, I can't disguise how breathy my voice is.

His eyes scan my face before dropping to my breasts and returning to my eyes. "As long as you're sleeping with me, I'll be the only one you sleep with."

"Excuse me?" I scoff and push against his chest, trying to sit up. But he's so much larger than I am, I can't budge him.

"Calm down."

"No. Let me up." He sighs and pushes off the bed to stand and I sit up. I get to my feet, close the distance between us, and poke him in the chest, indignant. "You don't get to demand exclusivity from me on a first date. I don't do exclusivity."

He takes a step closer to me. "And I don't share."

"*You* don't get a choice in the matter. All I promised you was tonight. You think because you claim you can rock my world and be the one guy whom I'll want for more than one night, you can deliver? Better men than you have tried, buddy." I fold my arms across my chest and glare up at his beautiful, cocky face.

He takes another step forward, and I'm forced to step back or have his bare chest touch my arms. And right now, I don't want to touch him. Because in spite of how pissed I am about his possessiveness, I'm more turned on by it than I'd like to admit. His eyes drill into mine, and where they were a bright blue earlier, they're much darker now and make me think he might be, too.

Ford continues to advance and I retreat, knowing full well there's a wall behind me. "Were you this difficult with any of the other men you've slept with?"

"None of the other men I've slept with have been possessive assholes."

He huffs an amused laugh and takes another step forward. When I step back, my shoulder blades collide with the wall. And maybe I should be nervous or alarmed, but for some reason, I'm not. Despite how Ford is bearing down on me, I'm not afraid of him. He plants his hands on either side of my shoulders but doesn't come any closer. "You like that I'm possessive. I think the idea that I want to claim you for only myself turns you on." He lowers his head and runs the tip of his nose along my jaw until his mouth is next to my ear. When he speaks again, his voice is low and husky and his breath plays over my skin, sending goosebumps down my bare arms. "Part of me thinks it's what's been missing from any other relationship you've ever had."

"I don't do relationships," I counter.

"You do now. With me."

"You're a cocky bastard; you know that?"

His lips brush down the side of my neck and I shiver, letting my arms fall to my sides. "Yeah, I do," he replies. "I see something I like and go for it; it's how I'm built. You want this only to be a physical relationship, that's fine. But it will be a relationship. And I will be the only man you sleep with."

"How about you go fuck yourself?" And I spit out the words, but damn, I'm aching with need.

"I think I'd rather fuck you, Josie. Would you like that?" He drags the knuckle of his index finger down my sternum, between my breasts, and down my stomach. He circles my belly button with the tip of his finger and just barely skims under the waistband of my jeans. "I bet, if I were to stick my hand inside these jeans, I'd find your panties soaked, wouldn't I? Is that pretty pussy aching yet, beautiful girl?"

My chest heaves with how hard I try not to react to his words. But, God, it's as if he's seeing straight into a part of me I didn't know was there. "It's okay if you like to let someone else tell you what you need. And I'd love to be the one to give it to you." Ford's hand hovers over the button of my jeans and he trails kisses down my jaw. "Just say the word, and I'll make sure you have it."

"And what word is that?"

"Tell me there won't be anyone else. If you decide you want out, that's fine. But if we're fucking, it's only each other. I don't sleep around. I don't give a shit if you date other people, but mine will be the only cock you suck. Mine will be the only cock allowed to get you off." He nips under my ear and my heart rate tics up. "Yours will be the only pussy I taste and get my dick wet with."

"You haven't even had me yet, and you're convinced it will be that good? So good you won't want to go home with other women? You think you'll be so good that the idea of other dick won't do it for me?"

He pulls back to look into my eyes. "First of all, I know it is. Second of all, call it a hunch. But sure, I'll give you this freebie. If, after tonight, you don't feel as satisfied as I know you will be, we'll go our separate ways. You're so convinced you don't do relationships; put your money where your mouth is." He grips my chin and drags the pad of his thumb over my bottom lip. "However, if one night isn't enough, you're all mine. Physically, anyway. Like I said, you want to date other men—as jealous as the thought of that makes me—I'm not going to stop you. But I will be the only man you fuck."

I open my lips and suck his thumb into my mouth and he huffs a sharp breath and yanks it away. I give him a smug smile. "Would the thought of me going on dates with other men make you jealous?"

His nostrils flare and he narrows his eyes. "I already told you, I don't like to share. But as long as I'm the one you end the night with—as long as I'm the one who gets to share your bed—I don't give two shits who buys your dinner."

"So, what, you'd be content to just be a fuck buddy?"

"No, ideally, it would evolve past that point, but that's all you want. And I'd rather have you on what you think you want the terms to be than not at all. I like you, Josie. I've enjoyed getting to know you over the past few weeks. I like how blunt you are. I like that you don't bullshit. Too many people in my life are fake and I like that you aren't. And I'd like to learn what makes you tick, but if all you think you want right now is someone to have fun with, I can be that, too."

I already knew, even with this back and forth, I was going to sleep with him. And the thought of him seeing me with someone else and being jealous fills me with more satisfaction than it probably should. I don't know who I am in this moment. I'm not the type of woman who taunts men. I'm not the type who agrees to anything more than *tonight*. But I find myself wanting to take Ford up on his offer. To see if I could do it.

His hand still hasn't moved any closer to the button of my jeans, so I tilt my hips until I'm pressed against his palm. His eyes search mine and I nod. And yet, he still doesn't proceed. I'm about to say something, and he opens his mouth again. "I have one other thing to discuss." I groan in frustration and he grins. "What, are you antsy, Freckles?"

"You're the one who's gotten me all worked up for this magic cock of yours and now you're stalling. So yeah, I'm antsy."

"Good." He pulls his phone out of his pocket and thumbs across the screen, and I frown. For a moment, I think he's going to take a picture or something, but he begins speaking again. "Are you on birth control?"

Confused, I answer honestly. "Yeah." I don't add, *the permanent kind.*

"And are you clean? When was the last time you were tested?"

I blink rapidly but, again, answer truthfully. "Yes, I'm clean. I was tested six weeks ago. I haven't been with anyone since then. Why?"

He turns his phone toward me and I squint at the screen. It takes a moment before what I'm seeing registers. They're test results. Ford's test results. "I was tested last week when I accepted my new job and haven't been with anyone since then. And as you can see, I'm clean."

Realization dawns with why he'd tell me. "You don't want to wear a condom?"

"I have no issues with wearing one; I just wanted you to know. That way, if at some point, things happen spontaneously and we forget, we're okay." He takes his phone out of my hand and lays it on my dresser. "Because like I said, as long as you're sleeping with me, you won't be sleeping with other people."

My nostrils flare in annoyance. Annoyance that he's so possessive and even more so that I like it so much. "Fine," I say, unbuttoning my jeans and shoving them down my hips. Ford's eyes fall to track my movement and I'm pleased to see the hunger that fills his gaze. I take a moment to work them down my calves and off my feet until I'm left standing in only my bra and panties.

Ford takes a step back and unbuckles his belt. And fuck, why is it so sexy to watch a man take off his pants? His movements are agonizingly slow and he doesn't take his eyes off mine as he unbuttons and unzips his jeans. He lets them drop to the floor before stepping out and pulling off his socks. And sweet Jesus, the sight of him in only his boxers has the ache settling in once again.

I start at his feet and let my eyes travel up his muscular calves and massive quads, over his narrow hips with that delicious "V" that descends into the waistband of his boxers. His broad chest and taut abs are dusted in dark, wiry hairs, and I can't wait to feel those hairs against my stomach and breasts as we move together. Both his arms are sleeved in colorful ink, along with something on his right side that I can't make out from this angle.

Unable to wait any longer, I step forward and close the distance between us, reaching up to wrap my arms around his neck and pull him down to me. Our lips collide, and it's as if a switch has been flipped. There will be no more discussion. There will be no more delays. He quickly takes charge of the kiss, as I knew he would. I get the feeling that there are very few instances where Ford would give up control. And tonight, I'm okay with it. I guess we'll see how long I can handle it past that point.

His tongue greedily invades my mouth and he wastes no time reaching around to unhook my bra and pulling my arms from around his neck to discard the lacy barrier on the floor. He shuffles me back to where I was against the wall and wedges his knee between my thighs as he kisses down my jaw and neck, and my breaths are already coming quicker. His stubble tickles my neck and chest, and when he bends lower to flick his tongue over my nipple, I gasp and can't stop from grinding my hips against his thigh.

Ford huffs a laugh and brings his hand up to cup my other breast. "Anyone ever tell you that you have perfect tits, Freckles?" He gives it a gentle squeeze. "Just right for burying my face in. Just right for watching them bounce when you ride my cock." He tugs my nipple between his teeth, and I hiss with the sting just before he swirls his tongue over it to ease the pain. "Just right to hold onto as I pound into you from behind."

"You talk an awful big game, Ford. Do you do anything with that mouth besides talk?"

He raises his eyes to mine and his lips curl into a wicked grin. "Oh, my beautiful girl. I'm going to do a lot with this mouth." He bends to trail kisses down my chest. "And just remember, when you call out for God, he's not the one who made you come so hard you see his son."

A bark of surprised laughter falls from my mouth, but it quickly dies as Ford's lips move lower, and his tongue skims under the waistband of my panties. He hooks his fingers into the sides of my underwear and drags them down my hips as he drops to his knees. He helps me step out of them before discarding them on top of the pile of our other clothes.

He plants a kiss above my knee before licking and sucking his way up my inner thigh. Lifting my leg to drape over his shoulder, he lifts his eyes to mine. "Fuck, this is a pretty pussy, Josie. Look at you, all wet for me. Can I have you?"

"You don't see me stopping you, do you?"

"No, but I want you to tell me you want this."

God, how I want this. Can he not see how my body is practically vibrating with need? Can he not see what a puddle he's turned me into with his words and his kisses? "I want this, Ford."

"That's my girl."

He leans in, and I grab his hair until he returns his eyes to mine. "I'm not your girl."

Ford removes my hand from his hair and presses a kiss to my palm. "You will be." And before I can say anything else, he spreads me wide with the index and middle fingers of his free hand, and his tongue flicks over my clit, causing me to let out a moan that I'm unable to bite back.

CHAPTER EIGHT

JOSIE

He makes slow licks up my center, giving me just enough sensation to ratchet my need even higher. He groans against my flesh, the vibration causing me to gasp, and I thread my fingers through his hair. When he sucks my clit into his mouth, the intensity nearly makes my knees buckle. "Fuck," I breathe. He chuckles, and I moan through gritted teeth, my breaths coming in ragged huffs. His tongue laps lower and he nuzzles his nose against my clit, and I can only let my head fall back against the wall and *feel*.

For several long minutes, I'm in the most unbelievably delicious torture as Ford seems to use every available tool in his arsenal to fulfill his promise of making me see Jesus. And when he slides two fingers into my pussy, I cry out as he crooks them while thrusting in and out, perfectly rubbing against my g-spot. "Ford, shit." I can't stop from grinding myself against his face or my toes from curling against his back, or the rapidly building orgasm threatening to explode any moment.

He pulls back a couple of inches, but I can still feel his huffs of breath against my skin. "Fuck, Josie. You're so fucking perfect. Come for me. I want to taste every bit of it. Let me have it." He returns his tongue to my clit, and I let out a high-pitched moan that sounds more like a squeak when the sensation hits the now overly sensitive bundle of nerves. It's exactly the trigger my body needs to go over that edge, waves of pleasure crashing into me so abruptly that I see spots and my legs shake. And I very much feel as though I've seen the son of God.

Damn this cocky motherfucker and the horse he rode in on.

Ford barely gives me a moment to collect myself before he's back on his feet and claiming my mouth with those same greedy kisses. And when he runs his hands down my body and over my ass, lifting me off the ground as if I weigh nothing, I have no choice but to wrap my arms and legs around him and hang on as he ferries me over to the bed.

He lays me on my back, and I untangle myself from around him as he shucks his boxers. And although I should be grabbing a condom from the nightstand, I am transfixed as he slides his thumbs into the waistband of his underwear and pushes them down his hips, his thick cock springing free. A small, audible gasp falls from my lips, and he gives me a smug smile as he pumps his fist over his impressive length. "You going to keep looking at it, or do you have a condom so I can do something with it?"

Snapping out of my trance, I open the drawer, fish a foil square, and toss it to him. He picks it up off the bed and examines it. "Not latex?"

I shake my head. "Allergic."

"Good to know," he replies as he rips the packet with his teeth and rolls the condom down before joining me on the bed. He wraps his hands around the outsides of my knees and yanks me farther down the mattress. Settling between my thighs, he brings his hand up to my face and grips my chin, forcing me to look him in the eye as he slams into me. I gasp with the invasion, and he grins wickedly. "Fucking perfect." He gives me a hard kiss, drops his hand down to my hip, and digs his fingers in as he pulls out nearly to the tip and drives back in just as brutally.

"Shit," I moan and rock my hips, wanting him even deeper.

"Too much?" he asks, and I breathe a laugh and shake my head. Pleasant surprise flashes through his eyes, and he begins to piston his hips in earnest. It's a slow, almost punishing rhythm that nearly steals my breath with each thrust.

I let my hands roam over his muscled back, shoulders, and arms, loving the feel of him under my fingers as he seems dead set on his goal of claiming me as his own. Because fucking hell, I'm not sure it's ever been like this before. And in this moment, I'm here for it.

As my eyes begin to drift closed, he grips my face again, forcing my attention back on him. "No, you watch. I want you to watch me fuck you, Josie. I want you to know exactly who is giving you the best fuck of your life." My chest heaves with his words. Although I'm indignant, it's because the words are true and he knows it. Determination flickers in his gaze as he continues to move above me, and I can already feel another orgasm starting to build. He kisses me, and it's a deep, claiming, harsh kiss meant to rattle every one of my senses, it feels like. Because God knows I can't see, hear, taste, smell, or feel anything but *him* in this moment.

When he breaks his mouth from mine, I gasp for breath, and he bends to kiss his way down my chest, his tongue circling my nipple before he draws it between his lips. "Ford, fuck," I moan and slide my fingers into his hair.

He shifts our bodies until he's bracing the back of my knee against his bicep, not even bothering to stop focusing his attention on my breasts or somehow lose his rhythm. But when he presses my knee back, increasing the depth of his thrusts even more, I scream with the change of angle as he hits a spot I wasn't even aware existed, and a climax stronger than my earlier one slams into me and tears spring to my eyes with the intensity and a sob wells up in my chest.

He brings his face level with mine, and his grin is smug as he thumbs away the tear that slides down toward my hairline. And somehow, he's still just as calm and collected as he's been all night. Sweet Jesus, is he some kind of robot?

Ford slows his thrusts and crooks my leg around his hip. "Have you had enough, Josie? Have I convinced you yet that mine will be the only cock you want?" I drag in lungfuls of air and try to think, but it's nigh unto impossible. "Or do I need to continue trying to convince you?" I shake my head. "No to which question? Use your words, sweetheart. You had no issue being mouthy earlier; why the difficulty now?" He reaches between us and presses the pad of his finger into my clit and I gasp.

"Fuck, Ford; I'm convinced," I choke out.

He chuckles. "Yeah, I'm not so sure." He bends his head and nips at my earlobe, his finger continuing to circle my clit. "Give me one more, Josie. I want to feel your pussy tighten around my cock again."

I moan and try as I might to hold off, he coaxes another release from me as surely as if he was stealing it. And when I come, I'm pretty sure my heart is going to burst from my chest, and my throat aches with trying not to scream. "That's it. Fuck, Josie. Shit."

"Please, Ford. I can't. No more."

"You've had enough?"

"Yes," I whine.

"You want me to come?" he asks through gritted teeth.

"Yes. Fuck."

"Tell me that's what you want. Tell me to come for you."

I don't even have the brain power to question what he wants me to say; I just do as he tells me. "Please, Ford. Come for me."

He smiles and dips his head in concentration. His forehead is damp with sweat, and he braces his forearms on either side of my shoulders, goes up on his toes as if in a plank, and furiously pumps his hips. I feel the muscles of his arms and back tense as he gets closer to his own climax, and somehow, watching him begin to come undone makes me want to follow him over the edge again.

I pull his mouth to mine for a deep kiss and reach down to work my clit, hoping to get there with him. When he realizes what I'm doing, he smiles into our kiss. Sensitive as I am, it takes me only seconds before I'm right on that edge. He breaks our kiss and presses his forehead to mine. "Now, Josie. Fuck." I let go as his hips buck one final time, and he lets out a low grunt.

I'm unable to move for what feels like hours, but is most likely only a couple of minutes. Ford is still above me, and he peppers my face with soft kisses as he pulls out. My brain and body are officially jelly as he rises from the bed. Somewhere in my mind, it registers that he says something about coming right back, but I'm still unable to process exactly what just happened. Except that I know I've never experienced anything like this before.

When Ford returns, he rouses me. "Come on, Freckles. Sit up and drink some water." He helps me to rise and sits next to me on the bed, supporting me as I come down and sip the bottle of water he's brought me. Grabbing the throw blanket from the end of the bed, he wraps it around me, pulls me against him, and rubs my back.

When I can finally form words, I look up at him. "Is it always like that for you?"

He huffs a laugh. "Sometimes."

"Jesus Christ."

He drops a kiss on the top of my head. "You'll be all right." His expression sobers, and he tilts my chin up, forcing me to look him in the eye again. "Or, was it too much for you? I know I asked earlier, but I probably should've checked in more."

I shake my head. "No, it was...Shit, I don't even know. But it wasn't too much."

Relief flashes through his gaze. "Okay. Finish your water and go pee."

I narrow my eyes. "So bossy."

He grins. "There she is."

And yet, I do what he says. I grab a sleep shirt from my dresser and slip it over my head before going to pee and brushing my teeth. When I return, I expect Ford to be dressed or even gone, but he's under the covers scrolling through his phone and I stop short. "What do you think you're doing?"

He frowns. "What? I'm checking my phone. Don't you check your phone one last time before you go to bed?"

I plug my phone up and stand at the edge of the bed. "You're not staying. I don't do sleepovers."

His brow ticks up. "Well, I do. Get in bed. I'm tired."

"This is my bed."

He heaves a put-upon sigh. "Josie, get in bed; it's late. I need aftercare, too. For me, that means cuddling." I fold my arms, and one of his brows lifts again. "Woman, if I get out of this bed, it will be either because this house is on fire or because you need me to fuck you again. Otherwise, get your ass under these covers and snuggle with me."

He folds down the covers on my side of the bed and pats the empty spot. I'm not sure whether I want to laugh because he's demanding I cuddle with him or if I want to continue to be stubborn in the hopes he'll actually fuck me again. But then I think better of it because my legs are still shaky from the four orgasms I've already had.

I don't move for a few seconds, and something like uncertainty flits through his gaze. If I pressed it, he would probably leave since consent seems to be something Ford genuinely values. So why aren't I? I was honest when I said I don't do sleepovers. But he's also taken care of me tonight—before, during, and after what I'm already considering to be the best sex of my life. If he needs this as his "aftercare," would it kill me to take care of him, too?

Sighing, I climb into bed, and he offers me a grateful nod. "Thank you." His tone is sincere as he tugs the covers up around me and reaches across me to turn off the light. He pulls me into his arms and curls his body around mine as he lies down.

And because I don't do sleepovers, I can't remember the last time I actually slept with someone. Not unless it was a drunken hookup where one or both of us passed out three seconds post-orgasm. And even then, they're always gone before I get up. Unsure how I'd feel to wake up next to Ford, I can't help but ask, "Will you still be here in the morning?"

"Yes." His answer is so matter-of-fact that it takes me by surprise. There's no, *if you want* or *maybe* or *uh, sure.* Just, *yes.*

"Okay," is all I can say, uncomfortable with how comfortable it feels to have his arms wrapped around me.

Sure enough, Ford is still in my bed when my alarm goes off. He's rolled away from me and doesn't stir as I sit up. I'm greeted with some appreciable soreness from the previous night's activities, and I hate to admit it might've been the best night's sleep of my life.

Climbing from bed, careful not to rouse him, I tiptoe from my bedroom and head across the hall to the bathroom. I'm greeted with the smell of fresh coffee and hear Jess moving around the kitchen. I hurriedly do my business, wash my hands, and walk into the kitchen. He's poring over something on his laptop, still dressed in his scrubs, and looks me up and down as I come into the room while he sips his coffee. A slow smile crosses his face and I shake my head. "I don't want to hear it."

"There's a car in the driveway," he says knowingly.

I pull a mug down from the cabinet, pour myself a cup of coffee, and join him at the table. "There's a boy in my bed."

"Would this *boy* happen to be a certain viking lumberjack who recently moved to town and whose ID you sent me last night?"

I take a long drink of my coffee. "Yes."

"And he's still here? You don't do sleepovers."

"I know."

He examines my face. "You're freaked out."

"Yes," I admit.

"That good, huh?"

"Better."

His brows draw together in curiosity. "Like, better how?"

"Like, he said, 'just remember, when you call out for God, he's not the one who made you come so hard you see his son.' And he wasn't joking." Jess blinks rapidly and I elaborate. "He wasn't joking four times."

His brows rise and he asks, "He was able to get it up four times? For a guy in his thirties, that's pretty impressive."

I shake my head. "No. Four times in one session. And after my third orgasm, he hadn't even broken a sweat. He only finished because I waved the fucking white flag."

"You said four."

I nod. "Yeah, watching him come got me off."

Jess laughs. "Shit. No wonder you let him sleep over; he earned it."

"He didn't give me much choice. He said cuddling was his required aftercare or something."

He nods and his smile is smug. "Well, I'll be damned. I never thought I'd see the day any man would best Josephine Campbell. But you're in trouble. You liked it." He holds my gaze. "So I'm guessing he knocks me out of the running for the best you ever had?"

I snort a laugh. "Only just barely, my friend." He joins in, and we drink our coffee for a minute.

"Are you going to see him again?"

"He said he's cool with keeping things strictly physical, so that's the plan. I think he thinks I will catch feelings, but you know how I feel about corporate types. The sex might be enough to keep me interested, but I don't care about anything more than that."

"I hope he makes you eat your words."

Rolling my eyes, I scoff. "You sound like Silas."

"Well, your brother and I are both intelligent individuals." He yawns and checks his watch. "What are your plans for the day? Isn't Hensley coming back soon?"

"Yeah. Tomorrow. I've got to go to her place today and make sure everything is ready for her return."

"All right. Well, I picked up a shift for tonight, so I won't be home again if you want to have another night with the viking."

"All you do is work anymore."

He shrugs. "What else do I have to do when Brooklyn's out of town? It's either work or stay home with you. And not that I don't love you, but if I can make money, I will." He yawns again. "Shit, I'm going to bed. If you decide to let him rock your world one more time before you kick him to the curb, try to keep it down? Also, I already took Gouda out."

"You're the best." I wave him off as he shuts his laptop and leaves the table. Refilling my coffee, I return to bed, where Ford still hasn't budged. I set my mug on the nightstand and crawl back under the covers. With how he's lying, I can finally make out the tattoo on his right side.

It's a pair of ice skates that look to be hanging from a nail by their laces. What does it mean to him? From how he speaks, I know he occasionally slips into a midwestern accent that makes me think of Minnesota or Wisconsin. And the only reason I'm even able to identify it is because of *before* since most of my assigned territory was in that region of the country. Maybe he liked to ice skate in the winter?

CHAPTER NINE

FORD

When I wake and see the sun streaming brightly through the windows of Josie's bedroom, I'm honestly surprised she didn't try to wake me the first chance she got in an attempt to kick me out. Not that it would have worked, but judging by how reticent she was to even let me sleep over, I'm shocked to find her awake and scrolling through her phone, sipping a cup of coffee as I roll toward her in the bed.

With my hand still under the covers, I slide it up her shin and over her knee and inner thigh. Josie doesn't look at me and simply keeps staring at her phone. Not even when my fingers brush over her bare pussy does she react. My cock sure does, though.

I yank the covers down, snatch her phone away amid her protestant scoffs, and drop it to the floor. "Put the coffee down, or you'll be wearing it in about three seconds."

Her façade finally breaks and she smiles, her eyes coming to mine as she sets her mug on the nightstand. I rise to my hands and knees and bracket her hips and shoulders. She lies down and I take in her face, free from makeup and her hair still wild from sleep. She's beautiful. "You let me stay."

She shrugs, her fingertips trailing down my chest. "I wasn't sure how far 'aftercare' extended." She puts the word in air quotes and I nod, bending to drop kisses onto her hip, stomach, ribs, breasts, and chest as I ruck up the hem of her sleep shirt. Shifting her legs to wrap them around my waist, she pulls me closer.

"And what if my aftercare needed to also include having you again this morning?" I ask and slide my hand up the inside of her thigh.

"We would have to be quiet. Jess is home, and he needs his sleep."

I nip at the underside of her breast and she inhales sharply. "Oh, I can be quiet, Freckles. Can you?"

"Debatable."

I run my thumb up her pussy, and her hips buck as I press into her clit. "Are you sore?"

She huffs a laugh and threads her fingers through my hair. "Yes. But not so much that I'm willing to deny you *aftercare*."

I smile against her skin, slide two fingers into her, and groan as an ache settles into my balls when she rolls her hips, a soft moan falling from her lips. "You're so wet already. Fuck."

"You're pretty sexy when you're asleep. And maybe remembering last night got my motor running." Josie pulls my face up to hers and gives me a soft kiss. And not even morning breath could stop me from kissing this woman, especially when she's as fucking sexy as she is.

Running her hands down my sides, she shoves my boxers down my hips before pushing them the rest of the way down my legs with her feet. Her breathing grows increasingly ragged, and she huffs into our kiss as she reaches over to open her nightstand drawer. She breaks her mouth from mine to rip the condom open with her teeth before extending it to me.

I reluctantly withdraw my hand to take it from her and roll it on. And although I'm sure she expects me to simply drive in, I reach between us to finish what I started. She scoffs, and I lift one brow and give her a smug smile when she moans. "What, you're going to complain about the fact that I want to give you more than one orgasm?"

"I don't have time," she says with a whine. She tries to push me away, and I capture her hands in my free one and pin them above her head. Her cheeks flush and her mouth falls open.

I bend to flick my tongue over her nipple, and her hips buck. "So make time. If you had something to do this morning, you would've said so last night. You don't. You're just afraid you'll like me if you let me stick around."

She narrows her eyes. "I don't like you." And yet, she doesn't try to pull away from me, and she's close to getting off, simply judging by how her pussy is pulsing around my fingers, and her breathing is growing more and more shallow.

Shaking my head, I chuckle. "You tell yourself that. In the meantime, come for me. You don't need to like me for that, do you?" She clamps her teeth down on her bottom lip as she moans, clenching down around my fingers. "That's my girl."

She huffs a ragged breath. "I told you; I'm not your girl."

I withdraw my hand and grip her chin, forcing her to look at me as I enter her. Fuck, she's perfect. Josie whimpers and rocks her hips, still not attempting to pull her hands from mine. "And I told you, you will be. You can tell yourself you only want my cock, and if that's the hook I need to catch you with, that's fine. But it won't just be my body you want; wait and see."

"You're a cocky shit, you know that?" she asks through gritted teeth.

"I do. But this cocky shit's going to make you come again." I shift to put her calves on my shoulders and brace my hand on the headboard as I deepen my thrusts.

"Fuck," Josie gasps and strains against my grip.

And like I do whenever I get into the zone, I push away my own discomfort and need and focus on the task at hand. The task, this time not being a hockey game, but a sexy and obstinate woman I'm determined to claim for myself.

I huff a laugh and pound into her as her pussy pulses around me. "Yeah, you can call me a cocky shit or arrogant motherfucker or whatever other names you want. And you know what? They'd all be true. I am arrogant. I am cocky. But I'm also good at what I do. Which right now includes fucking your sweet cunt. And if you want to get off, you'll have to ask nicely."

Josie moans, and I can tell she's getting close. Just before she lets go, I slow down, and indignation flashes in her eyes. "You asshole."

"Yeah, that's true, too, a lot of the time."

"You said you weren't a sadist, but I'm pretty sure that's a lie."

I give her a wicked grin. "I guess I can be. Like I said, all you have to do is ask nicely."

"Fuck you."

"You know, you keep sweet talking me, and I won't be able to contain myself." I release her hands to brace both her legs on my biceps, and she drags my mouth to hers for a hungry kiss. I press her knees back as I pick up my pace again and Josie cries out, most of the sound swallowed by our kiss.

I break my lips from hers. "You want to come?"

"Fuck, Ford."

"That's not an answer, Josie."

She moans and rakes her short nails down my chest, and I

grunt with the pain. "Oh, God. Ford." Her words come out a near shriek, and I cover her mouth with my hand to muffle the sound.

And again, just before she comes, I slow down, not letting her go over, and she lets out a frustrated groan behind my hand before she sinks her teeth into the side of my palm. "Ouch," I yelp, jerking my hand away.

"That's for denying me."

I huff a laugh. "I already told you what you had to do. It's up to you how long this lasts."

Her jaw clenches as she whines. "You know, I don't need you. I'm pretty good at getting myself off; been doing it for years."

I pull out nearly to the tip and slam into her, sweat popping on my forehead and chest, and Josie gasps. "Yeah, but right now, I'm the one in control of your orgasm. Beg me for it."

She chokes out a sob, drawing so close to that precipice again just before I back her off. Her forehead is damp with sweat, pieces of her dark hair sticking to her skin. She beats her fists against my chest, and I pin them above her head once more.

I see it in her eyes the moment she makes the decision, and I'm smiling before the words even leave her mouth. "Please, Ford. Please. I need to come."

And so, I give it to her. It only takes about thirty seconds to build her back up again, and for a moment, I can see she's afraid I'm going to deny her again, but I release her hands and guide one to her pussy. She ravenously works her clit, and I capture her mouth with my own as she finally goes over with a long moan. I let the beautiful sound settle in as I allow myself to let go, and with a final buck of my hips, I spill into the condom with a grunt.

Josie huffs ragged breaths as she comes down, and I raise

my head to examine her face. She's not nearly as out of it this morning as she was last night, so I press a kiss to her lips. "Okay?" I ask.

She punches me in the ribs, taking me by surprise, and I let out a whoosh of air. "What the fuck, Josie?"

"You're an asshole."

"And?" I ask, rubbing my ribs as I pull out and roll away from her.

"I don't like you." She jumps out of the bed and yanks her nightgown down over her hips.

"And?"

"Don't do that again."

I grab a tissue from the box on the nightstand and discard the condom in the small trash can next to the bed. "Okay. So, would you say edging is a hard limit for you?"

She blinks, confused. "What?"

"Edging," I repeat. "Is that a hard limit for you? You didn't like it?"

She opens her mouth and closes it again, her cheeks flushing. "I want a safe word."

"Okay."

Her brow furrows and she frowns. "Why are you so calm? I just told you I didn't like you."

"I know. You don't have to like me to want to fuck me. Even though I think you actually do like me. But for the sake of this argument, the two don't have to be mutually exclusive. You wanted a purely physical relationship; that's fine. But you didn't answer my question. You didn't like that I edged you? Or was it the fact I told you had to ask for permission to come?" She bristles, picking my boxers off the bed, and tosses them at me, hitting me in the face. "Ah, so the latter. Got it."

"Fuck you, Ford."

"You already did that, sweetheart," I say smugly and hop from foot to foot as I tug my underwear up my legs.

Her nostrils flare. "I think we're done here. You need to go."

I nod. "Okay." I pick up my socks and slip them on before pulling on my jeans and tee shirt. I don't bother donning my flannel and simply hold it in my hands. Her brow is still furrowed and she stands with her arms folded across her chest. "When you want to talk about why you liked that you had to give up your control, call me. We can discuss more about what you liked and didn't like about this. Or, don't. It's up to you." I pick my phone up off the nightstand and I'm almost to the door when I turn to look at her one last time. "It's okay if you need time to process what happened last night and this morning. Especially if stuff like this is new to you, it can be a lot. If you want, I can even send you a list or you can find one online with information on levels of interest in all kinds of different stuff.

"If you decide you only want vanilla, that's fine, too. I have fun with you, Josie, and I'd prefer not to have fun with anyone else right now. Like I said, you don't have to like me to want to fuck me. You only want to fuck, give me a call. The ball's in your court, Freckles." I give her a wink before stepping out of the bedroom and shutting the door behind me.

CHAPTER TEN

JOSIE

I stay rooted to my spot after Ford leaves. And for fifteen solid minutes after, I debate calling him to come back. But that part of me that refuses to give up control also refuses to let myself call him. I hate that he could read me so well. I hate that he was so rational. I expected him to argue and want to hash everything out. But no, he had to throw my own words back in my face. And yes, dammit, I like him. Fuck.

As I shower and go through my daily routine of checking my provider portal on the house helper app and taking Gouda for a run, and other duties around the house, Ford's words keep playing in my mind. *You can find a list online.*

I realize I'm probably way over my head with Ford. "Kinky" and "Josephine Campbell" are not synonymous by any stretch of the imagination. But the fact that I've liked everything Ford and I have done has me intrigued enough to pull out my laptop and do a quick online search for kink lists. Four hours later, I know way more than I ever wanted to know about certain things. Certain things I can't unsee and would never be comfortable with. Other things, though, I'm intrigued about.

An alarm goes off on my phone, reminding me that I need to do Hensley's grocery shopping and ready her house for her return tomorrow. I change into jeans and a sweater and work my hair into a braid before heading out the door.

It's after eight by the time I return home, throw together a sandwich for supper, and play with Gouda for a while. And because Jess has already left for work, I again find myself sitting at my computer, reviewing *the list*.

And as I tally up the things I'd be interested in or already know I like, I find many things I didn't even know were kinks. Doesn't everyone enjoy being told it's good during sex? I guess not. And if I'm honest, Ford had me pegged on both the edging and the fact that I liked having to ask for permission to come.

The more I think about it, the more turned on I get. Fuck. Am I really almost thirty-five years old and still don't know everything I like sexually? And I suppose, after examining my findings on the list, I'm not quite as vanilla as I thought. Full-blown kinky might be a stretch, but there are things I'm definitely interested in.

More of Ford's words play over in my mind. *Maybe your issue with having someone keep your interest is because they didn't know what you needed.* I wish I could say he's wrong, but apparently, that's the truth because even though he was here less than twelve hours ago, I'm already craving him like a fix.

But it's too soon to wave the white flag of surrender just yet. Maybe he'll break before I do and reach out. Something tells me he won't, though. Something tells me he'll be strong enough to wait me out. Will I?

Nearly a week later, I'm finishing up bottling a batch of Pap's latest distilling of moonshine and placing the jars into cases. I'm sweating my ass off in the stillhouse, and I'm nearly buzzed from simply smelling the homebrew. My phone dings with a text and I pull it out of my pocket to read the screen.

> Hensley: Come out to the bar with me. I already know you don't have plans. I ran into Ada at the drug store and she was getting cold medicine for Bea, so no excuses. Picking you up @ 7:30. Dress to kill. I need a wing woman. My Fiji buzz is wearing off and I need some fresh dick.

I sigh and roll my eyes. I rationalize that going out with Hensley will possibly get me out of my funk and make me quit thinking about sending the list to Ford with a text telling him to come and make me like the things I checked "mild interest" on.

Shooting her a thumbs-up emoji, I finish my task in the stillhouse before returning to the farmhouse to let Pap know I'm done. As usual, he's sitting on the porch, but instead of his shotgun draped over the arms of the chair, he's playing his guitar. Even with his arthritic fingers, he can still pluck a nice melody, and I kiss the top of his head before falling onto the porch swing with a sigh.

"What's with the theatrics, Jo-Jo?"

"What theatrics, Pap?"

He gives me a knowing smile. "You've got that look you always get when something's not going your way. You've always gotten it. When Cole and Silas were allowed to do something you weren't because they were older, you'd always pout. You're pouting now. Why?"

I fold my arms and push my feet off the porch, making the swing sway. "I met a guy."

He huffs a laugh. "Well, don't sound so happy about it." He

leans the guitar against the side of the house and rises from his rocker, sprier than a man who's nearly ninety should be. He joins me on the swing and drapes his arm across the back, giving me his full attention. "What's wrong with him?"

I shake my head. "Nothing."

"Okay, so what's the problem?"

"I like him."

"And why is that a problem? That's great."

"He's an asshole."

He narrows his eyes, the same brown as mine, and smirks. "What kind of asshole? The kind like Si is to Ada or legitimate, where he'd end up hurting you?"

I sigh. "Probably like Si. But he's so infuriating."

"The best ones are."

"He also has a kid."

"Okay."

I level him with a gaze. "You know how I feel about being a mother."

"All right, is the kid's mom not in the picture?"

"No, she lives with her. From what I gather, Ford—that guy —sees her a lot, though. He moved here to be closer to her."

"Sounds like a decent guy to me. And it sounds like this kid already has a momma, so you wouldn't be one. Next objection?"

"He's also a corporate type, Pap. You know I left that life. I don't want to be dragged back in, even by association."

"Does this Ford fella talk about his job when y'all are together?" I shake my head. "All right, so make it a rule that he can't talk about work. What else?" I'm quiet for a minute and shrug and Pap pats my knee. "What are you really afraid of?"

"What if I'm broken, Pap? I don't think I'm cut out for a long-term relationship. I've never been able to have one. I get bored. Ford said if I just wanted to have fun, he was okay with that, but he keeps calling me 'his girl,' and I don't want to like it."

"But you do." It's not a question, and I nod. "You never know until you try. Maybe this Ford is the one guy who makes you want to do it."

"Yeah, and what if just because things are exciting right now, in six months, after there are real feelings, I get bored again? What if he introduces me to his kid? It wouldn't just be him I'd hurt."

"Jo-Jo, you're the only one who can decide what you want. But if you won't even try because of 'what if'? That makes you a coward. And you are not a coward, Josephine. You come from a long line of risk-takers. Look at Silas and Ada. Do you think they'd be as happy as they are if he hadn't finally given himself permission to love her? It was a huge risk for both of them, but look at how well the gamble paid off.

"If you're still thinking about this guy, chances are, you won't get bored; not anytime soon, anyway. If you're worried about it, lay down some ground rules. Don't meet his kid. Don't talk about work. But at some point, if you don't dig deep, you're only left with the topsoil. And the topsoil isn't the good dirt. You want that good, rich stuff that's below the top layer. That's where the nutrients come from. You have to dig and till and mix it up to grow the best harvest." He nudges me and wiggles his bushy, white eyebrows. "And sometimes, you need some good fertilizer to spice things up."

I shake my head and laugh. "Thanks for the analogy, old man."

He wraps his arm around my shoulder, pulls me against his side, and presses a kiss to the top of my head. "You're the only one keeping yourself out of the game, Jo-Jo. Get in there. You might win big."

Right at seven-thirty, I'm checking my reflection in the hall mirror, swiping on some lip gloss when Hensley honks in the driveway. Grabbing my clutch purse, I drop in my house key, phone, ID, credit card, and lip gloss as I walk out the door. "Have fun," Jess calls after me.

I slide into the passenger seat of Hensley's Mercedes, and she doesn't even wait for me to fasten the seatbelt before she backs out of the driveway. "Damn, Jos, you look hot. We are some fine bitches tonight," she says excitedly as she shifts gears. "It's ladies' night, and so many guys will be there to buy us drinks. I hope you've hydrated."

In reality, I don't plan on drinking much, considering my luck with allowing someone to buy me a drink lately. I plan on supporting Hensley in her quest to find some willing bedfellow for the night. I will sit at the bar, content to only be eye-fucked. Because the only person I'm interested in letting fuck me for real, I'm not currently speaking to, even though I have *the list* saved to my phone and ready to go whenever I decide to stop being so damn stubborn. But as stubborn is my default as of late, I don't see it happening.

"So, what ended up happening with that guy who saved you from being drugged? You never did say. Did he move to town? Did y'all go out?" Hensley asks and shifts gears again as she weaves through traffic.

"Yeah, it was fine."

"How was he in bed? I'm guessing if he's already flamed out, he wasn't that memorable."

"Actually, he was good." *Best I've ever had.*

"So, what happened?"

"He thinks he can convince me to want more than just a fuck buddy."

Her brows rise in curiosity. "Ooh, a challenge. So, what's the problem? If you're convinced he won't change your mind, what's the harm in continuing to have fun with him? If it runs its course, no harm, no foul, right?" I don't respond and simply watch as the street lights pass by at warp speed as Hensley makes her way downtown.

Hensley and I have been at the bar for about an hour, and so far, she's the only one getting any kind of attention tonight. Two tequila shots and two vodka cranberries later, I'm just starting to feel fuzzy enough to contemplate letting someone offer to buy me a drink. Not that I'll actually let them do it, but I'm almost willing to consider it.

And really, who is surprised? Sure as hell, not me. Hensley could be a Victoria's Secret model. With her svelte figure honed by a lifetime of pilates combined with her naturally blonde hair, double Ds, and the tan she recently acquired on her trip to Fiji, she's a stunner. She's also a lot of fun. And tonight is all for her, so I'm happy to stay out of the spotlight.

But as she heads to the dance floor with yet another guy who I already know she won't go home with, I start in on my third drink. And as if *the list* were this physical thing I've been carrying around, it taunts me from its place on my phone.

Dammit, I miss Ford. A week without communicating with him has nearly killed me. I didn't realize how much I'd enjoyed our banter and light conversation. But radio silence? It's torturing me. And not in a good way, like Ford edging me until I begged for permission to come, followed by the most intense orgasm of my life.

Hensley's words play back in my mind. *If you're convinced he won't change your mind, what's the harm in continuing to have fun with him?* She has a point. I've never had anyone make me want anything more than "right now," so I'm not overly concerned Ford will be the guy to make me want more than that. And at this moment, I'm just uninhibited enough that my stubbornness is taking a backseat to my libido and I shoot off a text.

> Josie: I have something for you.

I'm not sure if he'll respond. For all I know, he's already moved on and is currently edging some other lucky woman into oblivion, and I've ruined my chances with him. The thought of Ford being with another woman makes something twist in my chest, and hot rage settles into my belly. And even though he said he doesn't sleep around, I kicked him out. I haven't reached out. He may decide I'm not worth the trouble; I'm too much drama. I'm about to drain the remainder of my third cocktail when my phone lights up on the bar top.

> Ford: Is it a conversation? Because that's the only "something" you need to have for me right now.

Even though I know I owe him a conversation, I don't feel like a fucking conversation right now. Right now, I only want to get laid, and my stubbornness rears its ugly head again.

> Josie: I don't have a conversation, actually. What I do have is a short dress, thigh-high stiletto boots, and the ability to find someone in this bar who will fuck me if you're not interested.

Almost immediately, the dots begin to bounce, and I smile. My grin widens even more when his next text comes through.

Ford: Where are you?

No way in hell I'm making it easy on him, so I open my camera app and take a strategic selfie. And by strategic, I mean my substantial cleavage, along with the bar logo in the background. I send it off without another word and order another drink.

For the next half-hour, my phone lights up with texts from Ford, but I don't open them. Let him think I've already made my choice for the night. And even though I'm trying to get a reaction from him, I can't deny the jolt that runs through me when I see him walk in. Positioned where I am at the end of the bar, I have the perfect vantage to view the door to the bar, and when he enters, his posture is tense and very much like some big cat on the prowl. Or, probably more accurately, a viking in search of a village to plunder. I will happily be that village tonight.

Dressed in jeans and a dark button-down with the sleeves rolled up to showcase all that beautiful ink I haven't yet gotten to appreciate fully, he's a horny girl's wet dream. And just the sight of him has me growing damp as I remember exactly what he's capable of.

As he winds his way through the dance floor, his eyes scanning the room, several women attempt to engage him in a dance, and he politely declines with a quick smile. But after he spots me, he starts ignoring the other women altogether and makes a beeline for the bar.

When he reaches my spot, he takes in my boots and short dress, showcasing a lot of thigh. Were I interested in dancing tonight, I'd have to be careful not to flash any bystanders with the goods. His eyes travel upward, stopping at the plunging neckline of the red mini-dress, his nostrils flaring in blatant possessiveness that has my skin prickling. And when his gaze meets mine, all I see is heat.

I uncross and recross my legs, and for a split second, he's unable to not look before bringing his eyes back to my own. He takes the stool next to mine and signals for the bartender. Unlike any other time we've had drinks, he doesn't order a beer. Instead, he orders a double shot of Maker's Mark and I'm not sure if I should be intrigued or alarmed by this change.

After his drink is delivered, his eyes don't leave me as he sips. "You come out by yourself tonight?"

I shake my head. "My friend, Hensley, is here, too."

"Will she be upset if you don't leave with her?"

"Why wouldn't I leave with her?" I ask, my tone challenging.

"Because you're leaving with me."

I shake my head despite the thrill that runs through me. "I don't think so."

He downs his drink in one gulp and wipes his mouth with the back of his hand before dropping it to my thigh and leaning into my personal space. "If you didn't want to come home with me, why did you tell me where you were? Why did you tell me you want to be fucked if you're not willing to leave with me?"

Wanting to get in his space, I lean forward until my mouth is next to his ear. I'm aware of my breasts brushing against his chest, and he must be too because the hand on my thigh inches higher, just under the hem of the skirt. "I said I could find someone in this bar to fuck me. I didn't say where."

I pull back and examine his face, a slow smile tugging at the corners of my mouth, and I lift one brow. His expression is unreadable, but he gives my thigh a subtle squeeze. I glance over his shoulder and jerk my chin toward the other side of the bar, knowing he'll look where I've indicated. I don't wait for him to respond and simply hop off the stool and begin making my way to the bathrooms, unsure if he'll actually follow.

I don't have to wait long. Less than two minutes after I've left the bar, the door opens to the single bathroom, and Ford steps in, locking it behind him. "You've got some balls on you, Freckles, thinking you can come out looking like that, and I wouldn't come to claim what's mine if you taunted me."

I plant my hands on my hips. "And I keep telling you. I'm not yours, Ford." I take a step closer to him. "If I want to fuck half the guys in this bar, you can't stop me. If I want to fuck half the men in this state, that's my choice. I don't belong to anyone, least of all, you."

He stalks forward and pins me against the sink, caging me in with his arms, his eyes drilling into mine, making my pulse soar with his closeness. "Then why did you text me? Was it simply to tease? You're the one who said you had something for me. Was that not an invitation?"

I lift my chin in indignation. "How do you know I didn't send that text to ten different guys, and you're just the first one to show up?"

Ford's jaw clenches, and I nearly want to smile seeing the jealousy roll over his features. He lifts his hand from the sink to wrap it around my throat, and my breath catches. He doesn't squeeze and fuck, am I so turned on that I'm practically a puddle. He leans even closer and drags the tip of his nose up my jaw until his mouth is next to my ear. "Is that true?"

"What's it matter? You showed up."

"Because I already told you I don't share, Josie. If I walk out of this bathroom after I fuck you and ten other guys are waiting their turn, it won't end well for anyone."

"You're such a caveman."

"And you're infuriating. Answer the fucking question."

I don't say anything and instead, run my hand up the inside

of his thigh and over the sizable bulge in his jeans. I stroke him through the fabric, and he huffs a breath. "I didn't text anyone else," I admit.

He tilts my head to the side and scrapes his teeth down the side of my neck before licking back up the same path, making me gasp. "And have you let anyone else fuck you since I did?"

"What's it matter?"

He increases pressure on the sides of my throat and I let out a small moan. "Because I don't share, Josie. I already told you, I didn't give a fuck who you date, but mine is the only cock allowed to get you off. That doesn't change just because you needed to figure shit out. Answer the fucking question."

"No," I reply honestly.

He releases my throat and takes my chin in his hand, forcing me to look at him. "Good." He crashes his bourbon-laced mouth to mine and, in the next breath has me lifted off the floor and deposited on the edge of the metal sink. Ford steps between my knees and runs his hands up the outsides of my thighs, squeezing and kneading almost painfully in his ascent.

I hurriedly work the buckle of his belt and fastenings on his jeans before dipping my hand into his boxers and giving him a rough stroke. Ford groans and breaks our kiss, bending to trail his mouth down my chest, bringing one hand up to drag the fabric of my dress off my shoulder and freeing my breast. He grips it and sucks the nipple with an audible *pop* as he pulls his lips off, causing me to cry out with the intensity of the sensation.

Ford nips and sucks the flesh of my breast, and I'm sure I'll have several hickeys tomorrow. "Take out my cock, Josie," he commands, and I quickly obey, continuing to work his length. He releases my breast to dig into his back pocket to retrieve his wallet. He fishes out a condom before returning the wallet to his pocket and ripping the foil with his teeth. I can't help but notice it's not a latex condom, and the thought that he remembered makes my chest fill with warmth, but I push it away.

He makes quick work of rolling it down over his cock and runs his hand up the inside of my thigh. He pushes my panties to the side just before slamming himself to the base, nearly causing me to fall into the basin of the sink. Only his other arm wrapped around my waist keeps me in place. I moan as he pulls out almost to the tip and drives back in, setting a brutal pace, and I can only hold on to the edge of the sink to keep from falling apart immediately.

Ford brings the hand not currently holding me in place up to grip my chin. "You want to be fucked in public? I can do that. You want to dance with other guys and let them get you hot? I don't give a fuck. You want to summon me to a bar just to get you off? Hey, if I'm free, I'll show up. You want to pretend like you've not thought about me for a week? You go right ahead, even though we both know it was the best sex of your life, and you've missed me."

"I asked you here to fuck me, not lecture me. Shut up."

He gives me a wicked grin. "Such a mouth you've got on you. If you can still talk, I must not be doing a good job." He drops his hand from my chin and hooks it under my knee, lifting it to press farther back. I nearly scream with the change in angle, and only Ford's mouth covering mine muffles the sound.

"Fuck," I whine, and he huffs a laugh.

He drags his mouth back to my ear, and his voice is low and husky when he speaks. "You want to only call me when you're horny? That's fine. You want to pretend like you don't like me? I don't care. But make no mistake; when you get off tonight, it'll be because I allow it. And you're going to beg for it. I'll let you scream loud enough for this entire fucking bar to hear how hard I pound into you; how well you take my cock. And as long as

I'm the one fucking you, you are mine, Josie. This body; this cunt? They're mine. Say it." I let out a high moan, and honestly, I'm not sure I could form words if I tried. "What's the matter, Josie; cat got your tongue?"

He slows his thrusts, and Ford kisses me as I gasp with the change. Wanting to keep this contact with him, I wrap my arms around his neck to hold him in place, my breaths coming in ragged exhales as I get closer and closer to my orgasm. "Say it, Josie," he commands against my lips.

"Please, Ford."

"Say it," he demands through gritted teeth and bends to flick my nipple with his tongue before sucking it hard enough to make me cry out.

"Fuck, Ford," I moan.

"Tell." *Thrust.* "Me." *Thrust.* "Who." *Thrust.* "This." *Thrust.* "Pussy." *Thrust.* "Belongs." *Thrust.* "To."

He brings his face back to mine, his brows pinched in concentration, a sheen of sweat popping on his forehead. His jaw is clenched in obvious frustration and he narrows his eyes. "You want to come?"

I give him a jerky nod. "Please." I'm aware I'm begging. With my mind so far gone with need, I don't have the where-withal to question it.

He gives me a smug smile. "Say it. Tell me what you already know, what you've known since I kissed you. Like I said, you can pretend you don't like me. You don't have to like me to want me to fuck you—to claim you. Because if you think I'm doing anything other than that in this moment, you are mistaken, Josie. You are mine. Right now, if that just means this sweet pussy, I'll take it. But you will admit it, and I want to hear you say it."

And fuck, he's right. Damn him. I do want him to claim me. My body, anyway.

"Fucking say it." His mask of control seems to be slipping, and I know from experience that I won't be able to see him get off without it triggering my own release. But I also know he's got some wicked reserves of control and must be able to come at will and could probably last hours. He'd probably keep me in this bathroom right on the edge of oblivion until he was satisfied I'd been punished enough.

At this moment, though, I only want to get off. My brain can't focus on anything else. No one has ever been able to seemingly scramble my mind the way Ford can. And the only thought I have, the word leaving my mouth in the same instance, is *yours*.

He smiles triumphantly before covering my mouth with his own for a deep kiss, his tongue sweeping against mine, seeming to claim this part of me as well. He presses my knee back even farther, and I scream into our kiss when he hits that deep, sweet spot that must've been created for only him to find. My orgasm explodes, and Ford breaks his mouth from mine. "Fuck, yes. Give it to me, Josie."

It seems like it will never stop, even as I dig my nails into his shoulder, my body quaking as he bucks his hips one final time with a grunt, his forehead falling to mine, his bourbon-soaked breath huffing across my face.

Ford pulls out with a groan and gently lowers my leg back to the edge of the sink. He discards the condom and does up his jeans before dropping a kiss onto my lips and giving my ass a possessive squeeze. He doesn't say another word and steps out of the bathroom, leaving me to have an existential crisis about what it means if I'm *his*, even if only physically.

CHAPTER ELEVEN

FORD

It is not my custom to abandon a woman after a fuck. Especially not one like that. It was risky for me to do it, knowing there was a possibility that someone might recognize me. I should've demanded Josie leave with me, but I could see it in her eyes that she wouldn't have gone. She has a defiant streak, and I'd be lying if I said I didn't love it. But I need her to know she's mine. Fuck if I know why I'm so determined to prove that point. But for some reason, I want to prove it to Josie. I want her, even if only physically, for now. And if all she wants is physical, that doesn't include cuddling in a bathroom after a bar booty call.

The past week without communication has been hell. I've been distracted and broody, and I don't like it. Part of me thought I'd blown it with her and she'd never reach back out, but when I saw her text pop up on my phone as I was dropping Emerson back off at Piper's after supper, I nearly wanted to throw my fist in the air in triumph.

But even after she sent me the photo of the bar, it took me a few minutes to locate the correct one online and another half-hour to make the trek across town after a quick stop at CVS to get some condoms; wishful thinking and all that.

And now, as I sit at the bar once more after leaving the bathroom, another double of Maker's in my hand, I wonder if I should go back to check on her. But I already know I won't.

Five minutes later, when Josie returns to her stool at the bar and orders another vodka cranberry, she pretends not to notice me. She's perfectly put together once again, and I'm now regretting that I wore a condom since the thought of her sitting at this bar for the remainder of her time here with my cum dripping down her thighs sends such a spike of territorial pride through me, it's enough to have my cock lengthening in my jeans again.

When the bartender delivers her drink, she gestures to me. "You can put his on my tab, Lou." Lou simply nods and returns to making drinks for other patrons.

I turn to face Josie then. "You're not buying my drink."

She lifts a brow. "It's the least I can do. You're sure as shit not getting your *aftercare* tonight, so let your bourbon comfort you." She lifts her chin in defiance, daring me to object.

I shrug. "Whatever you want, Freckles." I down my drink in one gulp and set the glass on the bar. "Thanks for the drink. And the fuck." I stand, and Josie's jaw clenches, but she makes no move to stop me as I back away from the bar. Sighing, I turn to go, brushing off offers of dances as I wind my way through the crowd toward the door.

As the seconds tick by and the bourbon settles more fully into my system, I realize I'm too buzzed to drive, despite only having two drinks. And although I don't plan on leaving until I'm sober, I still climb behind the wheel of my 4Runner. I drag my hand down my face before fishing around in my gym duffle until I come up with my water bottle, draining the half-gallon still left in it.

Knowing there's nothing left for me to do but wait, I lean my head back against the seat and close my eyes. A moment later, when my phone buzzes in my pocket, I'm alert, hoping it's Josie wanting to actually talk. Or, invite me back to her house. I don't much care which.

> Luke: Remind me that parenting gets easier. I'm currently running on day three with no sleep. Layla is a weepy mess, and my mother-in-law keeps reminding me how much I'm fucking up with the babies. Babies who I still can't tell apart.

Despite how things are going for me, I can console myself that I'm not currently raising newborn triplets. Knowing Luke wouldn't be texting me if he probably wasn't sneaking away for a few minutes of peace, I click his name to call him. He answers on the first ring. "Help."

"It gets better," I reply. "I'm not sure when, but that's what they tell me."

"You're no help at all; you know that?" He sighs. "Tell me something that will make me feel better about my life."

"I'm currently sitting in the parking lot of a bar because I'm too buzzed to drive home. I can't go back inside because Josie's there, and in spite of the fact that I fucked her within an inch of her life in the bathroom, she's pissed."

"Okay, that doesn't actually make me feel better. That might make me feel worse. Because while you're apparently having hot bar bathroom sex, I can't remember the last time I had sex, and it will probably be months before I'm fucking anything except my hand. So, you can fuck your story, Ford." After a beat, he asks, "Why is she pissed?"

"Because I made her tell me she's mine and wouldn't let her get off until she said it."

He snorts a laugh down the line. "Wow. I swear, you and

your kinks. So, she's not impressed with your need to be dominant?"

I sigh. "I don't know. Honestly, I think she likes it, and it weirds her out. She's so outspoken and opinionated, I think it's hard for her to reconcile liking that she has to give up control. Hopefully, she figures her shit out."

"What if she doesn't?"

"Who knows? I haven't met anyone else who's piqued my interest like her, though, so it looks like I'll be fucking my hand, too."

Changing the subject, he asks, "You have plans for Thanksgiving?"

"Piper and Conrad invited me over. Mom and Dad are going on a cruise, so I'll probably take them up on their offer so I can spend the day with Emmy."

"How is my goddaughter? You going to bring her out with you when you come to meet the babies?"

"Yeah, I've got a few days after Christmas between games, so we'll come out then."

"Good. Hopefully, we'll all be over the crying, and my wife won't hate me anymore. Pretty sure she'll never forgive me for knocking her up extra good."

I huff a laugh. "Well, get a vasectomy so she doesn't have to worry about it happening again."

"Trust me, I'm thinking about it." He says something else, but it's muffled, and a moment later, he sounds clearer again. "Gotta go. Talk to you later."

"Okay. Get some rest."

"Afraid that's a pipe dream, my friend." He disconnects the call, and I close my eyes again, willing my body to sober up.

Sometime later, I'm about to doze off when someone knocks on my passenger window. I jerk to alertness and blink rapidly as Josie's face comes into focus. I turn the ignition over to roll the window down and look at her, expectant. Her arms are folded and she's biting her lip, apprehension radiating off her. "What's wrong?" I ask, worry replacing my annoyance.

She sighs. "Can you take me home? Hensley thought I left and already went home. I don't like to Uber when I'm by myself. Normally, I'd call Jess, but you're here already. If you can't, I'll call him."

Knowing I'd never be able to live with myself if I left her standing out in the cold, I click the unlock button. "Get in." I roll the window back up as she climbs inside, but I don't start the car. "I'm still buzzed, so you'll have to wait a little while."

"Didn't picture you as such a lightweight. Two drinks are your limit, huh?"

"Actually, they were doubles, so more like four. Supper wasn't very carb-heavy, so I didn't have much on my stomach to absorb the booze."

"Do you want me to drive?"

"How many drinks have you had?" I ask, knowing full well she's probably tipsier than I am.

"Five. Plus two shots."

I scoff. "Then no. We'll wait."

She sighs and looks out the window. I take in how beautiful she is, even though I'd prefer her in simple jeans and a sweater, her hair falling down around her shoulders, not up in this severe high ponytail. And since we don't have anything better to do than talk right now, I ask, "Was it your plan all along to call me from the bar? Fulfill some fantasy of hooking up in the bathroom?"

She eyes me, her brow ticking up. "You think that's the first time I've ever had sex in a bar bathroom?"

"Yes," I say, no hint of arrogance or anything other than the genuine belief that this is the truth. "Am I wrong?"

"No," she admits.

A jolt of primal satisfaction surges through my system, but I do my best not to gloat. "You still didn't answer my question. Was it a plan?"

"No. I wasn't planning on reaching out to you again. But I was horny and buzzed, so I figured I could do worse."

"At least you're honest," I say with a snort.

She narrows her eyes. "You didn't have to come."

"What was it you said? 'I was horny and figured I could do worse'? That goes both ways, sweetheart."

"Don't *sweetheart* me."

"Then don't pretend like you want anyone besides me right now. Don't pretend I can't read you like a fucking book, Josie. Don't pretend you're not glad I was still here so you might have another chance for me to fuck you again when I take you home."

She folds her arms. "Yeah, I think not. I'm good for the night. There will be no *again*."

Exasperated and confused, I can't stop myself from saying, "I don't get why you're acting like this. I already told you that if all you wanted was a physical relationship, I was good with it. Even though I'd be happy to take you on dates and actually get to know you, if all you want is to fuck, I can do it. So, why do you fight against something you obviously want?"

"I don't *want* anything except to go home. Are you sober enough to take me home yet?"

"Why, antsy to get home so you can drag me inside and let me make you scream my name again?"

"Keep dreaming, pal."

Heaving a resigned sigh, I start the car. "Okay."

Ten silent minutes later, I'm pulling in at Josie's house. I don't cut the engine, unsure if she'd even let me walk her to the door, and I'm not really feeling up to being rejected. After a moment, when she doesn't get out, I turn to her. "Do you want me to walk you to the door?"

"No."

"Okay," I reply, and even though I was expecting the answer, it stings.

After a beat, she blows out a breath. "I don't know how to do this."

"Do what?" I ask, confused.

She gestures between us. "This. Us."

I snort a frustrated laugh. "You've made it pretty clear there is no *us*, Josie."

"Well, you said you're fine with only a physical relationship."

"I am."

"But in that same breath, you said you wanted to get to know me and take me on dates."

"Because I'd be fine with that, too."

"Well, I'm not. I don't do relationships; I already told you."

I heave a sigh. "Okay. So what do you want? Just to fuck? I told you it's fine if that's all you wanted. But if you're fucking me, there is no one else. That's a hard limit for me."

Her jaw clenches. "Well, I have some hard limits, too. And a safe word."

"Okay."

"I don't want to hear about your job or your kid. I don't need to know those parts of your life."

I frown. "Okay."

"And if it's not on my list, assume it's not on the table."

"What list?"

She pulls out her phone and taps on the screen, and seconds later, my phone buzzes in my pocket. "That list." Realization dawns and my pulse ticks up. "And outside the bedroom, I don't belong to you."

I huff an amused laugh. "That's never been up for debate."
When her brow furrows in confusion, I shake my head. "I don't
own you, Josie. What we do in the bedroom doesn't translate to
the real world. I have no issues with how confident and inde-
pendent you are during the day. I wouldn't be attracted to you
if you weren't.

"Make no mistake, it's a huge turn-on for me to watch you
give up control when we have sex, but I don't own you. If
anything, your giving up control proves that you have the
power in this dynamic. I can't do anything unless you let me,
and you have the power to stop things at any time."

She blinks, absorbing my words. After a beat, she searches
my face. "So you really don't have a problem with this only
being for sex? You won't get all alpha and possessive if you see
me out with another guy?"

I push down the jealousy that surges forth and shake my
head. "No. I told you, you want to see other people, I don't care.
But I'm the only one you sleep with."

She frowns. "Why would you be okay with that?"

"Because I like fucking you, Josie. I'm fine with it if that's
all you want for now. And unless and until one or both of us
decides this doesn't work, I can be content with knowing I'm
the only one who gets to share your bed."

"Okay."

"Okay," I echo.

Josie bites her lip. "Do you still want your aftercare? I think
you're owed."

I lift a brow and project nonchalance, even though I'd love
nothing more at this moment than to take her to bed again. "I
thought my bourbon was the only aftercare I was getting
tonight."

She rolls her eyes. "Shut up and come inside." She doesn't
wait for my response and hops out of the vehicle.

CHAPTER TWELVE

FORD

When I follow Josie through the front door, I'm greeted by a barking Gouda, whom I squat down to pet after toeing off my shoes by the door. As I stand, Josie gestures to the sofa. "That's Jess. Jess, Ford."

Jess gives me one of those universal guy head jerks. "Hey, man."

I dip my chin. "Good to meet you."

He narrows his eyes. "Have we met before?"

I shake my head, wondering if this is the moment when I'm found out. "Not that I know of."

Jess shrugs. "Maybe you just have one of those faces. I swear, you look so familiar."

"Maybe," I agree, although I know it's only a matter of time before I have to tell Josie who I am or someone in her life does it for me.

Josie clears her throat and grabs my hand. "Goodnight, Jess." It's not until we're halfway to her bedroom that I realize we've never held hands. I've fucked this woman and slept with her, but I've never held her hand. And knowing what she's in this thing for and what she expects from me, I like the hand-holding more than I probably have a right to.

"Goodnight," I hear Jess call as we enter Josie's room and she shuts the door.

She sighs and sits on her bed to unzip her boots and slip them off, flexing her toes as they're finally free from the confines of the heels. "So, that was Jess."

"I gathered," I say with a grin. "You know, from the 'that's Jess' part of things." I don't move from my spot against the door and fold my arms as I watch her shed the "club girl" façade. She pulls a makeup wipe from the vanity on the far side of the room and swipes it over her face, revealing those freckles I'm so fond of.

Once her face is clean, she pats on some moisturizer, pulls her hair down, and rubs her scalp. Lastly, she tugs the dress off her shoulders and shoves it over her hips before tossing it into a nearby hamper, leaving her only in a red lace thong, which she loses as well, affording me the sight of her naked; my cock swiftly reminding me of its need for her.

She moves around the room as if I'm not even present and retrieves a nightgown from her dresser and pulls it over her head before turning the covers down on her bed, crawling under the blankets, and plugging up her phone. It's only then that she glances up at me. "You going to stand guard all night, or are you planning on coming to get your *aftercare?*"

I nod and push off the door, unbuttoning my shirt and hanging it over the back of a chair before shucking my jeans and socks, leaving me only in my boxers. "Although, you can call it what it is, Josie: cuddling. It's okay if you want it, too."

Her jaw clenches, and I think she will protest, but she says nothing as I join her in the bed. "Do you have to be up early?" she asks after a beat.

I shake my head. "I don't have anything until the afternoon."

"You don't work in the mornings?"

"You're asking about my job?"

"Never mind. Don't tell me."

I huff a laugh. "Okay. Can I ask about your job?"

"No."

"Do you sell pictures of your feet on the internet?"

She laughs, surprised by my question. "No, but if I did, would it matter?"

I shake my head. "No. So long as what you do makes you happy, I don't care what it is. Does it?"

She looks up, thinking for a moment. "Yeah."

And when she doesn't elaborate, I nod. "Okay. So, is it only my job and my daughter you don't want to know about? Like, can we talk about other stuff?"

"Depends on what it is, I guess. I reserve the right to call an audible on the play."

"Football fan?"

She shrugs. "Not really. My dad and grandfather are. You pick up certain lingo. You?"

"Not really. My dad is also a football fan. Team?"

"University of Tennessee, duh."

I smile, nodding. "Ah, SEC. Of course. I should've known. So, no NFL teams?"

"Nah. You?"

"Well, considering I'm from Minnesota, it's safe to say we're firmly settled in Vikings territory. Dad has season tickets."

"I see. And do you go to the games with him when you're there?"

"Some. Not much. Not really a football fan. My uncle usually goes with him."

"So, your parents are still in Minnesota?" she asks, and somehow, I'm able to hide my pleasant surprise that she wants to know anything at all about me. But I'm not about to question it, and I'm curious to see how far she'll take her line of questioning.

"Yeah. Although they came to visit a lot when I was in San Jose. Did you go to college?"

"Yeah. University of Tennessee. You?"

"Yeah. University of Denver. Major?"

"Finance. You?"

I'm surprised since she doesn't really strike me as the banker type, but simply answer her question. "Leadership and organization."

She considers my answer. "Okay."

"Do you have any hobbies?" Josie laughs. "What?" I ask, confused about why she's laughing.

"It's just funny, is all. You seem to know how to read me, and you now have a list of all my kinks and yet, you know almost nothing about me."

I shake my head and almost tell her it's not for lack of trying on my part. "You're right; I don't. So fill me in. Hobbies?"

"Are you a narc?"

I frown. "What kind of question is that?"

"If you're a cop, you have to tell me. It's the law."

I snort a surprised laugh. "No. I'm not a cop."

"Okay, then I can tell you. I make moonshine."

"Moonshine? *That's* your hobby?"

She nods. "Yeah."

"Like, legit moonshine? Like what you'd see in the movies? With all the copper tubes and—." I gesture, trying to depict the large metal device I can't remember the name of. "What's it called?"

"A still?"

I nod. "Yeah, a still. You make moonshine. In a still? Do you put it in those jugs with the X-X-X on them?"

Josie laughs. "No. We store it in quart jars and put them in cases."

"We?"

"Pap. My grandfather. It's his still. I just pitch in, but I actually really enjoy it."

"Okay, but making moonshine's not really illegal, is it?"

"Not for personal consumption, it's not."

"But you all don't only make it for personal consumption, do you?"

"Sure we do," she says with a wink.

I can't help but grin. "Well, well. Who knew I was sleeping with an outlaw? Do you have any here? Will it knock me on my ass if I drink it?"

"The stuff Pap keeps back for himself will, no question. We also do flavored shine, too. Apple pie is a big hit." She reaches over the side of her bed, opens a drawer, produces a jar of amber-colored liquid, and extends it to me."

I take the offered jar. "Is this apple pie?"

"Yeah."

I screw off the lid and bring the jar to my lips, the stout scent of cinnamon hitting my nose. I take a tentative sip, tasting notes of apple, cinnamon, and cloves as the liquor warms the back of my throat. And while it's smooth, it still packs a punch, and I cough, making Josie laugh. I pass the jar back to her, and she takes a long sip before recapping it and returning it to the drawer.

"Man, that's pretty good."

"Apple pie is Ada's and my favorite. It's about seventy-proof, so it's definitely dangerous after the first few shots."

"And you can make all of it all by yourself?" I find the prospect of Josie manufacturing liquor to be fascinating.

"Yeah. Pap started teaching all of us when we were in our early twenties. There's still so much I don't know, but I think between Silas and me and now Ada, we could make a decent batch. Cole seemed to have it down to a science, but his brain was always so much better at stuff like that than Si's and mine." She smiles, but it's sad, and she pulls her knees up to her chest and rests her chin on her knee. After a beat, she sighs and turns her head toward me. "Do you have hobbies?"

I try to think of a hobby that doesn't revolve around Emerson or hockey, and it's a short list. "Reading. Cooking. Working out."

She snorts and rolls her eyes. "I would've had no idea you work out. What do you read?"

"Fantasy mostly. For the escape."

"I see. Because your real life is so terrible, you need to get away?"

I shake my head. "No, I love my life. But you have to admit, dragons are pretty badass."

"Touché," she says with a smile. Her hair falls across her face, so I reach to tuck it behind her ear, her smile falling as she pulls away.

"What?" I ask, entirely puzzled by her reaction.

"Don't do that."

I huff a laugh. "Don't do what? Touch you with anything but the intent to fuck you? I'm not allowed to show you any kind of affection?"

"No."

I nod, suddenly angry and more than a little hurt. "Okay. I won't do it again." I lie down, unsure why she wanted me to stay if I'm not even allowed to be nice to her when we're alone. She shuts off the light, and when she lies down, I pull her into my arms. She sighs, and I remind her, "Aftercare, remember?"

"I know. That's why I'm not complaining. This is the one exception to the affection rule. But only because you earned it."

I huff a laugh and bury my nose in her hair. "Would it be possible to earn other types of affection from you?"

"No, probably not."

"Noted."

Josie's gone when I wake up. But then I remember this is her house, so I don't have the right to feel as though she's fled or anything like that. Checking my watch, I see it's nearly ten, and I've slept much later than usual. I rise from the bed and pull on my clothes, not bothering to button my shirt as I go across the hall to pee and use my finger to brush my teeth.

Stepping into the kitchen, I spy a full pot of coffee and search for a mug; sure, at any moment, Josie will come into the room and demand I leave. But since I also don't see Gouda, I assume she's taken the dog for a walk.

"Bandit Brickman," a masculine voice I recognize as belonging to Jess calls from behind my back, and I sigh before turning around to face him. He stands leaning against an opposite counter with his arms folded across his chest. "That's you, right? I knew last night you looked familiar."

I nod. "Yeah. Bandit's my middle name. My high school coach thought it was more memorable."

"They weren't wrong. Does Josie know?"

I shrug. "Not that I'm aware of. She specifically doesn't want to know anything about my job. She said so."

Jess rolls his eyes. "Because she thinks you're some corporate goon."

I frown. "I never said anything like that."

"Didn't you tell her you were in management when you met?"

Understanding, I nod. "Yeah. She didn't seem to know who I was, and I rarely get to be anonymous; I didn't want to give it up. But I never lied; I am in management."

"You're the head coach of a minor league hockey team."

I sip my coffee. "Are you going to tell her?"

Jess shakes his head, holding his hands up defensively. "Nope, it's not my place. But you should. It'll be a lot worse if you all are out together and you get recognized. You don't want her having to face that, do you?"

"I don't think that will be an issue," I say, a bitter edge to my tone.

"Why?"

"You should ask your roommate. Speaking of which, do you know where she is?"

"Running with Gouda, probably." He picks up a cup and takes a drink. "Can I give you a word of advice?"

"I'm not sure," I answer honestly.

For a beat, he looks as though he's weighing his words. "Josie is sorta like a feral cat. She'd rather bite and scratch than recognize that someone is trying to care for her. She's always been that way." He rakes his fingers through his hair and heaves a sigh. "All I can tell you is, be patient. I mean, if you want more than just her nights."

I nod. "Okay." I drain my mug, wash it at the sink, and return it to the cabinet. I pat my pockets to ensure I have all my things before buttoning my shirt and heading for the front door. As I slip my shoes on, I still feel Jess's eyes on me. "Right now, Josie only wants my nights, man. I'm not running out on her."

He's nodding when I look back at him. "I know. You don't owe me an explanation; she's a big girl."

And yet, as I slide behind the wheel of my Toyota without telling Josie goodbye or giving her a kiss or any of the many things I'd prefer to do before I leave, I still feel shitty. When I send her a text explaining that I have to go, and all she sends me is a thumbs-up emoji, I feel even worse.

CHAPTER THIRTEEN

JOSIE

On my way home from my run, I'm energized and antsy and envision pulling Ford into the shower with me. But then I receive his text, and disappointment shoots through me. I remind myself that this is what I wanted; no strings, no commitment, no expectations. So I simply send him a thumbs up and pretend I'm not bothered.

And in truth, I'm not sure why I am bothered. I should be happy that Ford wants to play by my rules. I should feel relieved since it means he doesn't push me to go on dates or meet his kid or make him breakfast. I should be fucking ecstatic since it means I get to have mind-blowing sex pretty much on demand.

But on the flip side, I shouldn't enjoy waking up with him as much as I do. I shouldn't enjoy watching him sleep or letting my eyes roam over his inked arms or wonder about that pair of skates on his ribs. I shouldn't wonder why he majored in leadership and organization or want to know what his favorite thing to cook is.

Jess is sitting in his usual spot at the kitchen table, staring at his laptop as I enter the house. He glances up at me and sighs as I take Gouda's leash off and ensure she has water. He eyes me as I pull off my beanie, tug up my sleeves, and pour myself another cup of coffee. "What?" I finally ask, unable to stand him looking at me like he is.

"You realize if the situation were reversed and Ford was acting the way you are, people would say he's being emotionally immature. And they'd say that you were accepting less than you deserve."

"Why? Just because I don't want to be in a committed relationship? It's such patriarchal bullshit. A man can want no strings, and it's no big deal. The minute a woman decides she never wants to get married or have kids or do anything society expects of us and instead decides she's just going to have fun, we're seen as frigid, closed-off sluts. Last I checked, Ford is a consenting adult. If he doesn't like the arrangement, he's free to leave it."

"Josie, are you serious? That man is half gone for you."

I roll my eyes. "No, he's not. And even if he were, I told him I don't want a relationship. He knew that before he stayed over last night."

"He stayed over, and y'all didn't have sex," Jess remarks and raises a brow.

Shrugging, I ask, "So?"

"Have you ever had someone stay over and it didn't include sex?"

"First of all, we had sex at the bar, for your information. And if you must know, I was planning on dragging him into the shower with me, but he's gone, isn't he?"

"You like him."

"He's a good lay. He's fun. He's fucking beautiful."

"Josie, I know it would be scary for you to let yourself commit to someone. After—."

I cut him off. "Stop. That has nothing to do with anything. Just because you're happy, Si and Ada are happy, and everyone is in love doesn't mean I want it. I don't. All I want is to live my life my way. So that includes not doing anything I don't want to do, ever again. And that means no commitment."

"Well, I'm just here to tell you, you're going to run off a great guy if you keep him at arm's length," he warns.

"You don't even know him."

"I know enough. I talked to him while you were out for your run. He's a nice guy. And he likes you. He's successful and smart, and I love you, but you're an idiot if you push him away. Because eventually, he's going to want more. I'm guessing he already does, right?"

I clench my jaw and blow out a breath through my nose. "It doesn't matter. He knows I'm not open to that."

"Well, someone else will be. I'd hate to see you keep yourself from having happiness all because you think you wouldn't get to keep it."

"Aren't you supposed to be a guy? When did you start giving heart-to-hearts?"

He levels me with a gaze. "Now who's buying into the patriarchal bullshit, Jos? I'm allowed to be emotionally mature. You should try it."

For the next few weeks, Ford's and my schedule don't align to where we both have a free night. The fact that he's busy during the weekends and most evenings isn't lost on me. I recognize he could be going on dates, same as me, but considering he said he doesn't sleep around, I get the feeling that if he decided to move on, he'd at least have a conversation with me.

But after four weeks without sex with Ford—or anyone but

myself, for that matter—I'm going out of my mind. Not even nightly rounds with my vibrator help to scratch the itch. No amount of distraction that includes Thanksgiving and shopping with Ada for Bea's Christmas gifts and being a house helper and making moonshine help get him off my mind.

I go on a few dates or let men buy me drinks when Hensely and I go out, but even as they do, all I can think about is Ford. I finally stop going out altogether because none of them even remotely pique my interest enough to begin to take my mind off him.

A few weeks before Christmas, I'm sitting at a doctor's appointment with Pap and he nudges me. "How are things with your man friend?"

"I haven't seen him in almost a month," I admit.

"Y'all get in a fight?"

I shake my head. "Our schedules haven't lined up. We've both been busy."

"Too busy to have *fun?*" he asks, pumping his eyebrows lasciviously.

I snort a laugh. "Pap, don't even start."

He rolls his eyes. "Oh, please. I remember what it's like to be in my thirties. Those were the days, I tell you. Beatrice and I couldn't keep our hands off of one another. It's a wonder you don't have twelve aunts and uncles."

"Ford's on the road a lot for work, I think. He sends me these anecdotes about whatever city he's in and the local food. I send him pictures of Gouda when she does something cute."

"So, y'all are still talking, then?"

"Yeah, mostly texting. If we talk, it's in the mornings." My phone vibrates, ringing, and I pull it out of my back pocket. "Speak of the devil."

"Well, answer it. I'm not so far gone that I can't hear them call my name. Figure out a way to see your friend."

I sigh and swipe the screen to answer. "Hello?"

"Hey. You busy?" Like it usually does, the silky sound of his voice sends a thrill through me. And although I do my best to ignore it, I'm pleased to hear from him.

"I am at the moment; why?"

"What about tonight?" Ford asks and sounds out of breath. I can't stop my mind from drifting to times when he's sounded like that when we're together and my poor, neglected vagina reminds me of its presence as an aching warmth spreads low in my belly.

"Are you running?"

"Just finished a workout. I had a few minutes before I had somewhere I needed to be, but my schedule freed up for tonight, so I was going to see if you were doing anything."

I already know I have nothing planned other than sitting on the couch binging *Buffy the Vampire Slayer* for the umpteenth time and eating my horniness. "Not much. I could probably move some things around. What did you have in mind?"

"Well, we both have to eat, and I'd already planned on cooking, so I was going to offer to cook for you." When I don't immediately respond, he continues. "It's not a date. It's just food, Josie. It's not even anything romantic, I swear. It's just a pot of soup. And I don't know about you, but I could probably bust a nut from a strong gust of wind, so you know, two birds and all."

I snort a laugh. "Yeah, I feel you. Jess is working tonight, so I don't want to leave Gouda."

"All right, I can come over. The soup takes about an hour."

"Can you do six?"

"Sure. Is white wine okay with you? It's best for the soup."

"That's fine."

"Sounds good. See you at six." He doesn't wait for a response and disconnects the call.

When I slide my phone back into my pocket, Pap is looking on, a smug smile on his face. "I guess you're getting a ticket to fun town tonight?"

I roll my eyes. "You're terrible."

And even knowing it's not a date, I still rush around the house after I drop Pap back at the farm and ensure everything is in order. I also grabbed a full jar of apple pie for Ford to have for himself, knowing how much he enjoyed it when he tasted it. Was that really over a month ago? Sweet Jesus, I'm antsy.

As if sensing my apprehension, Gouda paces the living room as the clock moves closer to Ford's arrival time. When there's a knock right at six, she barks excitedly and jumps up, planting her front paws on the door.

"You're going to have to back up so I can let him in." She obediently steps back from the door and sits a few feet away, her tail wagging furiously. I steel myself to see him, knowing exactly how good he'll look as I open the door. He has a large grocery bag in one hand and a backpack slung over his shoulder.

"Hi," he says with that great smile and those blue eyes crinkling at the edges. His red hair is shorter, as if he's just had it cut, and sweet lord, he smells delicious as he passes me, like something clean and earthy.

"Hi," I echo, trying to disguise the fact that my heart is racing and I'm practically drooling as I watch him walk toward the kitchen after he removes his shoes and drops his backpack by the door. He's wearing faded jeans and a gray, long-sleeved henley with the first couple of buttons undone, and I immediately want to rip his clothes off so I can see what I've been missing for the past month.

After he sets the grocery bag on the counter, he squats to finally give Gouda some attention and she eats it up. She looks up at him, all dopey-like, and who can blame her? Dude's a lady killer. Once my pooch has had her fill of pets, she trots off and curls up in her bed, and Ford rises to wash his hands before unloading the grocery bag.

He spots the jar of moonshine on the counter and quirks a brow. "Got a delivery you have to make?"

I shake my head. "No, that's for you. I was at the farm today and thought you might want some to have at home."

He grins. "Well, thanks, Freckles. That's sweet."

I shake my head. "Not sweet. Just an even trade for you cooking supper." I'm not sure if I say it as a reminder to myself or him. Probably both.

Ford nods but looks as though he wants to say something. A moment later, his expression neutralizes, and he walks over to put the jar in his backpack before returning to the kitchen.

He moves around my kitchen as if he knows where things are, and I simply watch. I examine the ingredients on the counter as he searches for and finds a cutting board, followed by a large chef's knife. Spread on the counter is a large bunch of kale, two potatoes, an onion, garlic, ground Italian sausage, carrots, celery, Italian seasoning, chicken stock, and heavy cream. He'd also stored a bottle of wine and a baker's box in the fridge as he unpacked.

"Are you glad to be back in town?"

He begins washing vegetables and smiles at me over his shoulder. "Yeah. But I also don't mind being on the road since you get to meet a lot of interesting people. I've always had to travel for work, so I'm used to it." He brings all the clean veggies over to chop.

Noticing he's not gotten the soup pot out, I squat down next to the stove to pull it from a lower cabinet. My position puts me squarely in the range of his groin, and I have to force myself not to stare at him. I stand and plunk the pot onto the stove eye and Ford smiles. "Thanks."

"Sure. Anything I can do to help?"

He looks over his ingredients. "Yeah, actually. If you want to get the sausage browning and break it down, that'd be great."

"All right." I wash my hands and return to the stove, turn on the range, and add olive oil to the bottom of the pot before dumping in the sausage and breaking it up into chunks with a wooden spoon. "So, what were you supposed to do tonight?"

He looks up at me from where he's dicing the onion. "What?"

"You said you had plans but that your schedule freed up. Were you supposed to do anything fun?"

He shakes his head. "No."

"So, what then?"

He pauses his chopping and sighs. "You don't want to know."

"Why?"

He frowns, but his tone is matter-of-fact. "Because you don't want to know about my daughter."

"Oh."

He returns to his task and I feel as though I've already ruined tonight. Ford is apparently unaffected by everything because he just continues working, and when the sausage is browned, he instructs me to pull the meat from the pot to add it back in later. He dumps in the chopped onion, celery, and carrots and lets them cook down.

"Big plans for Christmas?" he asks as he dumps in the garlic and seasonings a few minutes later.

I shake my head and walk to the fridge to pull out a couple of beers to have something to occupy my hands and mouth. If I keep standing here like a bump on a log, I will start to fidget, and Ford will think I'm nervous. And truth be told, I am, but I don't want him to know that.

After setting his next to the stove, I take a long pull of my beer. "Not really. We'll all get together at Pap's on Christmas Day. Dad will drink too much eggnog and Mom will have to take him home and put him in bed. Bea's at the age where she really loves all the movies, especially *How the Grinch Stole Christmas*, so we watch all the versions. Then Pap reads her the book, despite the old animated version being the book. Silas will probably steal Ada away and try to get her pregnant again."

"And what about you?"

"What about me?"

"What do you do while everyone is engaged in their version of events?"

"I just enjoy watching everything unfold." I don't add that I used to play Chubby Bunny with Cole and Ada, and when he died, so did the only tradition I cared about. Ford examines my face but doesn't say anything and drops the chopped potatoes into the pot before dumping in the chicken stock and adding the sausage back to the mix.

"And what's your favorite Christmas movie?"

"*White Christmas*," I answer honestly.

His brows rise in surprise. "Really?"

I huff a laugh. "Yeah, why?"

He shrugs. "You just don't seem like the musical type."

I frown. "What *type* do I seem like?"

"I'm not sure," he says. "Maybe the *Die Hard* type? You don't strike me as someone who likes romance movies."

I shake my head. "I'm not. Can't stand them." *Anymore.* "*White Christmas* is the exception. I used to watch it with Meemaw. She loved Bing Crosby. It's a good movie."

"*Meemaw?* Is that like a grandma?"

"Yes," I reply, rolling my eyes, "a meemaw is like a

grandma. Meemaw was Pap's wife. She died about seven years ago."

He nods. "Sorry to hear that. Was it the same thing that your brother had?"

"No. She had cancer. Cole inherited his HCM from our mom's side of the family. Meemaw was my dad's mom."

"Gotcha."

"Do you have big plans?"

He looks up, thinking, and he's quiet for a long moment. "My parents are coming in for a couple of days. I have to work, so I'll really only get Christmas Day with the family. A couple of days after Christmas, I'm going to San Jose. My best friend and his wife had triplets, and I haven't seen them yet, so I get to play Uncle Ford for a few days."

I blink rapidly. "Triplets? Oof. Damn."

He laughs. "Yeah. It was a buy-one-get-two situation. Luke said he was only trying to pull the goalie, not build a whole damn team the first time out. Well, not really the first time out. They'd been trying for years, went through a few rounds of failed IVF, and finally just gave up trying. Six months later, Layla was knocked up extra good. The girls are their miracles," he says with blatant affection.

"That's great," I say with a smile. "So, how long have y'all been friends?"

"Since we were four. His family moved into our neighborhood, and that was it; instant best friends."

I consider his words. "Wait, so he lives in San Jose? And you all lived in the same neighborhood growing up?"

"Yeah, we also went to college together and then got jobs with the same company. He's my brother."

"Wow."

"Aren't you and your sister-in-law like that?"

"Pretty much." I don't add that we're not as close as we

once were since she and Silas started spending time together after Cole died. "I also have my friend Hensley. And Jess."

He stirs the soup and dumps in the pint of heavy cream, along with the kale. "Hensley is the one who left you stranded at the bar, right?"

I shrug. "I wouldn't say she left me stranded. She saw us go into the bathroom and assumed we'd probably go home together anyway."

"I see." He focuses on the pot, and a soft smile pulls at the corners of his mouth. "Jess cares a lot about you."

"Yeah, he's a good friend."

"How come it didn't work out between the two of you? Didn't you say you dated in high school?"

"Yeah, we did. We were kids, so it's highly statistically unlikely we would've made it this far anyway, even if we had stayed together. Plus, he's got Brooklyn now, and they're great together. Looking back, we were probably always better as friends." I drain the rest of my beer. "What about you and your ex?"

He seems surprised by my question and, after a final stir of the pot, lowers the heat and opens his beer, stepping back to lean against the sink. He crosses his long, long legs at the ankle and looks very relaxed in my space. I wish I didn't like it so much.

He takes a pull from his bottle and scratches his chin. "Piper and I were better as friends. When she got pregnant, we weren't married. But we wanted to do what we thought was the right thing to give Emerson the best home, so we got married. And it turns out, Emerson was the only thing keeping us together. Like I said, better as friends."

"Are you still friends, or did the divorce kill that?"

He grins. "No, she's still one of my best friends. I set her and her fiancée up. He's my accountant. They're great together. He's wonderful to Emerson, so I can't ask for more than that."

I can't help but think that Piper must be a lucky woman. She got to share her life with Ford, and even after they split, he still cared enough about her to help her move on. I don't hope it will be that way for the two of us. Most likely, once Ford grows tired of me, I'll never see him again.

CHAPTER FOURTEEN

JOSIE

"Wow, that soup was delicious, Ford." I push my empty bowl away and sip my white wine.

Ford smiles, dipping his chin in thanks. "Glad you liked it. I also brought pie, but I don't think I'm up for that just yet."

I shake my head. "No, my tank is topped for now. Maybe later?"

"Sounds good."

I stand to ferry the dishes to the sink, and Gouda walks in and sits, letting out a single bark. I sigh. "Just a minute, girl."

"Does she need to go out? I can take her."

"We normally play fetch for a few minutes after supper. I'm sure at this point, she's developed some sort of pavlovian response to me doing dishes."

"Well, if you want to go play with her, I can wash up."

I shake my head. "No. You cooked. The least I can do is clean up. It'll only take a few minutes."

"I'll get her." He steps past me, squeezing my hip and dropping a kiss on my cheek as he goes. The motion is so mundane, and it catches me off guard. It's such an everyday, couple-y, affectionate thing that I've seen Silas and Ada, my parents, and even Jess and Brooklyn do, but I don't like how warmth floods my chest to have it happen to me.

Trying to focus on the task at hand rather than on watching a gorgeous guy play with my dog in the backyard, I dump the remainder of the soup in a glass storage bowl and stick it in the fridge before beginning to run some dishwater. I'm well aware that Jess's kitchen is equipped with a top-of-the-line dishwasher, but I've always preferred to hand wash. Call me old-fashioned or sentimental, but some of my best chats with Meemaw or Mom have happened over a sink full of dishes.

I methodically wash the bowls, silverware and utensils, wine glasses, and the soup pot, movement in the backyard once again catching my eye. Gouda is chasing Ford, and he zigs and zags, trying to evade her before he turns, taking her by surprise and scooping her into his arms. He runs what looks to be a victory lap around the yard, the fifty-pound dog still in his arms. When he sets her down, she runs around frantically, and this time, he seems to be chasing her. The smile on my face would very much be considered goofy.

Until I think about what I'm doing.

I'm not a romantic person, not by a long shot. Not anymore. I don't envision my life with me, Gouda, *and*. I don't think about what it might be like to wake up next to the same person for the rest of my life. I don't think about more than *tonight*. I certainly don't let men cook for me or ingratiate themselves to my dog. I don't let them sleep over, especially not when there was no sex right before. I don't do giddy or sappy. I don't ever find myself wanting to ask about a man's childhood or his college experience or his family. Because the less I know, the less I feel, and the less I feel, the less it hurts when they're gone.

Needing to remember exactly what this thing between Ford and me is supposed to be, I dry the dishes and put them away before retreating to my room. I strip naked, hoping he'll be so overcome with lust that he won't want to talk anymore, and I can escape into the oblivion that sex with him promises. I turn down the covers and climb into bed, leaving on only the single bedside lamp.

The back door opens, and the water at the kitchen sink runs. "Freckles? Where'd you go?"

Damn him and his nickname. And double damn how it sounds to my ears when it leaves his mouth. "In here," I call.

"I gave Gouda some more water. I don't know if you saw us, but we got a good work—." His words die as he walks into the bedroom and sees me on the bed. Stepping into the room and shutting the door, he doesn't take his eyes off me. "Now this is a nice surprise."

"Is it really a surprise, though?" I ask, my tone smug.

He sheds his shirt and I try to keep my breathing even, despite the searing heat that settles into my middle. He tugs off his socks, discarding them on top of his shirt before he makes quick work of ridding himself of his jeans. "I read over your list," he says as he shoves his boxers over his hips, his cock springing free. I swallow at the sight of him, my mouth watering. "It was very informative."

I scoot to the edge of the bed as he steps closer. "Is that so? See anything surprising?"

He shakes his head. "Not really." I drag my fingertips up the outsides of his thighs, and he exhales, his dick jerking with my touch. Ford grips my chin, his thumb dragging over my bottom lip. I open my mouth and suck it in and swirl my tongue around the tip. He lets out a soft groan, his chest rising swiftly before he yanks it out, dropping his hand to my throat. "Did you decide on a safe word?"

I nod as he runs his thumb up and down the side of my neck. "Arson."

His brows rise. "Interesting."

I shrug. "Nothing puts a stop to a party quite like it."

"True." He bends to press a kiss to my lips and gives my throat a gentle squeeze, and my breath catches. He smiles against my mouth and pulls back. "I love to hear you make that sound."

"That's because you get off on control."

"Yeah, I do. And you get off when you let go of it."

I hate that he knows this about me. I hate that he figured it out so shortly after we met. I hate that I crave him controlling me. I hate that the thought of him telling me what to do and deciding when I can or can't orgasm is such a turn-on for me. So much so that the simple thought of him commanding me to come has me pressing my thighs together and eyeing his cock with such a need to taste it that I'm practically drooling.

"You want to suck my cock, Josie? Or are you just admiring the view?" I dart my tongue out to wet my lips and look up at him. He gives me a wicked grin. "I'd be lying if I said I hadn't thought about it. What it might be like to see those pretty lips wrapped around my cock. What it might be like to feel you choke on it. The sound you'd make when you gag. To watch you swallow me down. Fuck, I'm dripping just talking about it."

He brings his hand back up to my chin and thumbs my bottom lip once more. "Why don't you be a good girl and lick it off." His words make my skin prickle and my heart rate tics up. His smile widens. "You like being called a good girl?" I narrow my eyes and he huffs a laugh. "It's okay. I won't tell anyone. No one has to know how much you get off on doing what I tell you. No one has to know exactly how hard you came when you finally admitted you were mine."

He bends down again until we're eye level. "And make no mistake, Josie, you are mine. Now, be *my* good girl and suck my cock." I release a shuddery breath as he rises and slides his hand around to the back of my neck, threading his fingers into the hair at the base of my skull. I half expect him to pull me forward, to fuck my mouth, but he doesn't. He simply watches as I lean in and lick the salty bead of precum off the blunt head of his dick.

I wrap my fingers around his shaft and lick a line from base to tip, and Ford groans through gritted teeth. And when I take him fully into my mouth, he exhales sharply. "Fuck, that's a pretty sight." I glance up at him, and his teeth are clamped into his bottom lip as I begin to move up and down.

A thought occurs to me that he might think he controls this, but I could very easily bring him to his knees, even while he stands. I could make him lose control. I could remind him that I belong to no one. And he can call me his all he wants, but I am no one's except my own.

So, I relax my throat and take him deep and he grunts, his hips bucking. "Jesus Christ," he huffs. And when I slide back up, I hollow my cheeks with the suction, and his grip on my hair grows nearly painful. I bring my eyes back to his face; his gaze is dark, his expression unreadable, and I lift one brow in amusement.

His nostrils flare and he pistons his hips as he holds my head in place. Inwardly, I smile, knowing that in this, I've won. "You like this, Josie? You like me fucking your mouth? Because, fuck, you know how to suck cock."

I chuckle and he groans, his hips bucking. Pulling my mouth off, I bring my hand in to stroke him fully. "You call *this* fucking my mouth, Ford?"

His brows rise, and he lets out a deep breath and jerks my head back, the sting in my scalp immediate but not enough to cause me to do more than hiss with the discomfort. He bends until his face is inches from mine. "So fucking mouthy."

"Aww, what's the matter, Ford? Afraid I can't handle it? Stop being a little bitch."

Color rises in his cheeks, and his jaw clenches as he pulls himself to his full height, his eyes never leaving mine. "A bitch, huh? You realize you're playing with fire, right?"

"I'm not afraid of you."

He grips my chin with his free hand, and his touch isn't gentle. And honestly, I don't want gentle. Gentle would make me think of things like feelings or romance or anything more than what I'm capable of giving Ford. "Pinch my leg if you need to safe out."

"I won't."

And then, he truly does fuck my mouth. He holds me in place, his movements rough, and I'm not a bit dignified as I take him deep over and over. Saliva rolls down my chin to drip onto my chest as I allow him to use me, my eyes not leaving his, even as they water and tears slide down my cheeks. Even as the noises emanating from my mouth sliding over his dick are sloppy and wet and anything but ladylike. Even as my jaw begins to ache and my scalp stings from his grip, I don't safe out. I simply grip his hips or bring my hand into the mix and give his balls a gentle squeeze, feeling smug when he groans, his eyes falling closed.

I lose track of time after that, focused only on my goal of making him come undone. And if he were to slip his hand between my thighs, he would find me soaked and aching with my own need, but I push it away, needing to have this victory for myself.

"Fuck, Josie. This mouth. Nice to see you can do more than smart off with it. Such a good girl, taking my cock like you were made for it. You're going to make me come; you know that?"

And again, his fucking words settle into my system like some kind of drug, and I hate it. I hate that I love it.

"You going to let me come in this pretty mouth? You going to swallow me down like the good girl I know you are?" And despite my efforts to the contrary, I can't bite back a moan, and Ford huffs a laugh. "That's what I thought. I want to watch you. I'm going to come, and you're going to thank me for it. You want it?" I nod and he groans. Seconds later, he yanks me off of him but holds me in place as he pumps his fist over his cock. "Open that smart mouth and take this load." I obey and stick my tongue out, and Ford grunts as streams of hot, salty cum coats my tongue and the inside of my mouth. "Don't you dare swallow it yet." Once he's finished, he bends down until we're eye level again. "Such a good girl for me. Now swallow every drop, Josie." I obey and he grins. "And now say thank you."

"Thank you, Ford," I say with a smile of my own as I mop my hand down my chin.

He plants his hands on either side of my hips and leans in to kiss the side of my neck. "What shall we do until I'm hard enough to fuck you properly?"

"Decisions, decisions."

He drops to his knees and trails his mouth down my chest before gripping my breasts and flicking his tongue over one nipple and then the other, making me sigh and clench with need. When I press my thighs together, Ford grins, tugging my nipple between his teeth hard enough that I grunt before swirling his tongue over the sting. "Did getting me off make you wet? If I spread your legs, will you be dripping for me? Does my girl like it when she swallows me down?"

"I liked watching you get off," I admit.

He braces his hands on my knees and pushes them apart. I don't fight him, and when he kisses his way down my stomach, I plant my hands behind me and recline on the mattress. He nips at the skin next to my belly button and looks up at me. "Did you like sucking my cock?"

"Yes."

"Is that because even though it's considered giving service, you control the other person's pleasure?"

"Yeah."

He smiles and tugs my hips closer to the edge of the bed. "And now I get to be in control of yours." And because my aching need is so great, when he dips his head, burying his face in my pussy, I can only moan, my eyes practically rolling to the back of my head.

Ford groans against my clit. "Fuck, you needed this, didn't you? You're so fucking wet, Josie."

"Oh God, Ford. Shit."

He sucks my clit between his lips, and I gasp and thread my fingers through his hair. Thrusting his two middle fingers into me, he nips at my inner thigh. "You going to come for me, Josie? You're so close already, aren't you?"

"Yes. Fuck."

"Do you want to get off?"

"Please."

"Ooh, even a please. You know I like it when you beg." He raises his free hand and squeezes my breast, flicking my nipple with his middle finger. I'm so close; it would only take me seconds. But as soon as I'm almost there, he backs off, depriving me.

"Shit," I moan. He returns his mouth to my clit, and I nearly come off the bed with how close I am. I drag in lungfuls of air as I try to breathe when he crooks his fingers, rubbing over my g-spot. "Please, Ford. Fuck." Just before I go over again, he changes up his rhythm, and I whine.

He pulls his mouth off, and I gasp as he thumbs my clit and rises above me until we're at eye level. "Jesus, I love to hear you beg, Josie. Ask for it again, and I'll let you come."

I drag his mouth to mine, needing the extra point of contact. "Please, fuck. Please, Ford."

"That's my girl." He claims my mouth in a deep kiss, and this time, when I get close, he allows me to go over, my entire body seeming to shatter with the orgasm, and I scream, my thighs quaking with the impact. He slows our kiss and the movements of his fingers as if wanting to help me come down.

He steps back after a moment and joins me on the bed, pulling me with him when he lies down. His cock is hard again, but he makes no move to do anything with it. And even after I reach for it, my brain still foggy from endorphins, he stops my movements. "We have time."

As I come back to myself, lying in his arms with my head on his chest, hearing his heart thud steadily behind his ribs feels too nice, too couple-y, too feeling-y. So I roll away from him, shifting my hips back, grinding my ass against his erection. He slides his arm around my waist and kisses the side of my neck before nipping at my shoulder. Covering his hand with my own, I guide it between my legs and he groans. "You're insatiable, woman."

Wiggling my ass, I taunt, "What, are you tired?"

"You know better than that, Freckles."

"Then fuck me, Viking."

"Yes, ma'am," Ford replies with a chuckle. In one swift move, he has me rolled onto my back and pinned beneath him, his cock notched at my entrance. He searches my face, and for the briefest of seconds, I think about what it might be like not to have that barrier between us. I consider simply shifting my hips until he's inside me and how it might feel. Even though I can't get pregnant, I still don't have sex without a condom. Ever. And the fact that I'm even considering it has me snapping out of my trance and reaching to pull open the drawer to fish out a condom.

Disappointment flashes in Ford's gaze for only a blink before he rips the packet and rolls the condom down. And then, he's pushing inside me, and I sigh, my eyes falling closed. I rock my hips, and he groans, his hand coming up to grip my chin before he kisses me. "You feel so fucking good, Josie."

"Yeah," I agree. And, God, it feels good. Too good. Too much like I like him. Too much like it's real. Too much like wanting a future and dates and being happy to let him call me his. Too much like it would hurt if he weren't around anymore.

When his thrusts turn harder, I welcome it. And when his hand slides down to my throat, I welcome that, too. "Look at me, Josie."

I open my eyes, and his are hooded with need. He starts to pull his hand away, and I bring mine up to keep it in place, heat flickering in his gaze. "I trust you," I say, reassuring him. Because the truth is, I do. I trust him completely with my body, even if I'm incapable of trusting him with my heart.

Bracing my leg on his bicep, he pushes my knee back, hitting that deep, sweet spot and causing me to cry out. As I get closer to coming, the pressure on my throat increases. Ford's eyes stay on my face, his mask of control beginning to slip. "Fucking come. Now." His command is harsh, and it's the only extra push my body needs to come apart, the most intense climax I've ever experienced crashing through me with the power of a freight train. "That's right. Fuck, Josie."

I gasp as he releases his hold on my throat, and with a final pump of his hips, Ford grunts, his forehead dropping to my chest as he comes, his entire body shaking with his orgasm.

CHAPTER FIFTEEN

FORD

When I'm finally able to stand and go pee and return to the bedroom, I can tell something's up with Josie. But as sure as the mask of control I keep in place most of the time, one of indifference drops over her features, and she blinks up at me. "What kind of pie did you bring? And do you want to watch some TV?"

Caught off guard, I can only slip on my boxers and nod. "Okay. And it's chocolate cream."

"Sounds good." She hops off the bed and pulls a nightgown over her head. "I'm going to go pee. Do you care to serve up the pie?"

"All right. In the living room?"

"Sure." She leaves the room and heads across the hall, and I wonder if maybe I did something wrong. As sexed out as I am, I would've been content to simply pull Josie back into my arms and go to sleep. In fact, I'm not sure I'll be able to stay awake long enough to have pie, but she seems to have gotten a second wind, so who am I to argue? I'm happy to spend time with her, and maybe we can talk.

I dish out a piece of pie for us both and take them into the living room, and a few minutes later, she joins me on the sofa, pulling her slice of pie into her lap. Grabbing the remote, she flips through the channels until she comes to a rerun of *How I Met Your Mother*. "Have you watched this before?" she asks.

"Yeah. The whole series. You?"

"Yeah."

"So, what are your thoughts about the last season and how they tied everything together?"

She takes a bite of pie. "It's pretty accurate to life, I think. Guy spends his whole life waiting to meet *the one*, only to have her die and then end up with his best friend's girl."

Stunned by the bitterness I hear in her voice, I nearly flinch. "I think that's an oversimplification, don't you?"

"No, not really. You forget, I've seen that actually happen."

I nod, understanding. "With your brothers?"

She shrugs. "It wasn't like Ted and Barney and Robin, since Silas and Ada didn't get together before Cole and Ada. But in a way, yeah."

Josie sets her half-finished slice of pie on the coffee table and sighs. "Something wrong with your pie?" I ask.

"No. Lost my appetite. I'm tired." And without another word, she stands, takes her plate to the kitchen, and drops it in the sink before entering the bedroom. And while I'd love to find out why my question triggered her, I don't think she'd actually open up to me. And worse, she might ask me to leave, and I'd rather fall asleep with my body curled around hers than go to sleep without her, so I leave it alone.

This time, when I wake up in Josie's bed and roll over to see her still there and still asleep, I smile. And because I want to be just

Ford a little while longer before I have to slip on the Bandit mantle, I wrap my arms around her and pull her into my chest. She's facing me, and while she stirs for a moment, she drops back off into sleep, and I press a kiss to her forehead.

I'm almost back to sleep when my phone rings in the pocket of my jeans, and I sigh before rolling out of bed and fishing it out. Seeing it's Emerson, I swipe my thumb across the screen after clearing my throat. "Hey."

"Hey, Daddy. I'm supposed to take my driver's test today, and Conrad was going to take me because Mom has to work, but he had something come up. Are you busy?"

I glance at my watch to see it's after nine. "No. What time do you need to be there?"

"Eleven. I was going to see if we'd have time for one last lesson before I take the test."

I glance longingly at Josie's still sleeping form but answer, "Sure. I'll be there as soon as I can. Give me a half-hour."

"Thanks, Daddy. Love you."

"Love you, too." I disconnect the call and pull on my jeans and tug a clean tee shirt out of the backpack I brought with me into the bedroom when I finally came to bed last night, and swipe on some deodorant since I know I won't have time to shower with how long it will take me to get to Emerson. I shove my dirty shirt and socks into my bag and dig out my toothbrush before going across the hall to pee and brush my teeth.

When I return to the bedroom, Josie is beginning to stir, and I sit on the edge of the bed as I put on a clean pair of socks. "Leaving?" she asks with a yawn.

"Yeah. Sorry. I was going to cook you breakfast. Maybe next time." She doesn't say anything, and when I lean over to kiss her, she offers me her cheek. Hoping I hide how much the slight stings, I clear my throat and give her a tight smile. "All right. Well, I'll see you later."

"Sure. Be safe." She rolls back over, and I tell myself she's just still half-asleep and not that she didn't want to kiss me goodbye. God, I'm pathetic.

As I walk into the kitchen, Jess is sitting at the table nursing a cup of coffee. "Hey, man."

"Morning."

"Coffee?"

"No time. Gotta take my kid for her driver's test."

He blinks. "Driver's test? How old is your daughter?"

"Just turned sixteen. You know, the usual age for new drivers."

"Does Josie know how old she is?"

I sigh. "She specifically doesn't want to know about my kid, so, no. Why, you going to tell her?" My question comes out more annoyed than I intend, and I immediately regret it. Jess hasn't done anything wrong and doesn't deserve my ire.

"Hey, man, what's with the attitude?"

"Sorry. It's not you. I gotta go."

He gives me a sympathetic nod. "No problem. See you later."

"Maybe," I mutter as I slip on my shoes and walk out the door.

When I pull into Piper's driveway twenty minutes later, Emerson is waiting on the porch, scrolling through her phone. I park and climb from behind the wheel and leave the door open for her to get in. As I get into the passenger seat, I sigh but paste on a smile as soon as she's behind the wheel. "Thanks for this, Daddy. I know you like your sleep in the mornings. Sorry I woke you up."

I run my hand down her ponytail. "You didn't. And you know I'm happy to do whatever you need."

"Yes, I did," she says with a grin. "You had your sleepy voice when you answered the phone. Did you get in late? Mom and I were coming back from the movies around eleven and didn't see any lights on when we drove by your house."

"Something like that."

Her eyes widen. "Did you have a date?" she asks, hopeful.

No, definitely not a date. What Josie and I do is not dating. Despite how badly I want to do exactly that. "Just hung out with a friend." *Is Josie even a friend? Do I know enough about her to classify her as a friend?*

"Oh." She slumps, and I can tell she's bummed. "Have you found a date for Mom's wedding yet?"

"No. Like I said the last time you asked, I'll probably come alone. That way, I can dance with you all night."

She winces. "Sorry, Daddy, I have a date."

"I thought we decided we were going stag, kid? I feel betrayed."

Emerson shrugs. "Sorry, but when the cutest guy in the school shows interest, you jump on it."

"Just so long as you're not jumping on any part of him."

She screws up her face. "Daddy! I'm not talking about sex with you. Ugh."

"Well, you know what can happen when you're not careful."

She rolls her eyes. "Yes, yes. I'm aware. My very existence is a cautionary tale."

"My favorite one, kid," I say, squeezing her shoulder affectionately.

"But seriously, Daddy, you need to find a date for the wedding. You'll look lonely and pathetic if you don't have one."

Pretty sure I am lonely and pathetic at this point. Definitely pathetic. "I'll see what I can do."

Except for the everyday sporadic texts and photos we exchange, I don't hear from Josie for the next couple of weeks. And with the exception of a quick "*Merry Christmas. Be safe going to San Jose*" text, it's been radio silence. Well, except for the twice we've hooked up since then. And while still good, both instances were weird, daytime booty calls where I knew I wouldn't be spending the night.

I'm starting to feel used, and although I agreed to this only being a physical thing, it's starting to wear on me. Paired with the fact that Josie reveals practically nothing about herself or her family or her job, this thing is feeling more and more like I'm only good for seeking a release. Combine all that with the losing streak the team is on, and I'm in a fan-fucking-tastic mood as of late.

So, when Josie calls me instead of texts the day after New Year's, I almost don't answer. But considering I'm a pathetic simp and have accepted that I'm practically gone for her, I swipe the screen and project a chipper demeanor I don't currently feel. "Hey, Freckles."

"Hey. This might be a weird question, but do you know anything about ice skating?"

I would laugh if I weren't so caught off guard. "Uh, yeah. Why?"

She sighs. "Because Bea and I watched *The Mighty Ducks* last night, and she's now convinced she must learn to play hockey. I know it's presumptuous of me to assume you know anything about ice skating based on your tattoo alone, but here I am. I can't roller skate, let alone ice skate, so I know there's nothing I can teach her. I'm trying to score cool aunt points here."

"Aren't you the only aunt she has?"

"And your point is? She's only three, but I know this will be one of those core memories she will always look back on. And if she turns out to be the first woman in the history of the NHL, I want her to say it was all because I took her skating for the first time."

Yep, I'm totally gone for this woman. "So, for totally selfless reasons, I see."

"I'm so glad you get it."

"I do. But unfortunately, she wouldn't be the first female professional hockey player. There was a woman who played in an exhibition game back in the nineties. But she could be the second, for sure."

"Okay, well, thanks for squashing Bea's dream. Damn."

I can't help but laugh. "When are you wanting to take her skating?"

"Whenever. Silas and Ada come back from New York tomorrow, so hopefully before then, but I know it might be short notice for you."

"I don't have anything going on. Give me an hour? Or do you need more time than that?"

"No, that's fine. The rink is off Kingston Pike. Do you know the area?"

"I'll find it. See you then."

CHAPTER SIXTEEN

JOSIE

"Are we here?" Bea asks excitedly, from her booster seat as I'm pulling in at the ice skating rink. Thankfully, it's not busy at all. Maybe no one but Ford and Bea will be privy to the wreck I will be on the ice.

"Sure are, honeybee." I help my niece down from Ada's SUV and she obediently holds my hand as we cross the parking lot. I see Ford's 4Runner, so I know he's already arrived. When we get to the door and before I open it, I squat down in front of Bea. "Okay, honeybee. So, we're going to meet a friend of mine. He knows a lot more about ice skating than me, so he's going to give us a little lesson, okay?"

"Does he know about hockey? I want to know about hockey."

"I know; I'm not sure. We can ask him, okay? His name is Ford."

"Like Daddy's Bronco?"

I chuckle. "Exactly." I stand and open the door and we walk over to the rentals counter to get some skates. After paying and ensuring we have the right sizes, Bea and I walk over to a set of benches to change.

Looking out onto the ice, I stop short. Even in a ball cap and hoodie, I'd recognize Ford anywhere; as honed as I am to his body at this point. He moves across the ice like he owns it and glides at almost breakneck speed around the perimeter of the rink before spinning and skating backward just as quickly.

Bea tugs on my hand, bringing my attention back to her. "Are we going to put our skates on?"

"We sure are."

As I get our skates laced up after we step into the rink area proper, I shiver. I knew it would be cold, but I'm suddenly glad I'd insisted Bea wear her heavy coat, gloves, and knit cap. Ford smiles when he sees us and skates over to the entrance. When he's a few feet away, he skids sideways, shooting a spray of ice in our direction.

Bea squeals in delight and Ford squats down until they're eye level. "You must be Bea."

"And you're Bronco."

I snort a laugh and Ford stands and leans in toward me so Bea can't hear him. "Well, I appreciate the compliment, Freckles. That's the first time anyone's ever admitted I'm hung like a horse."

Heat licks up my neck, and my cheeks fill with color and I slug his shoulder. "Silas has an antique Ford Bronco. I told Bea your name was Ford. She's three."

He winks and squats back down to look at my niece. "Well, it's very nice to meet you, Bea. Your Aunt Josie says you want to learn to play hockey. Is that right?"

She nods enthusiastically, and he examines her skates. "Well, first, we need to make sure your skates are ready. If they're too loose around the ankle, you might get hurt. Can I check those laces for you?"

Bea backs up to a nearby bench and hops up. When Ford exits the ice, he pulls something out of a duffle bag right outside the rink. I realize they're blade guards and I frown. "You own your own skates?"

He shrugs. "I'm from Minnesota, Freckles; it's cold during the winter. What else are we going to do?" He jerks his head at the bench next to Bea. "I need to check your laces, too. I don't want to hear you whine if you twist your ankle."

"So bossy," I say with narrowed eyes, but I obey.

He takes a moment to tighten Bea's laces a bit more and ensure they're not too tight before doing the same for me, giving my calf a squeeze before standing. As we shuffle back toward the rink entrance, he slips off his blade guards and we all step onto the ice. "Okay, Bea, the first thing you'll want to know is when you fall, it'll hurt."

I pinch the bridge of my nose and try not to laugh. He points to his nose. "You see how my nose is all crooked?" She nods. "Falling on the ice hurts real bad sometimes."

Her eyes go wide and he smiles. "But that's okay. I won't let you fall today, all right?"

She nods again, and he positions his skates in a slight v-shape. "The next thing you want to know is that when you skate, you'll want to keep your skates about as wide as your shoulders and keep your knees bent." He points to his skates. "And you see how I have mine almost like a 'V'? You'll want to do that, too." He looks over at me. "You too, Freckles." I sigh and follow his instructions, hoping against hope I don't fall on my ass.

As he continues going over the basics, I'm struck with how patient he is with Bea and how well he explains things and doesn't seem to leave out any minute details. By the end of the lesson, I feel like I might actually know what I'm doing.

When Bea actually pushes off to skate, Ford skates backward right in front of her, keeping his promise to not let her fall and I can't resist taking my phone out to snap a quick picture and video to send to Silas and Ada.

Bea moves around like she's skated for months instead of only moments and after a few minutes, they skate over to where I'm glued to the edge, hanging on, still nervous to move away from the safety of the being able to reach out and grab the side.

"Come on, Jo-Jo; it's fun," my niece encourages.

"Yeah, Jo-Jo," Ford parrots. "Come on." He extends his hand out to me. "I won't let you fall either, Freckles." Jerking his chin out toward the ice, he grins.

I reluctantly push off the wall, trying to remember everything he's said, and he takes my hand in his. Apparently feeling brave, Bea skates a few feet ahead. "You act like you've done this before," I comment.

CHAPTER SEVENTEEN

JOSIE

"What, skated?"

"No, taught kids to skate," I clarify.

"I taught Emerson and some of her friends."

"You like it?" I ask, already knowing the answer.

"Skating? Love it."

"You can tell. You move across the ice like you own it."

"It used to feel that way," he says, and his tone is almost wistful.

"Thank you for doing this. I'm sure you had other stuff you'd rather be doing."

He lifts my gloved hand to his mouth and kisses the back. "Nope. Nothing else I'd rather do than hope you fall on your a-s-s so I can k-i-s-s it."

I laugh and he squeezes my hand before dropping it to skate a few feet ahead to where Bea is and he spins to skate backward in front of her. "Can you go real fast?" she asks him.

Ford nods. "I sure can. Wanna go fast with me?"

She looks up at him, an excited grin on her face. "Can I?"

"Of course." He skates toward her and scoops her up into

his arms and takes off, gaining speed, making her squeal with delight. Dear sweet baby Jesus, if I hadn't had my tubes tied, I might entertain the idea of having his baby. Good lord, he's looks good with a kid.

He probably wants more kids. He'll be able to find some great woman without shitty genes to give him perfect and gorgeous viking offspring. He'll find some great woman who isn't afraid of commitment and who works a respectable nine-to-five. That great woman will be happy to let him be affectionate with her and it won't make her feel weak. That great woman will be someone who's not broken. That great woman will never be me.

This is why I don't date and can't do anything more than hookups. This is why, when I've invited Ford over the past couple of times, it's not been at night. I can't *sleep* with him. It feels too much like something I'll never let myself have.

I really should break it off with him. He deserves so much better than me; someone who can be a mother-slash-stepmother. Someone who's content to be a corporate wife. He deserves someone who can be more than just a fuck. Because that's all I'll ever be.

By the time Ford and Bea have skated around the entire rink, I'm only a few feet farther than I was when they began. "Jo-Jo, did you see?" she asks when he sets her down. "We went super fast."

I nod. "I saw, honeybee. Was it fun?"

"So fun."

After another hour of skating, Bea's lips are turning blue and I can no longer feel my hands or feet. She whines as we exit the ice, but Ford nudges her as he dries the blades of his skates before changing into his street shoes and storing his skates. "You know what the best part of skating is?"

"What?"

"Hot chocolate," he says with a grin and wiggles his eyebrows.

Bea's eyes go wide and she looks at me. "Can we?"

"Sure. If I can close my hand around the cup," I say with a shiver. I turn to Ford. "Are you not freezing? All you have on is a hoodie."

He shakes his head. "Nah, I'm good." He stands and slings his duffle bag over his shoulder and holds out his hands. "Come on, ladies, hot chocolate's on me."

Once Bea and I put our shoes back on and return our skates, we sit at a table near the large roaring fire. Ford joins us with cups of cocoa for us all and hands my niece a smaller one with a lid. "I made sure hers isn't as hot as ours."

"Thank you," I reply, accepting my cup. I'm quiet for a while, content to let Bea and Ford carry the conversation, only chiming in when necessary and to laugh at appropriate times. All the while, I'm dying inside. Because all today proved was what I already suspected to be true: I'm in love with Ford. And fuck if I know what to do about it.

Hot chocolate drunk and unable to stall any longer, especially with how Bea is on her way to comatose in the chair next to me, I sigh. "Well, we should probably get going."

Ford stands when I do, and when I reach to lift Bea, he gets there first. "Here, I'll carry her out. I'm sure you're tired."

"I'm in good shape, but skating is a whole other animal."

He smiles and picks my niece up easily from her chair, laying her head on his shoulder. She wraps her arms around his neck and snuggles into him. Never have I been jealous of this little girl until this moment.

"It can be. But thanks for inviting me. I had a good time. Been a while since I gave any lessons."

"I'm sure if you needed a side hustle, they're always looking for excellent instructors."

He chuckles. "I'll have to think about that."

We make our way out to the parking lot and Ford looks around for my Mini and I point to Ada's Pathfinder. "I'm in Ada's SUV," I explain and click the fob to unlock the vehicle. I walk ahead and open the door so he can put Bea into her booster.

He buckles her in without needing any instruction and tugs her hat off her head and tosses it to the seat next to her before shutting the door. "Don't want her getting too hot."

"Thanks. You were great with her."

"She's a great kid. She looks just like you, by the way."

"Yeah, it does strangely appear as though Ada and I had the baby and not Silas and Ada," I say with a laugh.

"Well, she's beautiful, just like her aunt."

"Thanks." I don't know how to say goodbye after this. It's awkward because we're not dating. We're not really even friends, even if we're friendly. I sigh. "Well, I'm going to get her home."

He nods and shoves his hands in his pockets. "Sure. Let me know if she needs any other lessons; I'd be happy to pitch in."

"I will." I start to turn away, and he grabs my hand.

"Hey, I wanted to ask you something."

"Okay."

"Are you doing anything in a few weeks? On the twenty-third? It's a Sunday. In the evening."

When I pull my phone out, I see I am booked for a catering gig. Giving him an apologetic smile, I shake my head. "Sorry, I have to work."

He nods, dejected. "I understand. It was kinda short notice, anyway."

"Yeah. If something changes, I can let you know."

"Sure. That'd be great." He glances into the back window of the SUV and smiles at Bea's sleeping form. "I'll let you go."

He steps forward and drops a chaste kiss onto my cheek. "Be safe, Freckles."

And for some reason, this feels final, but I can't pinpoint why. "You, too, Ford."

He doesn't look back over his shoulder as he heads toward his SUV, and something in my chest twists as I slide behind the wheel. I know I won't call Ford again and I won't text him or return any he sends. I'll probably never find anyone else again, and that's okay. And broken I might be, but I know now I am capable of love and that is its own sort of victory, I suppose.

It's a quiet evening with Bea who, after supper and her bath, goes to bed like a dream, still exhausted from skating. I sit on Silas and Ada's couch in the house my brothers built for Ada with Gouda and their lab-mix rescue, Brutus, and a jar of moonshine. For tonight, I've opted for the fully leaded stuff and as I drink away my sorrows, I cry.

I look around this home. The home Ada sketched when she was a girl, Cole started as a surprise, and Silas finished as an enormous gesture to the two people he loved most in this world. My eye catches on the original sketch of the house hanging next to the fireplace that Cole took to the architect when he had the plans drawn up. Next to it is the painting Ada did of Silas up at Snowy's cabin when she started sketching again.

On the other side is a family photo taken in front of Pap's farmhouse, where so many of my childhood memories originate. Pap sits in a rocking chair with Bea in his lap, Ada and Silas behind the chair. Brutus looks on from beside the rocker. I'll never have a photo like this. Of me and a wonderful man and children. The best I can hope for is a long life for Gouda and many more years with Pap. But even those are dwindling.

He's nearly ninety. How much longer can I even hope to have him?

My phone dings from its spot next to me on the couch and it's a text from Ford. I clear it off without reading it, knowing if I open it, he'll see and it's best if I send a clear message that today was it. Does that make me a coward? Without a doubt. Can I do anything different? No.

On the coffee table is an old photo, and I pick it up. It's rare to see any photos that include both Cole and Ada, since it's probably weird now. I'm surprised to see that this is one of the four of us. Ada and I were about twelve, maybe, and Cole and Silas would have been around thirteen. We're all in bathing suits and standing in a line on the creek bank after one of our mud fights. Ada stands between Cole and Silas, and I'm on the end next to Cole.

It strikes me that although Ada and I were best friends and she was like a sister to me, once she and Cole got together, it was their show. Ada and I hung out, just like we do now, but she was no longer only mine. She was Cole's. And I suppose Silas felt that way, too, since he was in love with her that whole time. And now it's Ada and Silas's show.

And sure, I guess what I'm feeling can be called self pity, and I'd never resent Ada because she, more than anyone I've ever met, deserves to be loved. I love her dearly. But she and Silas got closure for Cole. They got their happy ending together. Because of Cole. All I got were these shitty genes and the knowledge that everyone you love dies and leaves you all alone.

The kicker is, I can't complain or wallow in the fact that I'm so jealous of what they have because then it sounds as though I'm unhappy for them when I'm not. And until we did the genetic testing when Cole got his diagnosis, I thought my life would look an awful lot like Ada's does now. I've accepted my lot in life. I've accepted that I'll never be a mother. So I'll be the best aunt this world has ever known. I've accepted that I'll probably never get married since most men want kids. Most men want women who aren't damaged and whiny because they didn't get a goodbye letter from their big brother when he knew he was probably not much longer for this world.

And I was fine. Perfectly fine with my acceptance of my lot in life until Ford had to step in and fuck up my *fine*. Because now that I know what it's like to love, how can I now be *fine* when the alternative is him? And how can I expect him to settle when he is so much better than that? When he deserves all his dreams—not a broken shell of the person I could have been.

CHAPTER EIGHTEEN

JOSIE

"All right, Josephine Campbell, you have wallowed in this bed long enough." Ada snatches the covers off of me and I have a sudden flash of me doing something very similar to her after Cole died. Guess our depression styles are pretty similar.

I jerk the covers back over my head. "Go away."

"Yeah. No. I think we both know that's not happening. If you don't get out of this bed and shower, I'll Jess and Silas come in and drag your stink ass across the hall."

She doesn't ask why I'm depressed because she already knows. I was so hungover when they got home the morning after ice skating—thank God they arrived before Bea was even out of bed—and I spilled everything to Ada. Well, not everything, because even hungover, I couldn't bring myself to say how jealous I am of what she and Silas have. But I told her how I was in love with Ford and how I needed to break it off with him.

And for the past two weeks, they've let me wallow. Aside from jobs I already had scheduled, I've stayed home and gotten drunk. A lot.

"Come on, Josie. We've got plans and you're coming. You even have a date."

I sit up and glare at her. "I do not have a date."

She nods. "Yes, you do. It doesn't have to be a 'real' date, but one of Silas's friends from college is in town and he has tickets to a hockey game and we're going. You're coming. You have got to get out of this house. I know what you're going through sucks, but it's a misery of your own making. If you called Ford, I'm sure y'all could talk this out. I'm sure he's as torn up as you that you've ghosted him."

"He'll be fine. He'll find some tall, viking princess to give him tall, perfect, viking babies."

"You don't even know if he wants babies, Josie. He already has one kid. Trust me, that's enough most of the time."

"You didn't see him with Bea. He was amazing and perfect. He was such a *dad*. I will not deprive him of that if he wants it. I l-love him too much to ask him to settle." Tears well in my eyes and Ada pulls me in for a hug.

"Oh, Josie. Again, you don't know what he wants because you haven't talked with him. You are a grown-ass woman and you're acting like a child. Now, get your ass out of this bed and get in the shower. You are going out. Over drinks after the game, we'll figure out how best for you to approach your problem. A problem you created."

And as much as I fought Ada and Silas about going out, I still showered and got dressed and did my hair and put on makeup to cover the massive dark circles under my eyes. Ada, Silas, Silas's friend, Wesley, who I'd met once when we were all in college, and me are all riding together in Ada's Pathfinder.

Wesley is perfectly pleasant company for an insurance

salesman. And not that there's anything wrong with insurance; I'm sure as hell glad we have it. But he doesn't seem to know how to take the salesman hat off. Or, apparently, the loafers. But I still smile and nod along as he explains the difference between whole and term life insurance. Honestly, to me, he sounds like the teacher from *Charlie Brown*.

Still, he's very nice. He opens doors and complimented me on my jeans and sweater and hair. When I said I was a glorified personal assistant and cater-waiter, he asked questions about my jobs and seemed genuinely interested. He bought over-priced popcorn and stadium beer and refused to let me pay him back. And despite how surly I've been, he's attempted to keep me engaged in conversation. Like I said, perfectly pleasant.

"So, do you know anything about hockey?" he asks as the players skate out onto the ice to warm up. I'm not exactly paying attention to more than my popcorn at the moment.

I shake my head. "No. Other than thinking it's kinda like soccer, but on ice?"

He laughs. And honestly, Wesley's a really good-looking guy. Maybe Hensley would like him. I make a mental note to give him her number. "Yeah, kinda. But it can get really violent. Lots of players have missing teeth, jacked up noses, perpetual broken fingers."

His mention of noses has me thinking of Ford's nose and its distinctive crook and I guzzle my beer. I realize a moment later, Wesley is still talking and I've been nodding along the entire time and I try to focus on what he's saying.

"But if you think about it, one of the most valuable players on the team is the goalie. Best offense is a good defense and all that. And honestly, Knoxville's got a pretty good team this season. They've gone through some coaching changes, but I think because their new coach was a goalie, he can think defen-sively, which Knoxville has lacked in recent seasons."

"You don't live here, but you follow Knoxville hockey? Not Nashville?"

He shakes his head. "Actually, I'm a San Jose fan, since that's where I'm from."

San Jose has me thinking of Ford and how he's from San Jose. Probably bad date etiquette to ask your current date if they know your recently ghosted fuck buddy, right? Right.

"San Jose's really struggling this season. Their goalie retired out of the blue to take a coaching position and their star center is out on paternity leave. Of course, who can blame him? His wife just had triplets a couple of months ago."

My ears perk up. "Triplets?"

Wesley nods. "Yeah, apparently all natural after they went through years of fertility treatments. When they did the press conference, he told everyone he was only trying to pull the goalie, not build half a damn team."

I choke on my beer, my stomach dropping. "What did you just say?"

He winces. "Sorry, that was a crude joke. I was just repeating what he said."

"What's his name?"

"Who, the player?" he asks, blatantly confused.

"Yeah, what's his name?"

Wesley frowns, surprised by my sudden interest in the player whose wife just gave birth to triplets. "Uh, Grenier. Luke Grenier."

My mouth goes dry and I try to remain calm. Ford's best friend's name is Luke and his wife just had triplets. And they live in fucking San Jose.

"Oh, yeah," Wesley continues, as if I'm not having some kind of existential crisis at the moment. "And the kicker is, the goalie took a coaching job here. Just out of the blue. Retired, making a shit ton of money because he was so good, to move to

Knoxville. He wasn't even injured or anything; just said it was time. Nothing against Knoxville, but you'd never catch me leaving the game before my time for a minor league coaching position. I'll tell you what, I won't be placing any bets on San Jose until they can prove that Brickman is replaceable. Not likely, if you ask me."

My heart trips over in my chest and I stop breathing for so long my head pounds. I gasp for breath and Wesley's expression morphs into one of concern. "Are you okay? Do you need some water? You're not looking so good."

"Did you say Brickman?"

He nods and looks at me as if there is something wrong with my ability to process information. "Yeah. Bandit Brickman. He's the coach." He gestures out toward the ice where the players are lining up and the announcer asks everyone to stand for the national anthem. "That's him. The guy in the suit. Tall, dark red hair. He's gotta be at least six-four."

"Six-six," I mumble as I look down onto the ice to see Ford standing with a clipboard, dressed in a suit and tie, looking entirely professional and fucking delicious. And I'm pretty sure I won't survive this night.

Ford is a hockey coach. He coaches hockey. Oh, my sweet Jesus, I told him he could get a side hustle as a skating coach. I am fucking dense. Ford isn't a corporate goon. He's a fucking hockey player. He's a goon of a completely different sort.

Silas nudges me on my other side as we sit, knocking me out of my thoughts. "Hey, doesn't that look like that guy from the bar? The one you've been—." His words die when he sees my face and realization dawns. "Oh. And you didn't know?"

"How the fuck would I know?" I hiss.

"You never talked about work? In almost three months, you never talked about your jobs?"

I shake my head. "I told him I didn't want to know; I

thought he worked for some corporation. He told me he was in 'management.'" I put the word in air quotes and Silas cracks up.

"Oh my God, this is fucking amazing. You've been sleeping with a professional athlete who's a multimillionaire and you had no clue?"

I slug his arm. "Keep your voice down. And no, I had no clue. Jesus Christ, I'm the most oblivious person on the planet." I put my head in my hands and my brother squeezes my shoulder.

"So, are you going to talk to him?"

"What am I going to say? 'Sorry I ghosted you, but I'm in love with you. And now that I found out you're not a corporate goon, we can be together?' He's going to assume it's because I think he's loaded. It doesn't change the fact that I'm not good enough for him, Silas. Most likely, he wants things I can't give him."

Silas's jaw clenches, and he shakes his head. "You're making a lot of fucking assumptions, Josie. You don't know what he wants because you haven't had the balls to talk to him because you're a fucking coward."

Tears spring to my eyes. "That's real easy for you to say, Si. You have everything you've ever wanted in your life. You have your dream girl, a beautiful, amazing kid, and the dream house."

His eyes turn hard. "And you know what it cost me. So don't pretend I have everything. I'd happily still be pining for Ada if it meant Cole could be here. Don't you fucking dare to pretend to be some martyr. Just because I chose not to let my grief stop me from being able to live doesn't mean I don't still grieve. You have no one to blame for your unhappiness except yourself, Josie. And if you let a great guy go because you're scared of *what if*, then you learned nothing from Cole's death."

"I didn't learn anything, Si. You and Ada got to have all the worthwhile lessons and get your fucking closure. I got fucking nothing. So, you go live your idyllic life. I'm so fucking happy for you and the amazing future y'all will have. I love you, but I'm allowed to be bitter; you should know what it looks like."

I rise from my seat and don't bother saying goodbye to Ada or Silas or Wesley and pull out my phone and summon an Uber. Because even the thought of a sketchy Uber ride alone is more appealing to me in this moment than watching the man I love be so close and knowing I'll never let myself have him.

CHAPTER NINETEEN

FORD

I thought my eyes were playing tricks on me before the game. As is my ritual during warm-up—which, since I'm no longer a player, has required some modification—I scan every section of the arena. I try to make eye connect with a few fans in each section and hopefully convey through a smile or nod that we're going to do our best.

It took me two passes to see her, and I thought I was imagining it. But I'd recognize her anywhere and when I saw she was talking to a smiling loser who was wearing a fucking polo shirt to a hockey game like some kind of dweeb, I nearly wanted to jump into the stands and pummel the prick. He must be why Josie ghosted me. Did she meet him before or after we went ice skating? For all I know, she stopped to get Bea and herself some supper that night and he was there.

And when I saw her brother and sister-in-law in the next seats, I knew for sure it was her. Jesus Christ, how I miss her. Even seeing her tonight at the game and not being able to speak to her or touch her was like being a drug addict and seeing your drug of choice almost within reach and having it torn away. It's worse than never even having the drug.

During the game, my eyes kept drifting up to the stands and her section. One minute, she was talking to her brother and the next time I looked, she was gone. And as far as I could tell, she didn't come back.

Somehow we won the game, and I didn't have to give a shitty pep talk in the locker room. I just pasted on a smile and congratulated my players on a good game and gave them pats on the back. Sitting in my office, attempting to think through the plays we made during the game, my mind keeps turning to Josie and I can't concentrate. There's always tomorrow, right? I can come back in the morning and re-evaluate for tomorrow's game.

As usual, when I leave the locker room, there are always a few fans who are there for me. And honestly, that part of things never gets old, especially when it's kids. Some of them are players themselves and they like to tell me about the plays they made and I try to listen attentively and respectfully until they're all done. Even when I don't feel like it. Tonight is no different. I spend about twenty minutes with some kids who are aspiring players before their parents whisk them away.

When they all step away, though, I let my mask fall and slump, a deep sigh working its way up my chest. "Wow, and here I thought Josie had it bad."

I snap my head up to see Josie's brother standing against a far wall, and I take a few steps closer to him. "Silas, right?"

He nods, extending his hand. "Ford? Or do you prefer Bandit?" he asks with a smile as we shake.

"Ford is fine. I thought I saw you guys here."

Silas lets go of my hand and sticks his in his pockets. "Yeah. Good game, by the way. First hockey game I've ever been to." After a beat, he adds, "Josie, too."

"Yeah. I figured that."

"I don't mean this to sound like a pickup line, but do you want to grab a drink?"

I can't help but laugh. "Sure. And even if it were, I'm kinda into your sister, so you know, one Campbell at a time."

Silas chuckles. "Touché. Did you drive? Because I let Ada and Wesley take the car so I could stay after and talk to you. My parents have Bea and Ada's antsy to pick her up."

"Yeah. And the guy? *Wesley?*" His name leaves my mouth like a curse, and Silas winces.

"Not really a date. He's a buddy of mine from college who came into town and had tickets to the game. He's from San Jose and came to see you, believe it or not. Ada and I roped Josie into coming because we wanted to get her out of the house."

I consider why Josie might be holed up at home. Maybe—hopefully—she's as miserable as I am. And yeah, it's shitty to hope she's miserable, but misery loves company and all that.

Silas and I get to my 4Runner a few minutes later and even though there's a bar right down from the arena, I'm not up to seeing any more fans. He directs me to a bar about twenty minutes away. "It'll be quiet here and I come here a lot. I'm not sure they even know what hockey is, if you know what I mean."

I should feel insulted, since hockey is my livelihood, but tonight, I'm nothing but grateful. I ditch my tie and jacket in the backseat and undo the top couple of buttons on my shirt before following Silas into the bar.

We take a booth in the back and a server stops by a few minutes later to take our drink order. Unsure how long I'll be here, I stick with beer and, when it arrives, I take a long drink.

"I don't know what Josie has told you about our family; about our brother, Cole."

I let out a bitter laugh. "Your sister is one of the most closed-off people I know. I'm in love with her, but I know next to nothing about her. You know, aside from the fact that she hates pickles and loves vodka cranberries. I know what her favorite Christmas movie is and that her hobby is making bootleg moonshine. She adores your daughter and has a tattoo that your brother also had. I don't know what she does for work or even her middle name." Taking another pull from my glass, I lift a brow. "I know other things, too, but I'll spare you that information."

"Thanks for that, I guess." He looks down into his glass. "Did Josie tell you how Cole died?"

I nod. "Yeah, hyper-something cardio-something. Sorry, it was just the once."

He shrugs. "Hypertrophic cardiomyopathy. It's genetic. After Cole got diagnosed, we all got tested. It comes from our mom's side of the family and when you're a carrier, there's a fifty-fifty chance your kids will have it. My mom is a carrier. Cole had it. I don't. I'm also not a carrier."

I swallow. "And Josie? Does she have it?" The thought of her having a heart condition makes me want to cut mine out and give it to her and I would if it would help.

Silas shakes his head. "She doesn't have it. But she's a carrier." Understanding, I nod. "And did she tell you about our grandmother, Pap's wife?"

"Yeah. Cancer, right?"

"Yeah, breast cancer. Also genetic," he says, leveling me with a gaze. "I don't have the markers for that one either. And neither does my daughter."

I swallow again, my throat tightening. "But Josie does? Is that what you're telling me?"

He nods. "Normally, I'd never get involved with Josie's love life and I've watched her sabotage every relationship she's ever been in. She'd rather push someone away than hope she can outwit genetics and shitty luck. But I've never seen her like this

—torn up over anyone. So that leads me to believe you're different.

"And she said y'all never talked about your job and until she saw you at your game, she had no clue who you were or what you did. So she's not one of those women who'd only want you because of your fame or career. That's not her."

"I know." I can't help but laugh. "She asked me to give your daughter a skating lesson because she saw a tattoo of a pair of skates I have. She even went so far as to tell me I'd be able to get a side hustle giving skate lessons."

Silas snorts in amusement. "Well, she's nothing if not pragmatic." He sobers and tilts his glass until the liquid almost spills over the rim. "I don't think I've been a very good brother to her since Cole died. You see, he sent me these letters—."

I nod. "Yeah, Josie told me about the tasks and how Cole's goal was to set you and Ada up—make you two fall in love."

"Yeah. And it never occurred to me until tonight that while Ada and I got closure, she didn't. And while Ada and I were going through everything with the tasks and letters, Josie was still there for both of us. She gave us both pep talks and helped us work things out, and we both took her for granted. And while I've assumed this entire time she was okay, she's not.

"She used to have a high-powered job. She was a shark and made about ten times more than I do a year and was excellent at it. But when Cole died, she quit. Just out of the blue. Said life was too short to waste it in an office—even a corner one. So now, she house sits and walks dogs and runs errands for other people. And I think she's happy with that, but I worry she's wasting her potential."

"She is happy in her job. Even though she wouldn't tell me what she does, I asked her if she was happy. I could see it in her face she was. And something tells me whatever Josie does, she could make a success out of it."

He gives me a tight smile. "Yeah, probably." Blowing out a breath, he sips his beer. "I'm wondering now if Josie's been 'not okay' since way before Cole died. You have a kid, right?"

I blink, surprised by his sudden change in subject. "Yeah, a daughter."

"Do you want any more?"

I open my mouth and close it again and take a sip of my beer. "I'm not sure. Emerson is sixteen. Starting over? That's a lot to consider. If it's up to me, I don't have a burning need for more."

Silas's brows rise. "Sixteen? You're what, thirty-five?"

I nod. "Yeah. Winning college championship hockey games at eighteen and doing tequila shots with your best friend who's a girl don't really mix."

"Ah. Gotcha."

"Why do you ask?"

"Just curious." Changing the subject, he asks, "Will you be moving? What I mean is, is this coaching job temporary?"

"Not if I can help it. I like it here. No telling what the owners will do, but my daughter is here for at least another two years for high school and has already started looking at UT, so that's another four years unless she gets a swimming scholarship elsewhere." He nods and I continue. "Even if I wasn't coaching, I don't have a reason to leave. I've been really smart with my money, so working isn't something I have to do at this point. My money makes money for me these days. Whatever Emerson decides to do for college, I've already got her taken care of. And like Josie said, I can always do lessons."

He chuckles. "True. I only asked because Josie has sort of become the primary caregiver for our grandfather. Ada and I pitch in a lot on the farm, but it's mainly fallen to her. She won't leave Tennessee. At least not while Pap is still around. Probably not even then. The farm is special to all of us, but even more so to her over the past few years. So, if you plan on making a go of it with Josie for the long term, that's something you'll want to be aware of."

"Does Josie know you're talking to me about any of this?"

His eyes widen, and he shakes his head quickly. "Fuck no. She'd probably have my balls if she knew."

"So why risk her wrath?"

He grins. "I live with Ada, and she's a hell of a lot scarier than Josie ever thought to be. Plus, it's like you said, she's closed off. She didn't use to be. She used to wear her heart on her sleeve and was a huge romantic. That's not her anymore, unfortunately. She no longer believes in forevers or happy endings. At least not for herself. And I'm not sure why I didn't put two and two together before now, but I think it all changed after Cole's diagnosis."

Silas blows out a breath. "When we were told he had HCM, we all knew there was a chance he could die or would need a heart transplant later in life. And after that, we all got tested. What was my clean bill of health turned out to be what Josie considers to be a potential death sentence.

"She watched Cole and Ada love each other for fifteen years. She watched him get sicker and then die and leave Ada. And yeah, I was there for her, but for a while, Ada was in a scary place. I think Josie worries about doing that—what Cole did—to someone else. Leaving someone who loves her all alone to deal with the fallout. I don't know for sure if that's the reasoning behind why she refuses to let herself have any sort of happiness, but it's not too big a jump to assume."

He drags his hand down his face. "Josie is a big girl. And lord knows she's got the attitude to back it up. But I think some part of her is still that sixteen-year-old girl who's just found out that her big brother is probably going to die. And then she also found out she carries the same genes that killed her brother and grandmother. I'm pretty sure a part of her died that day, since a lot of her dreams died when she got her results.

"And yeah, she's had almost twenty years to process those results, but Meemaw died a couple of years before Cole and then he dropped dead one morning as he was leaving for work. So even though we knew it was probably coming, she hasn't dealt with it. She's pushed it all down and been strong for everyone else. For Ada. For me. And we let her.

"Until now, I've never considered myself a selfish person. I mean, my brother called dibs on the girl I was in love with when we were fifteen and I let him. And if he was here, I'd still be happy to sit on the sidelines, even knowing what I'd have to sacrifice. But where Josie is concerned, I guess I have been selfish. I've been happy to let her bear the brunt of her own burdens when I should've been a good big brother. I was so concerned for my grief and Ada's and trying to do what Cole wanted, it never occurred to me that Josie didn't get any kind of letter or goodbye from him.

"She will fall all over herself trying to help other people. Take in stray dogs and cats and run all over creation trying to find the perfect mango if it's on someone's grocery list. She will drag her depressed best friend out of bed and make her shower and eat while neglecting her own physical and mental health.

"She will give up all the dreams she had so no one has to go through what Ada went through. What our parents went through. What Pap went through. And she will do it all with a smile and a smartass remark and never once complain because she feels like someone else always has more on their plate than she does."

My chest tightens hearing Silas talk about his sister. I'd give anything to know these parts of her, but I'm reminded I don't. I know almost nothing. In over three months, I know nothing about this amazing woman I've fallen in love with. I feel cheated of getting to know her since I'm not sure she'll ever let me know her.

I nod because, honestly, I have no clue what to say. Silas drains the rest of his beer and signals for the check. When I pull out my wallet, he waves it away. "You're giving me a ride home. Besides, brokenhearted men shouldn't have to buy their own drinks."

"Did you have someone buy your drinks and give you a pep talk?"

He smiles. "Yeah, actually. My dad. But I usually let moonshine be my sounding board. She's a great listener most of the time. My liver's not real fond of her tactics, but that bitch needs to earn its keep."

When I drop Silas at his house, I grab his arm just before he climbs down from the cab of the 4Runner. "Thanks for the insight. I'm not sure if Josie will ever tell me any of it herself, but I'm glad I know."

"Sure thing." He hops down and is about to shut the door. "Oh, and it's Hope." When I frown in confusion, he elaborates. "Josie's middle name. It's Hope. Josephine Hope Campbell."

CHAPTER TWENTY

JOSIE

"Didn't know women wore ties these days," Pap comments as I'm struggling to tie mine.

I lift a brow. "Sometimes they do, especially when they're caterers for a big, fancy wedding. All part of the dress code. But even if it weren't, I'd still make it look good."

When I unknot it for the third time, frustrated, Pap steps in front of me and bats away my hands. Even at eighty-nine and arthritic, he still makes quick work of the double Windsor. "You eat today?"

"Yeah."

"When? And don't say when you went to the stillhouse. Because if you tell me you took food in there, you're going to clean it from top to bottom with a toothbrush. You know how I feel about the purity of my product."

I huff a laugh. "Okay, Walter White. No, it wasn't in the stillhouse. It was on the way to the stillhouse. I had a sandwich. I'm fine."

"No, you're not. You're getting too skinny. Do I need to call Ada and have her make us a pot of dumplings?"

"No, Pap; I'm fine. I'll eat at the wedding. There are always a ton of leftovers with these things. I'll bring some fancy food home. How about that?"

He shakes his head. "No thanks. My body doesn't know how to process fancy food. I'm a well-oiled machine, no need to gunk up the works," he replies with a pat to his belly.

I drop a kiss to the top of his head as I pass him. "All right. I'm not sure what time I'll be in. Probably late."

"Sure." When I'm almost out of the room, he calls after me and I turn. "And you know I love having you here and I love our chats and you're a hell of a lot better at making coffee than me, but how long are you planning on hiding out up here?"

"I'm not *hiding*. You need a little extra help; I'm happy to be here to do it."

Pap lifts a brow and sets his jaw. "Josephine, I am not an invalid. I do not, at present, require someone to feed me or wipe my ass. So, yes, you are hiding. You've got the non-stop ringing phone to prove it. I'm not sure what happened between you and your hockey-player fella, but the fact that he's still calling after weeks of you not answering tells me he at least wants to have a conversation. Don't you think you owe that to him? You already assumed he was something when he wasn't. And you definitely put the 'ass' in assume with this one, Jo-Jo."

I sigh. "I know. Listen, I have to go. I love you and I'll see you later."

As this is not my first catering gig at a fancy wedding, I know how this goes. I carry around trays of hors d'oeuvres during cocktail hour and deliver plates of food during supper. I serve wedding cake once it's cut. Then I get paid and go home. Hopefully, with a bag full of leftover crab puffs and wedding cake. Today's wedding is no different except that there's also a champagne toast, so you know, extra fancy.

Maybe it's the cynic in me, but why do people go to all this trouble for a simple piece of paper that says that you will legally be responsible for someone else's debt and choices and can't be forced to testify against them in the event they commit a crime? At least when Silas and Ada got married, it was on the farm with only our family. And I guess we had our own sort of champagne toast with some apple pie moonshine, but that's hardly the same thing.

So tonight, when the catering supervisor goes over the protocols for this event, I tune out most of it, simply because I already know. Please, for the love of all things holy, point me toward my tray and turn me loose. I can push the appetizers no one wants, and it's the only time my background in sales comes in handy. I can talk up the most mundane, bland cucumber sandwich. Lord knows I relish the challenge.

"Hey, your tie's crooked. Let me fix that for you." Gideon, one of the other seasoned cater-waiters steps in front of me right as we're about to leave the staging area. He reaches to adjust my tie and offers me a smile. "So, what are your thoughts about all this? You think you'll ever go through all this someday?"

I snort a laugh. "No. Not in a million years. Not in the cards for me, I'm afraid."

He nods. "I know what you mean. Been there, done that, got the alimony payments to prove it. At the last wedding, did those salmon tarts upset your stomach?"

I shake my head. "No. But the fact that you ate twenty of them might be why they upset yours. I told you not to do that."

"Yeah, but they were so good." As we move forward toward our assigned trays, he keeps talking. "I don't know if you're doing anything after this, but there's a group of us going out for drinks. You should come." He jerks his chin in the direction of one of the other waiters. "I don't know if you know this or not, but Sean has had a huge crush on you for years. He'd never ask you out himself, but he's dying to buy you a drink."

I try to smile, but it's not successful. "I think I'm good. Sean's cute and all, but not really my type."

"Why not?"

Besides the fact that he's not a six-foot-six viking redhead hockey god who I'm still in love with? "He's too innocent. I'd totally corrupt him, and then he'd be ruined for all other women."

Gideon laughs. "I don't know; he might like that. Hell, I might like that. Come out with me. Just me," he says with a playful smile.

"Sorry, pal. I don't shit where I eat."

"Nice. Fine, but if you ever decide that you're done wasting your talents and you go back to your real world job, call me. I'd be happy to let you corrupt me."

I roll my eyes. "Not likely. Now give me my tray and let me push these," I look down at the tiny card on my assigned tray, "brie and jam puffs."

"Good luck."

"None needed, thanks." I paste on my most professional smile, knowing full well these people won't even look at my face. They never look at faces. I never noticed that was the case until I started this job. I attended countless numbers of functions exactly like this in my old job and I can't tell you what any of the staff looked like.

Now, though, I make it a point to look at the faces of the people who serve my food and try to be extra polite. And every once in a while, some guest will actually thank me for standing with a tray for them to pull snacks from and I'll feel like I've done something amazing.

I meander around my quadrant of the reception hall, taking in the crystal chandeliers and centerpieces that probably cost more than my car payment each. "Excuse me?"

I snap out of my daze and focus on the person trying to get my attention—a tall, blonde girl in her mid-to-late teens. She's so tall, it's hard to determine her age. "I'm sorry. Yes?"

"Do you know what kind of jam is in these puffs?"

Giving her a small shake of my head and an apologetic smile, I pick up the card on the tray. "I only know they're brie and jam. Sorry."

"No problem; I was just curious. Hopefully, it's not something super out there, like ghost pepper or banana."

I huff a laugh. "Yeah, not sure I'd like that either." She shrugs and pops one into her mouth and chews, a thoughtful smile crossing her face once she's swallowed. "Good?" I ask.

She nods. "Yeah. Cranberry. Great actually. I'll have to get my dad to try one. He's on a cranberry kick lately." After she eats another one, she asks, "Do you like your job? Is it fun?"

"Sometimes. Sometimes I get to take home leftovers. Why? You considering a career in food service?"

"No, I'm going to be an Olympic swimmer."

I grin. "I like a girl who knows what she wants. You any good?"

"Sure. But I come from good stock, my mom likes to say. My dad was a professional athlete, so maybe I'll have a shot, too." She spots someone across the room. "Speaking of moms, I've gotta go. Mine is summoning me." She sighs. "Maid of honor duties and all that."

"Well, I'll be here if you need any more puffs. Nice to meet you."

"You, too." She walks across the room to where the bride, a blonde woman in her mid-thirties, is standing with a tall man in his late thirties or early forties with medium-brown skin and glasses in a tuxedo who can only be the groom. They all laugh about something and I can't help but smile as I watch the exchange, even though it hurts. Someday, that'll be Ford. He'll be in the tux with a beautiful woman at his side in a gorgeous dress and he'll laugh with his daughter and they'll all live happily ever after. I gave him up so he can have that, I remind myself. And although it hurts as surely as any gaping wound, I'm not sorry.

After a few more guests pass, my tray is empty, so I return to the staging area for a refill before returning to my post. And even though I smile at the people who swing by, my mind is elsewhere. At least, until I hear a familiar voice. "I'm telling you, Daddy, you have to try these puffs. They're great."

"Come on, Ford; indulge this girl. She's been talking nonstop about these cranberry-brie things for a while. The least you can do is make all this money Piper and Conrad are spending worth it."

My stomach drops and my mouth goes dry and my ears ring. I don't even have to look to know who I'm going to see. And not only is it Ford, but the girl—the teenage girl—is his daughter. And he's not alone. He has a date. A beautiful, striking, tall amazon of a woman dressed in a gorgeous shimmery black evening gown while I'm in slacks and a tie and non-slip shoes with my hair pulled back in a bun. Her arm is hooked through his and she sweeps his hair off his forehead like it's no big deal.

I want this floor to open up and swallow me whole. Maybe he won't see me. Maybe he'll be one of those guests who doesn't see the help. But I already know he's not that kind of man. He makes eye contact with bartenders and keeps women from being drugged in bars. He's observant and genuine and will definitely see me.

Looking around, panicked, I spot no one. Not Gideon or

Sean, who've both been in my periphery all night. But I guess not when I truly need them. *Dear sweet baby Jesus, if you can hear this, please just send a swarm of locusts or a flood or any of a thousand natural disasters to help me avoid this moment. I know I don't call out to you unless Ford is reminding me who's making me call out for you, but please, for the love of Christmas and vodka cranberries, help a sister out?*

But the floor does not open up. A swarm of locusts does not descend. There is no flood or tornado or anything except this beautiful man accompanied by a daughter, who is definitely not an ankle-biter, and a woman who was born to walk a runway. And there is only me and a tray of hors d'oeuvres and my lack of an ability to abandon a job. Damn me and my sense of pride in a job well done. I can't be a flake just this once?

Apparently not, because here I stand, rooted to this spot as Ford and a girl I now know is Emerson and his date make their way over. Does he make her call out for Jesus when they're in bed? I bet she lets him hold her hand in public and sleep over and all the things normal women can do. She probably lets him take her out on dates and doesn't relegate him to only her nights. He probably knows all her trauma, and she lets him comfort her. This woman was probably happy to find out what he does for work. It's obvious she's already met his kid. I didn't even know his kid was barely even still a kid.

All these thoughts fly through my mind in a matter of seconds. Either that, or time has slowed to a crawl. Because they're still feet away and I'm forced to watch him—them—approach and it's like watching them ready the guillotine for execution.

Emerson is laughing at something Ford's date is saying and he's pulling Emerson into his side like a loving father and smiling down at her as they come closer. He's so attentive to her that he doesn't see me until he's two feet away and within arm's reach of this tray that will probably end up being my grave marker because this is the moment I die. This is the moment the guillotine drops, and my head rolls into the basket.

As recognition flickers in his gaze, I can't move. I can't speak. I can't breathe. And God, why does he have to look so good? He's wearing a tux and his hair is longer and styled perfectly and he's got stylish beard growth—you know, the kind where it's intentional and not just that he forgot to shave for several days.

"Josie." He says it barely above a whisper, as if he's afraid he'll spook me. And honestly, it's not far off. I'm about half a second from dropping this tray and making a run for it.

Emerson's face morphs into a mask of confusion while his date's eyes widen, as if something is falling into place. "Oh," she says and turns to Emerson. "Emmy, why don't we try some of the other great hors d'oeuvres? I think I saw some crab puffs over that way."

The girl frowns, but when she looks from her father to me, she nods. "Okay. Sure, Fiona." They walk away and I'm left standing like some sort of statue looking at this beautiful man.

"I didn't know this was the 'work' you were scheduled for when I invited you."

I nod. "I know. How could you have known?"

He opens his mouth and closes it again and his blue eyes— so open and honest and hurt in this moment—search mine. "Can you talk?"

I shake my head. "I'm working."

"I know. I mean, after."

"There's nothing to talk about," I reply weakly.

He steps forward, his jaw clenching, anger flashing in his gaze. "That's bullshit, Josie. You won't even have a fucking conversation with me."

I swallow, trying to dislodge the lump in my throat. "Like I said, we have nothing to talk about, Ford. I stopped answering your calls. Can't you take a hint? I don't want to talk to you."

He closes his eyes for a beat and blows out a breath through his nose. "Well, I want to talk to you. I don't care if I have to wait all night, but we will have a conversation. It's not up for discussion."

"You don't tell me what to do, Ford. I already said there's nothing to talk about, so we're done. So go back to your beautiful daughter and your date and let me work."

He's about to say something, but another guest approaches and he steps back to allow the woman access to my tray. Thankfully, she empties it and I have an excuse to leave. I tuck the tray under my arm and turn to walk away, but he grabs my wrist. "We're not done, Josie."

I yank it from his grasp. "Yes, we are. I have to work." I don't wait for him to respond and practically sprint into the staging area and find the head caterer standing at the end of the long table, going over her schedule. "Marie?"

She turns to me and her expression quickly morphs into one of concern when she looks at my face. "Josie, are you okay? You don't look well."

"I think I've come down with some kind of bug and I'm going to have to call it a night. So sorry if that puts y'all in a bind, but I don't think I can stay." I clutch my stomach, feigning a cramp, and her eyes widen. "I know I won't get my fee for tonight and that's fine, but I don't want to make anyone else sick."

"No, of course not. You never get sick. In almost four years, you've never called out or bailed. Go, don't worry about us. We'll make it. Feel better."

I nod and give her a weak smile. "Thank you. I'll see you later." Without another word, I escape out a back door.

CHAPTER TWENTY-ONE

FORD

I look for Josie for the rest of the reception and don't see her, and I conclude she must have ducked out when she went to refill her tray. And I'm pissed because I can't leave because I walked Piper down the aisle and we have to dance. Some modern family we've got here, I tell you.

Even as the music starts up and I try to keep my smile in place as I guide Piper out to the dance floor, she eyes me. "What's up with your face? You've got your constipated look."

I roll my eyes. "I'm not constipated."

"Then what is it? This is the happiest day of my life and you're being a wet blanket."

"Ouch. Thanks for that. I thought the happiest day of your life was when you married me," I retort.

She snorts a laugh. "I don't actually remember that day much. I was so sick from the morning sickness, I barely recall what the judge said. And as much as I love you, you and I both know this was inevitable and that we'd both move on to our forevers. I just wish yours would show up."

"She did, but she's gone now," I reply, my tone wistful.

Her expression morphs from amused to perplexed. "What? What are you talking about?"

Blowing out a frustrated breath, I give her a halfhearted shrug. "I'd been seeing someone. I fell in love with her and then she ghosted me. She was here tonight; one of the caterers. But she ran away, I think."

Piper frowns. "Okay, I'm confused. She ghosted you and you're still in love with her?"

I sigh. "It's complicated. But for the first time in my life, I found someone who had no clue who I was. She didn't like me because I was famous or rich or any of that. Hell, until last week she didn't even know I had anything to do with hockey."

"Okay, so what's the deal?"

"I don't know where she is. She's left her house and her roommate has no idea where she's gone. And because she doesn't work a nine-to-five, it's not like I can track her down at work. She's not answering my calls or texts and she hasn't been going out to bars. I don't know how to find her."

"Wow. You must really like this woman if you're stalking her," Piper says good-naturedly. "Is she your Conrad?"

I nod. "I think so, but I don't know if she'll let me be hers."

"Ford, you are a good man. You are a good father and a good friend. If this woman can't see that, it's a her problem, not a you problem. And I know you hate to lose, but this time, you might not have a choice. You can't catch someone who doesn't want to be chased. But I know you. I already know you're going to do everything in your power to go after her. Because that's what you do. You don't know how to quit, even when it might end up hurting you. The doctor told you that you needed to take a few weeks off the ice to let your nose heal and did you listen? No. And now look at this once-beautiful mug of yours."

I scoff. "I'll have you know, lots of women find my crooked nose intriguing. It's quite the conversation starter. And just because you're shallow and divorced me after I became horribly disfigured means that you're the vapid one."

She laughs, and her forehead falls to my shoulder. "I love you, you know that?"

I nod. "I know. And we have a pretty great kid, so I wouldn't take back our tequila-fueled hookup for anything."

She shakes her head, her eyes growing glassy. "Me, neither. And the fact that we're still *us* after everything proves that this was how it was always supposed to be. You are one of my best friends, Ford, and I want you to be happy. Emerson wants you to be happy. If this woman makes you happy, I say go after her. But you are too good a man to not have everything you deserve. If this woman can't love you and let you love her the way you deserve, you need to let her go.

"We got married because we thought it was what was right. And I'd never trade our time together because we both grew up so much during that time. But sometimes, you can't see the forest for the trees. You want to do the right thing, sometimes for the wrong reasons. You wanted us to get married because you thought it was the right thing to do. But it was for the wrong reasons. We would've still been good parents to Emerson, regardless of whether we got married. We've proven that.

"This woman may not be in a place where she can accept your love. You might want to be there for her and 'fix' her and you might get your heart broken. So just be careful, okay?"

I nod and the music dies down and I give Piper a kiss on the cheek as I pass her off to her new husband before heading back to my table and ordering a drink.

After lying in bed for hours when I return home from the wedding, I don't sleep. I can't. I can only see Josie's face and the tortured look in her eyes. The look that says, *I love you but won't let myself have you.* The look of a caged animal who only wants to bite the hand that's trying to feed it. The look of a scared little girl who still isn't over the death of her big brother.

In this, I can't empathize. I don't have a clue what she must be dealing with since I don't know what it's like to lose anyone; let alone someone like that. I don't know what it's like to find out you have genes that might kill you or ones you can pass on to children.

I do know what it's like to love someone. To love a child. To love a wife—which, now that I've loved Josie, the way I loved Piper is completely different. It's the love of a friend. A friend whom I felt attracted for for a period of time, sure, but only a friend nonetheless. But this kind of love hurts and part of me wishes I didn't know what it was like; that I didn't burn with the way I want her. I wish I didn't wonder what it would be like to wake up beside her for the next fifty years, and I wish I could still imagine my life without her in it. Alas, that's no longer the case.

Like I have every morning for nearly the past month, I go to her house. At this point, Jess expects me and is standing on the porch with his cup of coffee. Today, he has one waiting for me as well and I'm not sure if it's good news or bad. "She's not coming back. She asked me to rent out her room. The movers will be here later today to get her stuff to put in storage."

"Do you know where she's moved?" I ask, both alarmed and even more heartbroken.

He shakes his head. "No. And I only know about the movers because she texted me. She must have come while I was gone to work last night to pack up her clothes. I'm sorry, man."

I nod. "It's not your fault. I just wish I knew where to look; that she'd at least have a fucking conversation with me."

Jess sighs. "Feral cat, remember?"

A thought occurs to me. "Can I ask you something?"

"Maybe? I don't know."

"When did you and Josie date?"

"High school. Junior year. Why?"

"And why did y'all break up?"

He puffs up his cheeks in thought before blowing it out. "Damn, that was so long ago, I don't really remember. We'd been together for a few months and I told her I loved her and we slept together. A week later, she dumped me. No warning. I thought we were happy. I was pretty broken up about it and worked my way through the girls' volleyball team trying to get over her."

"You think she was happy? You know, before she dumped you?"

He nods. "I thought so. And until I met Brooklyn, I always thought Josie was kinda the one that got away. I see now she's great and all, but I love Brooklyn. But I used to really wonder what the catalyst was for our breakup. As far as I know, I didn't do anything wrong. We never fought and I don't think it had anything to do with us sleeping together because we didn't have any issues or anything. Sorry if that's TMI."

"No, that's fine. I'm just trying to figure shit out." I drain my mug and hand it over. "Thanks for the coffee. And I know it's a long shot, but if she comes by, can you tell her to call me?"

"Sure. Good luck."

Sliding back behind the wheel of my car, I drive aimlessly for nearly an hour. It's not until I pass the ice rink for a second time that I pull in. If I can't have answers, I can at least wear myself out enough to sleep until I have to be at the arena, right?

I step inside, skate bag slung over my shoulder and slump

when I see there's a class already on the ice and weaving through small humans isn't going to do it for me today. I sigh and figure I can get some skate time in at the arena, I guess, and turn to leave.

"Ford, right?" I snap my head to my right where a woman with long, almost jet-black hair sits at a table drinking what looks like hot chocolate. She looks familiar, but I can't exactly place her, even as I make my way over. Seeing my confusion, she gestures to herself. "Ada. Josie's sister-in-law."

I nod, understanding. "Bea's mom."

She smiles. "That's right. Care to sit? They're about to wrap up the class and I think it's free skate after that."

"Sure. Thanks." I take the seat opposite her and drop my bag on the floor. "So, you've got Bea in lessons, huh? Her coach any good?"

She considers. "He's no NHL legend or anything, but he's all right." She sips her cocoa, eyeing me. "How are you?"

"Besides the fact that I'm hung up on your sister-in-law? Peachy."

"Those Campbells weave a spell, that's for sure. I should know; I've loved two of them."

Furrowing my brow, I'm unable to not ask, "What's that like? I'm sorry if that's an insensitive question; I'm just curious. Do people give you weird looks?"

"They used to," she admits, her tone matter-of-fact. "But even though Cole and Silas were twins, they were as different as night and day. Cole was this calm, calculating, know-it-all who was the life of every party we were at. Silas is playful and spontaneous, but he's quiet and reserved and shy. And Silas and I are at each other's throats all the time, even now. But it's mainly because we don't take each other's shit and aren't afraid to tell the other person what they need to hear, not just what they want to hear. It wasn't like that between Cole and me. We had a very peaceful relationship. So, although the men were twins, they were most definitely different men.

"And the thing about these Campbells is, they are the most loyal bunch of people you'll ever meet. They're compassionate to a fault and have been my family since I was ten years old. I didn't come from the best home and Josie took it upon herself the first day of fifth grade to be my best friend. She brought me home, and that was it. They're the best people I know. But they also keep their cards close to their vests. It took months of Silas and me spending time together before I even knew how much Cole's death affected him. I'm not sure I've ever seen how it affects Josie."

Ada looks out toward the rink, and I follow her line of sight. Bea is skating like she's a natural and I can't help but smile. "It's one thing to not know you want something until the option of it is right in front of you. It's a completely different thing altogether when you know—you've always known—you want something and it's taken away or you know you'll never have it. I think it probably changes a person on a fundamental level. It causes you to grow callous and makes you think that because you can't or choose not to have *everything*, you should have *nothing*."

"Do you know where she is?" Ada nods. "Are you allowed to tell me?"

"Probably not, but I will anyway. Another thing about these Campbells is, they butt in and make you face things even when you don't want to. I figure I'm a Campbell now, so I can butt in, too. I can't promise you'll be successful, but I'm happy to let you try."

She opens a notebook I hadn't noticed and flips past several colorful sketches to a blank page and tears it out. She jots something down and hands it over. "A word of advice?" I shrug. "Keep your hands where he can see them."

I frown. "That's your advice?"

She laughs. "It'll make sense when you get there."

An hour later, after leaving the main highway some twenty miles ago and driving through enough switchbacks to give the most seasoned rollercoaster enthusiast motion sickness, my GPS finally alerts me to a gravel driveway. As I slowly make my way up it, once I clear a stand of trees, the landscape opens up to reveal a small white farmhouse that borders a forest. An ancient red barn and recently turned garden plot sit off to the right of the house down a small hill. I know this must be Josie's grandfather's farm, and she must have moved in with him. When I see Gouda lift her head off her paws on the porch, I know for sure I'm in the right place.

Exiting my vehicle, I remember Ada's warning and keep my hands at my sides. Gouda barks and hops off the porch and I squat down to give her a belly rub when she reaches me. She whines and wags her entire body with excitement. The front door opens and an elderly man in overalls and a flannel shirt—still rather spry for his age, judging by the way he moves—steps out with a shotgun cradled in his arm, pointed at the ground. "Something I can help you with?" He's around Josie's height with sun-leathered skin, short, thinning white hair, and a slight paunch that pushes out the front of his overalls. Shrewd eyes focus on me from under bushy white brows as he awaits my response.

"Yes, sir. I'm Ford Brickman. I was wondering if Josie was available."

"Ford, huh? You the hockey fella?"

"Yes, sir." I should probably be glad he's heard of me.

"Well, Josie's not available."

Disappointment drops like a weight into the pit of my stomach. "Oh. I see. Well, if you can tell her I stopped by, I'd appreciate it."

He presses his brows together in confusion and frowns. "You can tell her yourself. She'll be back directly. She's in the woods. And don't be asking me where she is back there, 'cause you'd never find her and I'm not up for tracking down city folk in my woods. You can come inside and have a cup of coffee and tell me about this hockey business. Never had much use for it myself. More of a football fan. No offense."

Relief floods my system, and I nod. "Yes, sir." I follow him into the farmhouse and he pulls two mugs from a cabinet and pours us each a cup of coffee from an ancient percolator coffeemaker on the stovetop.

"So, who do I get to fuss at for giving up my address? The only people who know how to find me are people I trust and I figure if it was Jo-Jo, you would've been here weeks ago."

"Yes, sir. It was Ada, actually. I hope that doesn't get her in trouble. She took pity on me when I ran into her this morning."

"Well, Ada Mae gets a pass. If I fuss at her, she won't make me chicken and dumplings, so I'll let it slide. I'm Fred, by the way. Or, Pap. Whichever you prefer. Now, is it Ford, or what is it, Bandit or some such?"

I huff a laugh. "Ford is just fine. Bandit is my middle name. My dad picked it after his childhood dog, so don't I feel special a lot of the time? My high school coach saw my full name and thought Bandit sounded better over the loudspeaker and would be more memorable. Bandit Brickman kinda stuck, I guess."

"Well, it's a good hockey name, I suppose. They named Josie after her uncle; my oldest son, Joseph."

"I didn't know Josie had any uncles." Just one more thing I didn't know, I guess.

He waves off my comment. "No reason for you to. He

passed when he was ten. Miles, Josie's daddy, was only about six, so it was a long time ago. But you know, a name has a lot of significance. And where you get a name gives it history. Even though Josie's never met her uncle Joseph, she's a lot like him.

"The reason he died was because he was trying to help me out. I had fallen off a ladder in the barn and hurt my back, but the garden needed to be plowed. Joseph must have heard me talking to Beatrice, my wife, and I'd been complaining about hurting. So, he went and climbed up on that tractor." Fred sighs, his tone turning wistful. "He got to going too fast down the hill and the brakes failed and it rolled over with him."

"I'm so sorry. I have a daughter and can't imagine what that must've been like for you."

"Thank you. But I said all that to say that Josie is a lot like that. She'll see someone needing help and jump in, even without being asked and do whatever's needed; even to her own detriment. And over the last few years, she's made herself so busy; so booked up with these jobs she does that she's never alone with her own thoughts.

"I'm under no illusions about my grandchildren. They all spent so much time here growing up, most of the time, I felt like they were my own kids. Cole would work in the garden and learned the land. He was so smart and had such an amazing memory, he could tell you every bug, flower, and tree on this mountain from memory.

"Silas is a fixer. He tinkers and likes to work with his hands and be physically active. I could always count on him to pitch in with the plowing and planting. And although biologically, Ada Mae's not mine, I've always claimed her. She and my Beatrice would bake and cook together and they had such similar spirits, you'd never know they weren't blood.

"Josie, in her own way, was like my Joseph. She'd do whatever needed doing and work herself to death to keep someone else from having to lift a finger. She's the epitome of an acts-of-service love language. After Cole died, she ran around and checked on her momma and daddy, Silas and Ada, and me. She ran errands and cooked and cleaned. She never slowed down and never once broke down that I know of. Part of me thinks she's afraid if she stops moving, she'll have to feel something.

"And in that, she's like me. After Joseph died, I kept myself too busy to even grieve. And when I wasn't working the land, I was getting blackout drunk. I was trying to stay so strong for everyone else, I didn't realize it was killing me. And not just physically. It was killing my heart—the emotional one.

"Josie's doing that, too. She dates around and, unlike Cole and Silas, who only ever had eyes and hearts for Ada, Josie tries to fill the void left from not dealing with her grief by running around town 'having fun.'" He puts the last words in air quotes and sighs. "And I'm not—what do the kids call it today—slut shaming, or whatever. I grew up way before the sixties and I'm familiar with free love and all that. Your generation didn't invent sleeping around."

I can't help but chuckle. I like this old man. He doesn't bullshit, and he's still sharp as a tack. "No, I guess we didn't."

"And until the day she met you that night you stepped in to keep her safe—thank you for that, by the way—all she's done since high school is 'have fun'. She'd never admit it, but she's been committed to you since that day. She's gone out, but only to satisfy her friends or kill time. When she visits here and I know you've texted her, she gets this look on her face I've not seen since she was probably about sixteen. But I think you scare her.

"I don't mean in the physical sense. Not that you're not scary, of course. Do they grow y'all different up north or something? Shit." I laugh and he takes a sip of his coffee. "But the way she feels about you scares her. Because she watched her brother and her best friend fall in love and she watched how it destroyed Ada when Cole died. And despite how happy Ada and Silas are—how much their love helped them heal—she's still stuck on the loss of it. She's afraid to have the good for fear of the bad."

CHAPTER TWENTY-TWO

JOSIE

I should've known it was only a matter of time before someone ratted me out. Whether it needs to be Silas or Ada whom I murder, only time will tell. Even knowing he's in the house and within reach doesn't make me feel anything but anxious.

Not like I wasn't already having a shit day or anything. Not like I've been in the stillhouse all day crying and mourning because of the finality of last night. Because he's moved on and I'm just me. And now, he's here to sever things once and for all. Because he doesn't sleep around and if he's going to be sleeping with the brunette beauty from the wedding, he won't be sleeping with me ever again.

And now he and Pap are sitting at the kitchen table having a fucking cup of coffee like it's any ordinary day. Not like today will be the thing that finally shatters my heart into dust, with no way to repair it. Not like today will be the reminder of exactly how broken I am and how I've pushed away this great guy who's finally decided he's done pushing back.

Pap's eyes lift to mine, but Ford doesn't look my way as I expect he will. My grandfather continues talking as if he hasn't seen me and, for a moment, I wonder if he's offering me a means of escape; that he won't tell Ford I'm here and let me sneak away. But when he rises from his chair and walks to the door, he calls out to me and I know my time's up. I flinch and sigh and hang my head. "Josephine, you have a visitor. And your legs work better than mine these days, so let 'em carry your cowardly ass into this house and talk with your fella."

I fold my arms and somehow find myself walking toward the porch. "Old man, none of this is any of your business."

He grins down at me. "Jo-Jo, I'm a Campbell. We are born and bred buttinskies. You're no different from the rest of us, except this time, you're the one being butted in on. So you will get your behind in this house and talk to this young man."

I heave a sigh as Pap steps off the porch. "I'm going to go to the barn for a bit. Don't go throwing any of my dishes and I expect all my furniture to be in working order when I get back." He calls for Gouda, who trots after him, and I'm left utterly alone on the porch. And because I've apparently run out of places to hide if he's found me here, I step into the house to face the music.

Ford still sits in the same place at the table, but when I enter the room, he stands, a tentative smile on his face. His beautiful, unshaven, tired face. He wears those faded jeans that look like they were made for him and that stupid long-sleeved henley that he leaves unbuttoned and hugs every muscle on his torso. Why does he have to be so fucking gorgeous? "Hey, Freckles. I've gotta tell you, you Campbells are quite the loquacious bunch. Well, all of them except for you."

I fold my arms tighter across my chest and make no move to close the distance between us. "My family lives for a good heart-to-heart. At least the ones with a good one." The fact he's not confused by what I'm saying means he probably knows about the testing. I drop my hands to my side. "Why are you here, Ford?"

"You know why I'm here."

"No, I really don't. Have all those pucks to the head damaged your ability to take a hint?"

"I'll have you know I always tried to wear sufficient protective equipment, so my brain is mostly intact. I've been trying to talk to you for weeks and I know you know that. You haven't blocked me because it still rings when I call. Are you just trying to torture me at this point so I'll know you're seeing my calls and purposely avoiding me?"

"I don't know what you want me to say, Ford."

"How about you tell me you love me? That you miss me."

I swallow and blink back tears. "I don't."

He takes a step closer to me and I retreat, my back hitting the door. "You are a lot of things, Josie, but a good liar is not one of them. How about you tell me you can't live without me? That seeing me across the room and not touching me is killing you. That seeing me at the wedding last night made you want to die."

I shake my head, even as a tear rolls down my cheek. "I can't say any of that."

He closes the distance between us and thumbs away the tear and cages me in with his free hand. And suddenly he's too close, and he smells too good. I can hear him breathing and I'm reminded of how he breathes and what he looks like when he sleeps. I'm reminded of how it feels to sleep next to him. It's all too much. "Oh, well, that must just be my train of thought, then."

"I can't do this, Ford."

"What, talk? Why?"

"You have a girlfriend."

His face screws up in confusion. "What? Since when? The

only woman I've been seeing for months is you. You know that."

"You had a date last night. Y'all were awful cozy. You didn't act like you just met her. How long have you been seeing her?"

He blinks and bursts out laughing. "Fiona? Is that who you're talking about?"

I shrug. "I don't know. Is that the name of the woman you were with? Tall, brunette, gorgeous and would give you tall, gorgeous viking babies."

He snorts a laugh. "Fiona is one of my oldest friends and my agent. She and I are friends like you and Jess are friends. She and her *wife* bought my house in San Jose. We kissed when we were sixteen and she came out of the closet the next week." Relief floods my chest and I open my mouth and close it again when I realize he's not finished speaking. "When you said you had to work, I called Fiona to come with me to the wedding. Emerson was adamant I bring a date. I would've preferred to bring you. She flew in yesterday and flew back home this morning."

He bends until we're eye level. "You assumed we were together. The same way you assumed I was some corporate asshole. The same way you probably assumed my kid was a lot younger than she is. The same way you assume I'm probably interested in having more. You've *assumed* a fucking ton, Josie. When, if you had asked me anything at all, I would've told you. I would have given you my entire life's story. But you never fucking asked because you didn't want to know."

He works his jaw and his throat bobs with a swallow. "When we met, and I realized you probably didn't know who I was, it was awesome; not going to lie. Back in San Jose, I wasn't anonymous. Any woman who was interested in me always saw 'Bandit' first. They knew nothing about 'Ford'. And most of them never cared to know about 'Ford'. I never had anyone who wasn't after me for my standing or my money or my celebrity.

"And the fact that you had no clue how hot shit I am made me love you even more. Because yeah, I am hot shit. I'm a great player and a good coach. But because you knew none of that about me, I never had to question who you were with."

He blinks and his eyes glisten with unshed tears, making my stomach knot up. "But let's be honest, you were never *with* me. And not because you didn't want to be. The thing is, I could see it; the morning it changed. It was after that night when you told me you trusted me. I knew I was probably on borrowed time after that. Because you'd started catching feelings and just from what little I knew about you, you'd never let yourself fall for someone.

"Then you only started calling me during the day when there was no way we'd really be able to do more than just hook up. Even knowing you were pulling away, I went to you because I wanted any part of you that you'd let me have. Even if it was only for an hour and you made me leave after and I felt like some comfort item you'd pull out whenever you needed it.

"And pathetic simp that I am, when you asked me to come give Bea a skating lesson, I ran to do it. I thought that day you might actually let me in. You let me meet your niece, which for you is the equivalent of meeting your kid. And it was a great day." He pushes off the door. "And then you fucking ghosted me, Josie. You went radio silent and ran away from home like some immature child. Like a fucking coward."

I step forward and shove my hands into his chest, pushing him back. "You know, it's so easy for all of you to call me a fucking coward when every single one of you has gotten everything you've ever wanted. You have this great career and an amazing and beautiful daughter and you can have anything in life you want.

"Silas got Ada and Bea and Ada got not one true love, but two. And all I got was a chance to pass on a death sentence to any kids I might have and have my ticket punched in a long, drawn out illness that drains every good moment I could ever hope to have, every ounce of my strength, and every penny I could earn.

"So no, I'm not a fucking coward. I am a realist who is choosing to live. Right now. Right this minute. I am choosing to live however many days I might still have left without needing to worry about burdening someone else with losing me. I've watched what losing someone does to the people who love them and I'm not doing it to someone else."

Ford shakes his head, a look of disgust on his face. "You think you're the first person to face hardship or indecision? You think the life I have was handed to me? Hell no. I worked my fucking ass off. I had a kid when I was nineteen and still managed to graduate college and be at the top of my game. You know how I did that? Because I had people who loved me. People who were there for me. People in my fucking corner who showed up for me and helped bear my burdens.

"I never would've made it if I had pushed people away and turned myself into some kind of martyr for a reality that might not even happen. You don't know for sure your kids would get HCM or that you'll get breast cancer. You are placing a lot of stock in a fucking *maybe*. And the fact that you would deprive yourself of happiness on the grounds of a maybe tells me that yes, you are a coward."

"You're right about one thing. My kids won't get HCM because I won't have kids."

He sighs. "You don't know that. Silas asked me if I wanted more kids and I said I didn't know, but if you wanted kids, I would do that for you. Because I love you, Josie."

Tears, hot and unbidden, spring to my eyes. I would've

been okay if he hadn't said it. I would have survived this day if I hadn't heard him say those words I already knew he felt. But it's so different once they're out in the open. I shake my head. "I won't have kids; I made sure of it. After Cole died, I had my tubes tied. So, no, my children will not get HCM because there will be no children."

Ford blinks. "But you wanted them, didn't you?"

"It doesn't matter."

"It does fucking matter. If you had to mourn not only your brother but also your dreams, it's no wonder you're terrified to want anything for yourself. And it's even worse if you haven't let yourself grieve. If you've pushed it all down or bottled it up and haven't let yourself think of a life past those things. If you're not thinking about a future where you're happy—even a future five minutes from now—can you really say you're living? Because it sounds to me like you've put yourself into some sort of *Groundhog Day* type of loop where you keep doing the same things over and over and over again, hoping to never have to break that cycle and move on to February third.

"You go on dates and find someone to take you home and you don't let them spend the night and you don't let them hold you. You house sit and run errands for other people. You foster animals who will move on to their forever homes. Silas said you used to have this big corporate job, and you left because you said life was too short to spend it in an office. But the thing is, you're not living. You are doing all this shit for other people so they can live their lives. You have no life outside of helping other people make sure their plants are watered and their mail is collected and they get the right fucking watermelon when they get home from their vacation."

He takes a step toward me and raises a tentative hand to my face. I should pull away from him or demand he leave or run out of the house—anything except let him touch me. And yet, his large hand cradles my jaw and I stay exactly where I am. "Let me help you live, Freckles. Letting me help you doesn't make you weak. Letting someone love you doesn't mean you're weak. And even if you got cancer, I'd rather spend whatever time I was fortunate enough to live with you than have to do life without you.

"I can't fix you. I can't tell you how to get over losing your brother and the dreams you had. Few people can. And I'm not sure these are things one 'gets over' anyway. But if you'll let me, I will promise to help you bear it. Because I love you. I know that's hard for you to hear, and I know you don't want it. I know you think if you can't have everything, you shouldn't get to have anything. But everything can be whatever you want it to be."

Ford rakes his teeth over his bottom lip. "Dreams change, Josie. Sometimes they're everything you've asked for. Sometimes, take what you're given and make your dreams fit around your circumstances."

He looks away for a moment and weighs his words. "I've played hockey since I was four. The first time I laced up my skates and picked up a stick, it was like someone handed me my purpose in life. When Piper got pregnant, hockey suddenly didn't seem so important. I offered to quit and get a job so she could stay home with Emerson. I was prepared to leave hockey behind, but she wouldn't let me. She knew how much hockey meant to me and although it was hard, we made it work.

"Some might say that Piper saw my earning potential, and that's why she made sure I stuck it out, but they don't know Piper. We divorced right before we graduated college. And even though I'd already signed with San Jose before then, Piper wasn't entitled to any of my earnings. I've still taken care of her and Emerson, don't get me wrong, but that's not why she wanted me to stick with it. She never wanted me to have cause to wonder what my life could've been. To never have an inkling of resentment for her or Emerson. Piper is one of my best friends. She's been in my corner since we were fifteen years old. But there were so many times I wanted to walk away from the game because getting a day job would've been so much easier.

"But if I had done that, I would've never gotten to experience the things that I have. I'd never be able to set the example for Emerson that I have; that dreams and hard work matter. That if you want it and have the talent to achieve something, you can. That you find a way to make your dreams come true, even if those dreams change over time. I would've never been able to help the causes I donate to and volunteer with. I would've never met you, Josie. And meeting you was one of the best days of my life."

Tears continue to roll down my cheeks and Ford swipes them away. "I'd never take back all my sleepless nights and two-a-day practices. I'd never take back the shitty motels and long bus rides and subpar equipment that gave me blisters the size of silver dollars or the four A.M. conditioning sessions. I'd never take back seeing Emerson in the stands at both my first and last NHL games. I'd never take back all the fights that landed me in the penalty box or all of my many, many injuries. I'd never take back the millions of seemingly inconsequential things in my life because every single one led me to you.

"Dreams change, Josie. I know this because mine have. Until I met you, I was content with the life I was living. I was content for my existence to be me, Emerson, and our small group of friends who have become my family. I was content with being a hockey coach. I was content with my serial monogamist life and never settling down. I was content with my house being empty half the time I'm there. I was content in my aloneness. Now, none of those things are enough for me.

Now that I've met you, I need all those things and. I need you, Josephine."

It's the first time he's ever said my whole name, and no one has ever said it the way he does. As long as I live, the way he says my name will forever be my favorite way to hear it said. Sure as if it were some physical thing, my resolve begins to crumble.

"You want to have a family, you want kids? You, more than anyone, should know that blood doesn't make a family. Ada's been your sister almost your whole life. Luke is my brother. He doesn't share my DNA, but is just as much my family as Emerson or Piper or my parents. Families are built with love and hardship and fighting and hope. They're built on choices and actions and selflessness. They are built around dinner tables and on bar stools and during road trips, practices, on ice, and in beds. They're built in the mundane and day-to-day and they're built on the grand gestures and once-in-a-lifetime experiences."

He lets his forehead fall to mine and I breathe him in. That clean, earthy smell I could pick out of a lineup because that smell is Ford. "I want to be your family. I want you to be my family. I love you. It will never be easy because my life is fucking complicated and messy and exhausting. I am exhausting. And truth be told, you are exhausting."

I huff a watery laugh and he smiles. "Be exhausting with me, Freckles. I'd rather have one good year with you than fifty mediocre ones alone or with anyone else. And I don't know what will happen, but I know whatever does, I will be at your side helping you face whatever comes. Because that is what people who love each other do.

"And, God, how I love you. In spite of the fact you hate pickles and think *White Christmas* is the best Christmas movie when everyone knows it's *Christmas Vacation*. Despite the fact you'd rather push me away than let me hug you. In spite of the fact that you'll only let me hold you when I call it my aftercare. In spite of the fact that even now, you'd wish I'd never come, so you wouldn't have to hear me tell you I love you.

"Despite everything—every reason someone should give up —I can't. Because there is no one else for me, Josie. I'm sure I could find some woman to share my bed with and even love me. But no one challenges me like you do or makes me want to chip away at that hardened exterior for any little piece of yourself you'll give me. And I will happily chip away at it for the rest of my life if you'll let me."

CHAPTER TWENTY-THREE

FORD

For a long moment, Josie says nothing. I begin to think my speech has had no effect on her other than to strengthen her resolve to not be mine. Despite what I feel like is the Stanley Cup level of effort on my part, I'm aware it might not be enough. She still may not let herself have what she wants. And in truth, it might not surprise me if that's the case.

She steps back and wipes her eyes and blows out a breath and I know this is the part where she says it doesn't matter and I should go and to not call her again and to not come back. I steel myself for that to be the case simply so I don't fracture into a thousand pieces on the floor of this farmhouse if that's what she says.

I try not to stare at her, to spook her like the feral cat Jess claims her to be. But this is Josie and I've never been able to take my eyes off her when I'm in the same space as her. Even dressed in overalls and a flannel, almost a twin to her grandfather, she's still breathtaking. Her dark hair is up in this crown of braids, like some sort of milkmaid, with pieces falling at the nape of her neck and around her ears. Her face is clean of makeup, but flushed from probably both my proximity and whatever work she's done today.

And even though she's covered from her neck to her toes, my body nearly hums at her closeness. My need for her is so great, it's all I can do to not simply grab her face and crash my mouth against hers. To drag her to the nearest available flat surface and bend her over. To claim her and remind her whose she is. To make her beg for her release and watch that ever-present control she keeps firmly grasped fall away. But I do none of those things. I simply stand and wait for her to speak. *Please speak.*

"You know, for someone who's not a Campbell, you're pretty loquacious yourself."

Her expression is neutral and I'm afraid to hope for anything more than this moment; than for a simple conversation.

That was all you asked for, remember?

"What can I say? I'm a fast learner. Hopefully, it means I'd fit in. And if you think I can be chatty, just wait until you get to know Emerson. She could talk the bark off a tree."

Josie huffs a laugh. "She's great, by the way. From the few minutes I spoke with her. Gorgeous."

"Thank God she looks like Piper. Could you imagine if she'd inherited this nose?" I ask, pointing at my face.

She gives me a small smile. "Pretty sure she has your original one."

For her to know what my original nose looks like means she would've had to dig. I try not to let the hope bubble up with this knowledge. I try to keep my voice even. "Possibly."

She starts to say something, and the door opens and we both snap our heads in the direction of the sound. Josie's grandfather, followed by Gouda, steps inside and gives us a wave.

"Getting cold out there. I trust I gave y'all enough time to get to the good, rich soil?"

I frown in confusion and she huffs a laugh. "We're getting there, Pap."

"Well, good. Ford, do you have a game tonight you have to rush back for?"

I nod. "Yeah, unfortunately. I've got to be at the arena in a few hours, actually." Turning to Josie, I ask, unable to hide my hope. "Would you want to come?"

Biting her lip, she shakes her head. When my face falls, she holds her hands up. "It's not that I wouldn't want to, but I'm in the middle of cooking a batch of mash and I can't leave it." She rocks back on her heels. "Otherwise, I'd love to," she says softly.

"Okay."

Fred clears his throat and we both turn to him again. He gestures toward the back of the house. "I'm going to go catch an episode of *Gunsmoke*. My ears aren't what they used to be, and I'll probably have it up pretty loud. Josie, why don't y'all step into the other room to finish your conversation? It's too cold to be standing outside and y'all won't be able to hear one another talk if you stay in here."

Josie blushes, and I blink rapidly. I'm trying to wrap my head around her grandfather wanting us to be in a room with a bed and practically telling us he won't be able to hear anything we say or do.

"Go on, this man's got a game to get to. Finish your conversation so y'all can get to the good stuff." He wiggles his eyebrows and I nearly choke.

"Jesus, Pap, you old coot." She grabs my arm and tugs me toward a hallway and into a bedroom and shuts the door. "I swear, I'm going to kill him."

The television in the living room comes on and sure enough, it's loud enough to wake the dead, let alone drown out any conversation we might have. I jerk my thumb in the direction of the sound. "And let me guess, there's nothing wrong with his ears?"

She shakes her head. "Nope. Hearing as well as a sixty-year-old at his last appointment."

"He's sweet. Had a lot to say about you." She sighs and drops onto the edge of a twin bed. I look around and realize this must be her room. There are touches of her and Ada all over this space. "Your room?" I confirm.

"Yeah. The boys were in the attic. Now, that's where Ada and Silas stay. Bea usually stays in here with me." She examines something across the rooms. "Spent most of my weekends here growing up."

I sit on the twin bed next to hers, our knees only inches apart. If we both leaned our elbows on our thighs, our faces would nearly touch. "I can picture you here. Listening to Backstreet Boys or NSYNC or whatever girls listened to. Reading whatever girls read."

She huffs a laugh. "Actually, I was more into The Cure and The Clash, thank you very much. And I was obsessed with *The Sisterhood of the Traveling Pants.*"

"The Clash, huh? You still like them?"

Grinning, she nods. "Of course. They're classic. What did you listen to as a teenager?"

I think for a minute and scrunch up my face in embarrassment. "Promise not to laugh?"

Her grin widens. "Oh, never. I will most definitely laugh."

"The soundtrack to *Tarzan*. You know, the Disney movie."

Her mouth falls open. "No way."

I nod. "Yes. I watched it for the first time when I was, like, ten and my mom loved the soundtrack. I mean, come on, it's Phil Collins. You know he went way harder than he needed to on that thing. But it's got some bangers."

"Okay, I'll give you that." She rubs her hands over her thighs and slumps. "I don't know how to do this."

"Do what?"

"This. Us. I don't know how to be an 'us'. I've never had to consider how to be one and I don't know if I'd be any good at it. It's like you said; I'd rather push you away than let you even hold my hand. I know that makes me fucked up. I'm broken, Ford. There's no part of me that hasn't been shattered by everything that's happened.

"And the kicker is, I know I'm lucky. Most people don't know if they have stuff in their genes that could kill them. I know with a fairly high level of certainty what could take me out. If I'm lucky, I'll be like Meemaw and I'll be in my seventies when I'm diagnosed. If I'm not, I could find a lump tomorrow.

"I look at Ada, who has suffered more than any one person should have to in their lives. Her dad was a drug addict who would spend all their grocery money on meth and when he was high, he'd beat on her.

"And that's not even mentioning the repeated bouts of lice and lack of basic hygiene since he couldn't be bothered even that far. My mom was the one who taught her about periods and combed the nits out of her hair. My mom was the one who took her for her first gynecologist appointment after she and Cole started dating.

"Her mother abandoned her to run away to Texas and when she was fourteen, her mom asked her to come visit for the summer. She was so excited because she thought it meant she was finally going to get to have a relationship with her mother. Turns out, her mom's boyfriend had a little kid, and they didn't want to have to pay for daycare during the summer.

"When she was fifteen, her dad got so high and paranoid that when she just happened to be walking through their living room, he thought she was out to get him and he stabbed her seven times. She almost died.

"So when I say I know how lucky I was to grow up in the family I did, I'm fully aware of that fact. But as much as I love Silas, Cole was the brother I always turned to. You're not supposed to have favorites, and I didn't, but my relationship with Cole was different than the one I had with Silas. I can't tell you why.

"And when he got his diagnosis, I knew he wouldn't live to be an old man. It was like somewhere in my mind or heart or gut told me I'd never see him have all his dreams. He told me a few days after he got his results and after we'd all done our testing but hadn't gotten ours back yet, that he'd never have kids. He said he'd done the research, and he knew there was a high likelihood that he'd pass it on to his own kids. And with the medications and how careful he had to be about exerting himself physically and watching his diet, he couldn't see shackling someone with that sort of existence.

"He said as much as he loved Ada, even then, he would never marry her since, if his condition progressed like he suspected it would, he'd eventually need a transplant and he wouldn't put all that medical debt on her. Even at seventeen he was this super pragmatic type-A planner.

"And even though I knew it was a possibility, and I'd had almost fifteen years to prepare for that day, When Silas called me from the hospital and could hardly get the words out, I already knew what he was going to tell me. I was at work. I was in my corner office on the fortieth floor and had just closed a twenty-million dollar deal for a commercial real estate firm. It should've been my biggest career achievement. And all I thought was, I wasn't there when my brother died. I'd had the opportunity to see him a couple days before that and turned him down to get ready for the deal I'd just closed. I lost so much time with my family because of my need to do more, be more in my job.

"Part of it was possibly Meemaw and watching her get sicker and sicker. I was terrified to come to the farm while she was sick. She couldn't do chemo or radiation because she was almost eighty and because she was already stage four, they opted for palliative care. She wasted away to nearly nothing and was in so much excruciating pain at the end, she begged for death. I worked longer and longer hours so I wouldn't have to hear her scream. And I will regret that for the rest of my days; that I wasn't brave enough to be here for her."

A tear rolls down Josie's cheek and I'm having a hard time keeping my emotions in check listening to the anguish in her voice. I want so badly to hold her and comfort her, but I want to let her talk and I'm afraid if I move, she'll spook and this spell will be broken.

"I knew from the genetic tests, I already had the breast cancer gene, so I started getting mammograms when I was twenty. Every six months. That's something I can do to try to catch it as early as I can. And if I end up getting it, I'm comfortable with the steps that will need to happen if I'm diagnosed. Part of me has even considered doing a preventative mastectomy, but I'm not mentally prepared for that yet. And maybe that makes me vain. I'm sure it probably does.

"But watching my parents have to lose their son and their mother. Watching Pap lose his wife and then his grandson. Watching Silas and Ada lose them, I'm not brave enough to do it. Knowing what those sicknesses look like, I'm not selfish enough to bring a child into this world if there's even a chance it could suffer the way Cole or Meemaw suffered. The way my entire family has suffered. So I made sure I wouldn't.

"And yeah, it was a dream of mine to be a mother. Not that I wanted to be a teenage mother or anything, but it was the biggest aspiration in my life. I wanted to be a mother like my mom and my meemaw. I wanted babies to spoil and kids to love. I wanted to encourage my kids to love on those other kids in this world who might not get enough of it at home.

"But when I got my results, and they explained there was a high probability I'd pass my shitty genes on to my children, I knew it would be risky for me to have kids. And I think part of me started shutting down that dream the day I got the news.

"I threw myself into school and then college and then work. I wanted to climb as high as I could as fast as I could. Because maybe if I filled that void I was going to fill with babies with work and success and money and sex, I could forget how much I was hurting.

"When Cole died, I made the decision to not have kids permanent. I made sure that I'll never lose a child. And an argument can be made that for me to make a permanent decision based on a 'what if' is selfish. I'm fully aware I could have a genetically flawless child. But I can't face another loss in my life. I'm not strong enough to survive it. It would literally destroy me. I'm already trying to mentally prepare myself for the day I walk into this house and Pap's not here anymore. I can't do more than that." A sob wells up in her chest and tears pour down her face and mine.

"So, no, I don't know how to do this. I don't know how to give someone my heart when it's already broken into so many shards and held together by Elmer's glue and the paper-thin layer of armor I've built around it. I don't know how to give someone the power to break it even more than it already is."

And although I should probably stay exactly where I am, I can no longer be more than an inch from her. Not with her sobbing the way she is. I reach over and scoop her up into my arms and pull her over to my lap and when she wraps her arms around my shoulders and buries her face in my neck, I hold her like I've longed to hold her for months.

"I've got you, Josie." I press soft kisses into her hair and rub her back and attempt to soothe her. I'm under no illusions that this one talk will have fixed her or us. Most likely, Josie needs professional help to work through her trauma and fears. But for now, I will simply hold her.

CHAPTER TWENTY-FOUR

JOSIE

I cry for forever it seems. It's probably longer than I've ever cried in my life. Ford simply cradles me in his arms and rubs my back and lets me snot and cry all over his nice, fitted henley. When I've cried enough tears to fill a bathtub built for two, I pull back and sniffle, occasional hiccups working their way up my chest.

Ford wipes my cheeks and ignores the snot that I wipe onto the cuff of my flannel shirt. His expression is warm and gentle and he gives me a soft kiss on the lips before pressing his forehead to mine. "Your broken heart is not a weakness. But regardless of the state of your heart, I want it. I want every shard, every fragment. I promise to wrap it in mine and protect it and never do anything to damage it. And I promise when things come your way that might hurt you, I'll bear the brunt of whatever you need to do to make it so you can feel strong again." He leans back and takes my face in his hands. "I don't know if you know this about me, but I can protect a goal pretty well. I don't let things get by very often and I have the record to prove it."

I huff a laugh. "So cocky."

He grins. "It's only cocky if you can't back it up. Like I said, records."

After a beat, I say, "I love you and I missed you."

He smiles. "I know. Now the rest."

Snorting a wet laugh, I obey. "I can't live without you. Seeing you across the room and not touching you kills me. Seeing you at that wedding last night made me want to die." The last words come out shaky and I close my eyes as another tear rolls down my cheek.

Ford thumbs it away and presses a kiss to my forehead. "I know." Somewhere in the vicinity of his pocket, a phone rings. "Damn." I stand and he digs it out and sighs. It's not ringing; it's an alarm, I realize.

"You have to go, don't you?"

He nods. "Sorry."

I shake my head. "I understand. Someone's gotta pat the butts as the players go out onto the ice, right?"

He laughs. "Not really an ass patter myself. More a pound-the-top-of-the-helmet kind of coach."

"I have a lot to learn, I guess."

He stands and pulls me into his chest. "Yes, you do. But I'll be happy to show you the ropes."

Once Ford leaves and I handle things at the stillhouse, I make a quick supper for Pap and me before taking a long shower and falling into bed. Replaying the events of the day over in my mind, I'm not sure I'll ever feel completely "better" but I do feel lighter. I have no reason to think today fixes things between us. I still don't know how to be in a relationship, but damn if Ford's confidence in us doesn't make me want to try.

As sleep evades me, I pick up my phone and examine the

screen. Somehow, in the busyness of the evening, I've missed a text from Ford.

> Ford: After tonight and tomorrow's games, I have to be on the road for a little over a week. I always try to spend a couple days with Emerson when I come off the road, so the next couple of weeks are going to be a little crazy. After that, though, I'll have a nine-day rest. So, free your schedule for a week. Don't ask questions, don't make excuses. Make it work. I'll send you the dates and tell you what kind of weather to pack for.

A thrill runs through me at the thought of a week of uninterrupted time with Ford. An even bigger rush of excitement hits me when I see none of what he sent was a request.

> Josie: So bossy.

And even though it's late, his response is almost immediate and I smile.

> Ford: You like me bossy, Freckles.

> Josie: I like you every way, Viking.

For the next two weeks, I survive on crumbs of time with Ford. We've had no time to do anything more than meet for a quick supper or lunch between pitching in at the gym with Silas when their front desk attendants come down with the flu back to back and Ford's games and road trips.

Now that I've given myself permission to want him—us— I'm even more ravenous for him than before. I can't get enough of his stories and anecdotes and his 'I love you'. Whether it's rushed at the end of a conversation just before he heads out to coach a practice or game or as he's coaxing an orgasm from me, even through the screen of a phone.

God, how I miss his body. Much like the month we spent apart and only sporadically texted, I am nearly buzzing with my need for him. My vibrator and his voice just ain't cuttin' it anymore. And since the only alone time I've had with him was that day at the farm, I feel like until we can consummate our reconciliation, we're not truly back together. Or, maybe together at all would be a better phrasing. Since, before he busted through that flimsy layer of shell around my heart, that day was the day we actually began to be an us.

So this trip—whatever he has planned—cannot come fast enough. And as I sit at the kitchen table with Pap waiting for Ford to arrive, I'm as antsy as a long-tailed cat in a roomful of rocking chairs, as Meemaw would say. "Josephine, something wrong with your chair? You seem to be having an awful lot of trouble sitting still."

"No, Pap. I'm just ready to go."

"Well, good. I'm ready to be rid of you for a few days."

I scoff, but there's no venom in the sound. "I love you, too, old man."

He sips his coffee and pats my hand across the table. "Truth be told, it's good to see you excited about something. Been a long time since I've seen that emotion on you. Too long."

Giving him a soft smile, I nod. "I know. It's feels nice."

"I like Ford; he's good for you. Reminds me how it was between Beatrice and me. No one pushed my buttons like her. But no one was my safe place like her, either. You need to have both in the person you love."

I look down into my coffee mug, currently empty. "If you

knew how things would end with Meemaw, would you still do it again?"

"In a heartbeat," he replies without hesitation. "The bad days come whether you have someone there to share them with you or not. But knowing you have that other person there to help shoulder your bad days makes every bit of it worth it." Pap's eyes grow glassy and my heart lurches because I've never, in my thirty-five years, seen him cry. I'm not so jaded to think he never cries, but it's not something I've witnessed.

He clears his throat. "Without Beatrice, I wouldn't have gotten to be a daddy to Joseph or Miles. Or Pap to you and your brothers. Having y'all helped me in my grief when I lost the one person in this life who gave me reason to live some days. And I'd never trade any of y'all to rid myself of all the pain I've ever experienced.

"I know you worry about what might happen. I know it eats at you and scares you. But don't let that fear keep you from what could be the greatest and most rewarding adventure of your life. I had the privilege of loving my Beatrice for over fifty years. There's not a day goes by that I don't miss her like a part of my very soul. But look at everything she gave me. How could I ever wish to be without that for the sake of my own pain?"

"What if I'm too broken to let him love me? Really love me? Not just how it is now; all sweet and passionate. What if I can't do this? What if all my damage is too much for him?"

"Oh, Jo-Jo. You will never be too much for the right person. Something tells me Ford's not scared of your damage. If he were, he would've never been able to get past you pushing him away all those months. You think he's going to walk away just when you're finally letting him in? You think he would've been as good at hockey as he was if he was a quitter? You don't get to the level he was in his career with a quitter's attitude. And as much as he loves hockey, I'd say he loves you more." He gives my hand one last pat and jerks his chin up to signal out the window. "But only one way to find out."

I turn to see Ford's SUV rolling to a stop in the driveway and I scramble from my chair, running out the front door. I close the distance between us and I'm in his arms three seconds later. He lifts me easily off the ground and I wrap my legs around his waist and my arms around his shoulders and assault his face with kisses.

He laughs into my mouth and holds me tight against him. After a moment, he pulls his face back. "Jesus Christ, you're a sight for sore eyes." Giving my ass a possessive squeeze, he wiggles his eyebrows. "And sore hands. Fuck, I've missed you."

I nod and look into his dark blue eyes, free of any doubt or fear that he can't be affectionate with me. They are clear and happy and genuine. "I've missed you, too."

Ford lowers back to the ground and takes my hand in his. "Are you ready?"

"Well, considering you sent me a whole packing list, sure. You realize how confusing that was, right? To tell me to pack a winter coat and a swimsuit. Especially considering you won't even tell me where we're going."

"All in good time. Have some patience. Let's go say goodbye to Pap and Gouda. I'm sure she's missed me, too."

When we've been on the road for a bit, I finally ask, "So, how was your time with Emerson?"

He smiles. "Good. She's got a big swim meet coming up, so she's pretty nervous, but she'll do great. Scouts are already looking at her colleges and while I want her to go wherever she wants, the idea of her possibly moving across the country makes me want to puke. Other than road trips, I've never been apart from her. So thinking about being apart from her for months at a time is devastating."

"I'm sure. But college is still a couple years off. You'll just have to make the most of your time with her before then."

"Yeah, except now, she has a boyfriend." The last word comes out almost like a growl and I laugh.

"Wow, tell me how you really feel about it."

He sighs. "I know she's sixteen and smart and knows how to be safe. I know Piper and I have raised her to know her worth and not expect less than she deserves. But I also know what I was like at sixteen; what boys are like at sixteen. Wanting to fuck everything in a skirt and rack up as many notches on their bedposts as they can."

"First of all, if you and Piper feel you've done everything you can to raise Emerson to make the best choice possible for herself, you have to trust her to make those decisions. And second, you are generalizing about all boys. Good lord, my brothers were almost virtuous. I was the one who got around in our family.

"Cole and Ada were each other's first, and Silas was only with a few women before he and Ada got together. So, not all boys are rabid sex maniacs. Maybe Emerson's boyfriend is one of the virtuous ones."

Ford blinks. "Wasn't Silas in his thirties when he and Ada finally became a couple?"

I nod. "Yeah. He always said he didn't like no-strings sex and because he'd always loved Ada, it was hard for him to not picture her when he was with someone else. He said even if Cole had lived, he was sure he would have eventually settled for someone simply so he could have the things he wanted in life, but part of his heart would always belong to Ada. It made me sad for him, watching how he pined for her all those years."

"You knew he had feelings for her?"

I huff a laugh. "Yeah. Men think women gossip, but no one gossips more than two horny teenage boys who realize they have the hots for their sister's best friend. The summer Ada was gone to Texas, they both thought they were so slick asking about her. Since it was long distance to call, she and I emailed all summer, and both Cole and Silas would ask how she was doing and stuff.

"And Ada's always been beautiful; with that black hair and gray eyes, almost like something out of a fantasy novel. I noticed before they did how they'd started watching her. And granted, they both teased her, but it morphed in the months before she left for Texas. It wasn't as ruthless, more flirty. Cole knew, of course, how Silas felt about Ada. And as a brother, it made him sad to know Silas carried a torch for a woman he couldn't have—even if that woman was Ada."

Ford squeezes my hand before lifting it to his lips to kiss my palm. "Well, I'll tell you this right now. If I had a twin brother and we both wanted you, he'd have to fight me for you. And I've never lost a fight."

"Good to know." He turns on the blinker and it's only then that I realize we're headed to the airport. "Okay, can you tell me where we're going? I mean, as soon as we get into the airport and go through security—which, good thing I didn't bring any of my switchblades—and get to our terminal, I'll know where we're going. Save me the suspense?"

"What's the fun in that?" He parks the car and turns to me without shutting off the engine. He reaches to drag a knuckle up my jaw and down the side of my neck, setting my skin on fire. It makes me wish we didn't have anywhere to be but some place where we'd have room to get each other naked and remember what our bodies feel like pressed together. But we don't have time or space because we apparently have a flight to catch and Ford is six-foot-six and unable to fit in anything smaller than a king-sized bed.

"I promise, though," he says, leaning in to retrace the path his finger just traveled with his lips, "by the end of this week, you're going to need a vacation to recover from your vacation."

His mouth sears across my skin, forcing me to press my thighs together and focus on breathing. "Promises, promises."

Ford nips at the juncture where my neck meets my shoulder, and I nearly moan. "And I keep my promises, Freckles." He pulls back and my body reflexively follows his, even with my eyes closed, and he chuckles and drops a kiss onto my lips. "Let's go. If you're good, I'll let you pick our in-flight movie."

CHAPTER TWENTY-FIVE

JOSIE

After making it through security, Ford leads me to a terminal and I glance up at the destination. "Atlanta?"

He grins. "Yeah, for an hour layover, and then on to San Jose. Luke's got his first home game since coming off paternity leave, so I figured we'd catch it tonight. He's been dying to meet you, and he and Layla invited us over for brunch in the morning before we fly out again."

"So, we're only going to be in San Jose for tonight? Where do we go from there?"

His grin widens. "Well, Fiona and Val will also be at brunch, and I'm picking up the keys to their house on Tybee Island." He leans over and presses a kiss to the side of my neck. "I hope you're ready for vacation sex, because there will be so much vacation sex."

I snort a laugh. "You had me at Tybee Island. I can't believe you planned all this. Fiona is just going to let you borrow her beach house?"

"I'm pretty sure I paid for it," he says with a chuckle.

Once our boarding is called and we make our way onto the

plane, we're motioned into first class and my mouth falls open. "First class?" I ask in a whisper.

"Yes, Freckles. Money has its perks. The primary one being leg room. Have you seen how cramped economy is?"

I roll my eyes as he stores our bags in the overhead compartment. "Yes, actually, because that's how I typically fly."

He takes my hand after we're seated. "Well, not with me."

"You know you didn't have to do anything. I would've been content to simply spend a week in bed at your house."

Ford feigns annoyance. "Now you tell me." He tucks a stray hair behind my ear. "I know that. And while I was sorely tempted to keep you in my bed until neither of us could talk or move and we wasted away due to starvation and dehydration, you do so much for other people. I wanted to do this one thing for you. Don't get it wrong, getting to take you and show you off to my friends is a huge perk, but I wanted to spend time with you away from our normal lives. Time that's just for us. Time that I get you all to myself and for us to really talk and be together."

I flush with happiness and thankfulness at Ford's sweet gesture. As I intertwine our fingers, I ask, "So, should I get used to being swept away to an island every time we break up and reconcile?"

He raises a brow and levels me with a gaze. "First of all, we would've had to actually have been in a relationship for it to be considered a break up. And if I'm not mistaken, we were firmly in the 'fucking only' camp. Second of all, there will be no breaking up, so there will be no reconciliations. Third of all, we can go anywhere you want, anytime our schedules allow."

"Noted. Do you have a favorite place to visit?"

He considers. "I've been to a lot of places, but I don't get to visit them, if that makes sense. With road trips, you're on a plane and at a hotel, then to the arena and back to the hotel and plane. You don't get to really enjoy the cities. And when I'm home, I love home."

"So, you never go on vacations? You and Emerson don't go anywhere?"

Nodding, he smiles. "We went to Disneyland and Universal Studios for Emerson's thirteenth birthday. Piper and I always tried to coordinate our schedules so we could go as a family. We also do beaches and skiing, stuff like that. Personally, I'd be happy to spend a week in a secluded cabin with no cellphone service."

"I can do a cabin. It has service, but it's spotty."

His brows pull together in confusion. "What?"

"Pap's best friend owns a cabin on a river in Georgia. Silas and Ada go all the time. I think they're going in a few weeks. I bet we could crash. You could even be a lumberjack if you wanted."

He considers. "Okay. Send me some dates, I'll see if I can make something work. Does it at least have running water?" he asks, his tone hopeful.

I laugh. "Yeah. Power, too."

"Oh, thank God. I'm not that country just yet."

The pilot comes over the intercom and announces we'll be taking off soon, so we ensure our luggage is secure and buckle our seatbelts. Once we're in the air, I turn back to him. "Can I ask, how are you and Piper still so close? What happened? I mean, if I can ask that."

Ford nods. "Sure. You can ask me whatever you want. Piper and I have known each other since freshman year of high school. Her parents passed away, and she had to go live with her aunt in St. Paul, which is where I'm from.

"I'm not exactly shy," I snort-laugh and he smiles. "I know, shocker, right? Anyway, her first day, she was terrified. New city, new school, she'd lost her parents; it was a lot. And not going to lie, she's beautiful. I would've had to be blind to not notice her. Luke and I were sitting with some of our teammates and she looked like a deer caught in the headlights and I couldn't take watching her stand there with her brown bag lunch looking so sad. So I went and invited her to sit with us.

"For weeks, she didn't talk. She'd sit and keep her eyes focused on her peanut butter and jelly sandwich and bag of Funyons. But one day, we got to talking about *Boy Meets World* because it had just gone off the air. Do you remember that show?" When I nod, he continues. "Everyone was talking about their favorite episodes and someone made some joke about how the episode where Cory and Shawn dressed up as girls was stupid because they were too ugly as girls for them to have been taken seriously enough for guys to want to hit on them.

"Piper's head snapped up, and she actually looked like she had some life in her. She told them that wasn't the point of the episode to begin with. That it had been about girls not being heard or taken seriously simply because they were pretty. She went on to say that Rider Strong actually made a very pretty girl and if we'd remembered the episode correctly, we see that Shawn was hit on by a guy and the guy tried to put his hand up the dress he was wearing, teaching him a crucial lesson about consent."

I nod, impressed. "Wow. That's impressive for a fourteen-year-old."

"Yep. And then the guy who'd made the comment made some crack about how she certainly was too pretty to take seriously and asked her on a date and she'd rolled her eyes. She got up, and he grabbed her ass and Piper punched him in the nose and told him if he'd missed the lesson on consent, he might need to rewatch the episode."

My eyes go wide. "Wow. I think I might be a little in love with her."

He laughs. "Right? But after that, she was pretty vocal about her opinions and no one messed with her. And I crushed. Hard. Even though I dated other girls and she dated other guys, we hung out and we were friends. We never happened to be single at the same time, which might be why we never dated in high school.

"Coincidentally, we both went to Denver for college and ran in a lot of the same crowds. I'd converted her to a die-hard hockey fan at that point, so she came to all the games. I'd been seeing this girl freshman year of college, but she broke up with me a few weeks before the end of the season.

"But that season was great. We kept advancing in the championship brackets and actually won the whole thing. It was... amazing. Luke, Piper, and I all went to this party to celebrate, and I found out Piper had broken up with her boyfriend and I thought, now's my chance. Apparently she had the same idea, because lots of tequila shots later, we woke up together.

"Then it kept happening without the tequila and a month later, we found out she was pregnant. Our best guess is that 'tequila Ford and Piper' didn't use a condom. And honestly, neither of us even remember that night. But it was good after that and I never hesitated to step up when she told me about the baby. I loved Piper; the sex was good. I thought it was the right kind of love; you know, the kind that can sustain anything.

"And while she and I were still best friends, and I asked her to marry me and she said yes, there was something missing. And even though we were attracted to each other and loved one another, it wasn't the kind of love either of us deserved. I would've stayed in it, simply for the sake of Emerson, but Piper said it wasn't fair to her.

"She said that one day, we would both find our forevers and Emerson would see what true love looked like. That she should be able to recognize what love is supposed to look like. That she loved me, but not like that. And I expected when we divorced, it would change things between us, but it didn't. And even after we divorced, we'd occasionally hook up just because we were both single and horny, but we always made sure Emerson never found out since we didn't want to confuse her.

"When Emerson was about five, Piper met someone and we stopped hooking up. And when she introduced me to him—he hadn't met Emerson yet—I could see it was different with him than it was with me. And you'd think when your ex-wife introduces you to her new boyfriend, you'd get all torn up or jealous. Especially with me, because I'm possessive—in case you hadn't noticed."

I laugh, and he grins. "But I just felt happy for her. It made me see that we really were just friends. It didn't work out with that guy, and Emerson never ended up meeting him. But Piper and I didn't go back to hooking up because she was ready to settle down and I didn't want to complicate things for her.

"About five years ago, I changed accountants and met Conrad. He was divorced, no kids, a great guy, and I knew he'd be perfect for Piper. It was like something just told me he was Piper's guy. So she got her happily ever after. And truly, I couldn't be more pleased for her."

"She sounds amazing."

"She is. And she'll still always be one of my best friends. I couldn't have picked a better person to impregnate on a drunken one-nighter."

I laugh. "Nice."

He shrugs. "What about you and Jess? Seems like he was probably your most serious relationship. I know it was high school, but did you love him?"

"I think so," I answer honestly. "Jess is great. He was popular and cute and everything any girl could ever want. And he chose me. I felt lucky to be his girlfriend. And he actually liked me. He wasn't my first kiss or even the first guy I fooled around with, but it was different with him, and I think I loved him. We slept together and the next week I found out about Cole's HCM.

"And my parents weren't all about waiting until marriage for sex or anything like that. They knew all of us were active. My parents have always been open and communicative about sex and relationships. I'm pretty sure I won the parent lottery, to be honest. They're amazing.

"But somehow I thought because I had sex, Cole got HCM. I know it's stupid and makes no sense, but I thought I'd caused it. And so, I broke up with Jess and didn't have sex again until college."

He gives me a sad smile. "Oh, that's awful."

"Yeah, teenagers are dumb. But after I got my test results, I didn't want to fall in love. Ada and Cole were so in love, and all I could think about was what it might be like if his HCM killed him. What that would be like for her. So, I didn't have relationships after that. I had a long string of hook-ups for a damn long time. Really, until shortly before I met you."

"Well, lucky for me, you did meet me," he replies, leaning over to give me a kiss.

"Lucky for me, too, Viking."

Ford nods. "You know, I thought by now, we would've come up with more creative nicknames."

"Eh, Freckles has kinda grown on me."

"Good, because I was going to tell you that you were stuck with it anyway."

I roll my eyes. "Well, fine, because you're stuck with Viking."

"Not an insult by a long shot. I'll gladly claim it." He kisses me again. "I'll gladly claim you, too. Over and over and over again."

"I might be on board for that." My voice has gone a bit breathy and my heart rate has started to pick up. "Um, how long until we get to San Jose? And how close is our hotel?"

"We have about an hour layover in Atlanta and then it's about another five-and-a-half hours until we're in San Jose. But with the time change, it'll only be two hours later than when we leave Atlanta. And we're staying in Luke and Layla's guest suite. They built it for when their parents visit. Really, it's their entire basement and is like an apartment. Two bedrooms, a full kitchen, huge soaker tub."

"So, what you're saying is, we won't have time for a quickie in Atlanta because the airport is so big and it'll probably take us a half-hour to find our terminal. And then, it'll be at least five-plus hours before you'll be able to get me naked? Any chance you'd be interested in joining the mile high club?" I ask in a whisper and wiggle my eyebrows.

Ford laughs. "While I appreciate your enthusiasm, I barely fit in airplane bathrooms by myself. If I add you into the equation, we're liable to get put on some kind of no-fly list, and that would make it awfully difficult for me to sweep you off on grand adventures if we can't fly."

I feign exasperation. "Fine. Party pooper. Don't say I never offered you anything, though."

"Never."

Changing the subject, I ask, "Will we have time before the game to get settled? And by settled, I totally mean naked."

"Damn, sweetheart. Unfortunately, no. We'll have to go straight to the arena." He leans in and moves my hair off my shoulder and kisses a trail down my neck. "But I will make your wait so very, very worth it. You have no clue how much I'll be looking forward to making use of every available flat surface in Luke's guest suite. I hope you've hydrated."

I let out a soft, frustrated groan. I'm about to say something about how I'm willing to risk the no-fly list for the sake of a much needed orgasm, when a flight attendant stops by to ask if we'd like a drink. Because I'm feeling fancy, I order a glass of champagne and Ford orders a whiskey.

After I take a sip, the bubbles tickling my nose, I smile. "I going to be spoiled and never want to fly economy again."

"If you're with me, you won't have to. And you will be with me."

"Bossy."

He quirks a brow. "You like me bossy."

"I already told you. I like you every way. Any way. All the ways."

CHAPTER TWENTY-SIX

FORD

Even in a ball cap pulled down low over my forehead, we make it fifty feet toward the exit doors at the San Jose airport before someone recognizes me. Josie seems caught off guard for a moment, as if she's forgotten that people know who I am and I want to laugh. I keep her close to my side and sign the autographs and take a few selfies before politely extricating us from the crowd that's beginning to form.

As we pick up our rental car and pile our bags in the backseat, Josie shakes her head. "I know you said you were a celebrity, and you had no anonymity here, but I'm not sure I actually believed it. You walk around Knoxville mostly unbothered, right?"

"Yeah. It's pretty nice."

"What's it going to be like at the game?"

I blow out a breath. "Probably a lot like the airport. I'm sorry, I should've warned you."

She shakes her head. "I don't have any issues with crowds and this city was your home for a lot of years, so I get you needing to kiss the babies and shake the hands and stuff."

"You make me sound like the mayor."

"For all I know, you were the mayor."

"Nope. Definitely not the mayor. I don't have any political aspirations."

"Is that because you have a lot of skeletons in your closet?"

"No. I just don't like having to be 'on' all the time. At least with hockey, there are off days; there's an off season. With politics or other kinds of celebrity, you have basically no private life. I've really enjoyed that since I've moved to Knoxville. Lets me know all the more I made the right decision."

I give her knee an affectionate squeeze. It's so different from how it was when we first started seeing each other. Now, she doesn't push me away or shy away from my affection. She relishes it. She seems to crave those small touches now as much as I always have. And 'relationship Josie' is so much more open than 'fuck buddy Josie' and I can't say I hate it. Honestly, I fucking love it.

As we enter the arena, it's a bittersweet for me. The rink was my home for my entire professional career—thirteen years. I could make the argument that I had more seasons left in me, but knowing Emerson and Josie are in Knoxville, there's no part of me that regrets leaving.

I keep Josie's hand gripped firmly in my left one as we wind our way through the crowd toward the ticket line with the e-tickets Luke sent me. I probably could have spoken with the front office and secured a suite, but I want Josie to experience hockey the way it's meant to be: right in the action, next to the boards.

It's been so long since I was simply a spectator at a pro game, it's a bit surreal. We used to go to Avalanche games when we were in college, but that was probably the last time I sat in the stands like a regular fan. And even now, I'm not a regular fan since I begin gaining the attention of other attendees as we wait almost immediately.

Within minutes, we're swarmed, and flashes from cell-phone cameras blink, questions are shouted at me, programs and Sharpies are thrust in my direction. I periodically glance to Josie at my side and she gives me a reassuring smile each time, no trace of annoyance or impatience in her gaze or posture.

And same as when we were at the airport, I politely extricate us from the throng, get some pre-game snacks, and finally make it to our seats. After a few of our section mates greet us and I sign even more programs, jerseys, and pucks, I turn to face the ice and blow out a breath. I wrap my arm around Josie and press a kiss to her temple before resting my forehead on the side of her head and whispering in her ear. "Sorry about all the autographs."

She looks up at me. "I told you, it's fine. After the airport, I expected it. Makes me feel like I'm with some big shot," she says with a playful smile.

"You are with a big shot. I'll show you just how big when we get to the house."

Josie bites her lip and lifts a brow, and I want to bite that lip myself. I want to suck it into my mouth and feel her tongue against mine and hear the way she moans. I want to run my hands all over her naked body until I've claimed every inch of her.

"You must think I have a faulty memory, Viking. I am well aware of how big your shot is." I huff a laugh, even as heat and need settle into my groin and I'm glad I'm sitting down.

A tap on my shoulder breaks the spell of me being unable to take my eyes off this gorgeous woman and I turn to see a boy who looks to be about ten years old standing on my other side. I give him a warm smile. "Hi."

"You're Bandit Brickman, right?"

I nod. "That's me." I lean in conspiratorially. "Can you keep it a secret, though?"

He grins like I've given him the keys to some candy-coated wonderland and nods enthusiastically. He furtively glances around and pulls a puck and silver Sharpie from the pocket of the hoodie he wears and asks in a whisper, "Will you please sign this?" I take it from him and quickly scribble my signature and hand it back over. "Thank you." He's still whispering and quickly darts off toward his parents a couple of rows back.

Josie loops her arm through mine. "Now, those autographs you can sign all day long. That was adorable. I swear, it's a wonder a thousand women don't offer to let you father their children. You are damn sexy with kids, mister."

"Oh, I've had plenty of offers."

"Do I need to be concerned about crazed female fans wanting to burn me in effigy? Have you ever had a girlfriend you brought out in public? Are there—what is the hockey equivalent of a groupie?"

"A puck bunny," I supply.

"Okay, are there any *puck bunnies* I need to worry about?"

I shake my head. "No. I tried my best to never sleep with any puck bunnies. Not going to say it never happened, but they were rare."

"So, how did you meet women?"

"Friends outside of the organization. Or friends of friends. And puck bunnies are pretty indiscriminate. They don't care who they bag as long as he wields a stick. A lot of them don't even care if the player is single."

"Well, you are very much not single," she reminds me, her tone smug.

"Thank God you finally admit it." Josie laughs and tucks into her nachos and beer. I point out Luke during warm-ups and he shoots us a wave just before the puck drops. I try to explain the rules of the game as it progresses and I'm up on my feet when Luke scores a goal. And when San Jose ekes out a final winning goal at the end of the third period, it's a satisfying victory for my former team.

It takes almost an hour to get out of the arena once the game is over and a news crew catches wind of my presence. I do a quick interview and life update for the local news's sports segment and all the while Josie waits patiently, reminding me just how much she does for others; how selfless she is. God, I love this woman.

Nearly twelve hours after leaving Knoxville, and closing in on midnight local time, we finally pull in to Luke's driveway. Having sent him and Layla a quick text before leaving the arena that we were going to grab a bite to eat and head over, they sent me the code to the basement entrance and said they'd see us at brunch. Although I would have gladly shot the shit with them for a bit before Josie and I retired for the night, I'm thankful we don't have to.

As we drag our bags into the house, we're both dead on our feet as our bodies are still on east coast time. We barely have the energy to undress and brush our teeth before falling into bed. By unspoken agreement, we simply curl up under the covers and I pull her into my arms without fear she's going to stiffen or roll away from me and I'm out in seconds.

I'm having the most vivid dream of my life. Wet heat and suction envelope my cock and sweet Jesus, I'm so close after only seconds. But when I hear the moan, I know it's not a dream. Pulled gradually from sleep, my eyes flutter open to see Josie looking up at me from between my knees, her lips wrapped so prettily around my dick. Her hair is mussed from sleep and she's naked.

And dear lord, it's too good and I'll be damned if the first time I come after we've made us official is anywhere but inside her pussy. Gripping her shoulders and pulling her off me, I sit up quickly and crash my mouth against hers with a soft groan. Josie licks into my mouth and her fingers are in my hair and she's straddling me and her pussy is hot and right there.

"Fuck, I've missed this," I breathe and run my hands over her breasts, kneading and teasing; down her waist and around to her back and down to her ass. I can't stop myself from grabbing that glorious backside and holding her in place as I grind up against her, nearly losing it when she gasps. "Jesus, Josie."

"Ford. God. Please."

Bringing my hand up to grip the back of her neck, I tilt her head as I kiss my way down her check and jaw and the column of her throat. "What do you want, Freckles? Tell me."

"I want you. Please." Her voice is a breathy whine, and my cock jerks hearing the pleading in her tone.

I nip at her shoulder. "You can do better than that. I want to hear it."

"Fuck me. Hard. Fast. Please. I need it so bad." She snakes her hand between us and grips my cock and gives it a rough stroke and I grunt with the effort of not busting a nut simply from her hand and the proximity of my promised land.

"How do you want me to fuck you?"

She shifts her hips and starts to guide my cock past her entrance and I grab her hand and grip her chin with my free one and look into her eyes. "Are you sure? I brought condoms. I'm not so far gone that I'd forget."

She resumes stroking me, but makes no move to sink down

onto me. "I'm sure. I can't get pregnant and I've not slept with anyone but you since we first hooked up."

I shake my head. "I haven't either."

"And we're both clean."

"Yeah."

"Is it okay?" she asks.

I wrap my arms around her and roll us in one smooth motion and Josie lets out a small squeak of surprise. I notch my cock at her entrance and keep my eyes on hers. "You trust me?"

She runs her fingers down my arm and lifts my hand from the mattress and brings it to her throat. "I trust you. I love you."

For some reason, this makes us feel the most real. This moment. I hold her throat, but I don't squeeze. It's a simple point of contact that lets me feel as though I'm claiming her. And as I enter her, inch by inch, I savor the hot, wet slide of this homecoming. Because that's what Josie feels like: home.

We let out a simultaneous moan that makes me smile, and Josie's eyes fall closed. I give a gentle squeeze to her throat. "I want to see your eyes." She opens and focuses hers on mine. "Good girl." Her pupils are blown wide and when she rocks her hips, driving me even deeper, her mouth falls open with a soft sigh.

I drop my forehead to hers as I relish the way our bodies fit together. And even though Josie asked for hard, for fast, I'm not ready for that yet. "So fucking perfect. Jesus Christ, beautiful girl, I've missed this so much."

She whimpers and I pull back and look at her. Her face and chest are flushed and she's panting and I want to memorize this moment. How gone she looks. "Please, Ford."

I drop my hand from her throat to settle onto her hip and dig my fingers into the pliant, soft flesh and increase the power of my thrust, and Josie gasps. "That what you want? You want to be able to feel how well I fuck you for hours later?"

"Yes. Please. Fuck, Ford."

I'm not sure I'll ever get over the way it sounds when my name leaves her lips. Especially when she's pleading. Fuck, it's like some kind of drug. I bend my head to suck her nipple into my mouth as I continue to pound into her. She moans and sinks her fingers into my hair and she's close. So close, her pussy is pulsing and her moans begin to devolve into these short, high exhales of breath.

And I debate edging her. The thought crosses my mind. In spite of how she claims to hate it, she doesn't. Her list says so. Fuck knows I memorized everything on that damn list and got off thinking about it on multiple occasions. But edging her also means edging myself and I'm not sure if, after all these weeks without her, I can deprive myself of my own release.

So instead, I brace her thighs on my biceps and press her knees back, fucking her deep, the way she likes. Josie shrieks, her eyes going wide and drilling into mine. "Yes. Fuck. Ford. Jesus. Please. Please."

Her eyes are glassy as tears well in them and I'm so close I'm about to die. "Get there, Josie. Fuck. Now," I command through gritted teeth. She reaches between us and works her clit and I feel it the moment she lets go with a gasp and my breath catches with how tight she gets and I can't hold my own orgasm at bay as electric jolts of pleasure shoot through every molecule of my being as I spill into her with a long grunt.

I'm huffing ragged breaths as I lower her legs to the mattress and drop my face to Josie's neck and simply try to come back to myself. After a beat, I collapse on the bed and pull her into my arms. She comes willingly, her head resting on my chest, and I nearly sigh in contentment.

Short of breath, she asks, "You think Luke and Layla heard us? Will they think I'm some kind of nympho?"

I can't help but laugh and wrap my arms tighter around

her. "I guess we'll find out at brunch. If Luke gives me the stink eye, it's a pretty safe bet. He's still flying solo these days, even though Layla's been released from her doctor. I think the idea of getting back into the swing of things post-baby is a little intimidating for them both."

She presses a kiss to my chest. "I think it was like that for Ada and Silas, too. I can imagine it's a bit nerve-racking."

"Yeah."

Josie rolls until she's nearly on top of me and folds her arms on my chest, propping her chin on them so she can better see my face. I look down at her, one of my own arms folded behind my head for support. I sweep her hair off her face and tuck it behind her ear. "Did you and Piper ever talk about having any more kids?"

I shake my head. "No. With my career and hers and how much we wanted to focus on Emerson, there was never a good time. Before she was born, I never thought about kids, period. Not that I didn't think I wouldn't want them at some point in the far distant future, but hockey was the only thing I was focused on, so kids were this abstract thing. Until they weren't. Why?"

She shrugs. "I don't want you to have regrets."

I frown, my brows drawing together. "Why would I have regrets?"

She bites her bottom lip, shrugging again. "I know Emerson is older, but if you want to have more kids, I want that for you."

"Josie, I told you, blood doesn't make a family. If we decide we want kids, we'll figure it out. We can foster or adopt or look into finding an egg donor if you decided you wanted to experience pregnancy. There's more than one way to skin a cat, Freckles, and anyway you wanted to skin it, I'll help you.

"But if you don't want anything—if you've decided you truly don't want to be a mother—I'm cool with that, too. If

Gouda and fourteen other animals are what you want, we'll do that. When I say it's whatever you want, I'm not simply telling you what you want to hear. The idea of Emerson being an only child doesn't fill me with regret or anything. The idea of her having siblings doesn't either. I'm adaptable. And for you, I'd adapt to just about anything."

"I can't promise life with me will be easy."

"Sweetheart, you are the antithesis of easy. I like you that way. If I wanted easy, I'd find a puck bunny."

She pinches my ribs, and I laugh. "No puck bunnies for you."

"Dually noted."

My phone dings on the nightstand, and I pick it up to see a text from Luke.

> Luke: If you guys are done bringing the house down and making the rest of us jealous, Layla and I are up and have coffee made. Brunch is in an hour.

I laugh, and Josie lifts a brow. "What's so funny?" I show her the text and the color drains from her face. "God, that is such a terrible first impression. I am mortified."

I give her a smug smile. "I'm not."

CHAPTER TWENTY-SEVEN

JOSIE

After knowing Luke and Layla—whom I've yet to meet—heard us having sex, even from upstairs, I'm a nervous wreck. Even with Ford reassuring me it's no big deal, it's definitely not the way I want to be remembered by Ford's best friend.

After we change the sheets and remake the bed and shower to prepare for brunch, I'm fidgeting with the sleeve of my sweater as Ford rolls the cuffs of his flannel. "Stop fidgeting. It's fine. We're all adults. Pretty sure Luke knows we have sex. In fact, I know he does. He knows about the bar."

My mouth falls open. "You told him about that?"

He nods. "Well, yeah. I was miserable because I was buzzed and you were being stubborn. He was miserable because the babies wouldn't sleep. We were commiserating. Plus, he's my best friend. You talk about shit with Jess and Ada and probably even Silas. Don't get all prudish on me."

"I'm not prudish. And I know they know we have sex. Public sex is a different story."

He levels me with a gaze. "So no one knows about the bar?"

"No. I mean, yes. Jess knows, and I guess Hensley assumes."

"Okay then, don't get all freaked out about it." I sigh and bite my lip and Ford steps away from where he's been examining his appearance in the mirror to stand in front of me. He takes my face in his hands and drops a kiss on my lips. "I know this relationship thing is new to you. I know you're not used to having to 'meet the family' or whatever. But Luke knows how bananas I am over you. Whatever you think he or Layla are going to think about you, it's going to be through the lens I put in front of them. They're going to love you because I love you, Freckles."

I almost hold my breath as we walk up the stairs to the main floor, the smell of coffee and bacon and something else wafting down from the kitchen. My mouth waters and the thought of coffee almost makes me forget my anxiety over the fact that people I've never met before have heard me banging my boyfriend.

Ford opens the door and I take a steadying breath before crossing the threshold behind him. When we come into the kitchen, it's empty and I calm down a bit more. I take in the warm gray hardwood floors, white walls, and black cabinets complete with concrete countertops. The space is modern and a bit industrial, with clean lines and stainless steel appliances. As I've not been to Ford's house yet, I'm not sure what I expected a professional athlete's kitchen to look like. But while the appliances are obviously top of the line, it's not over the top or flashy by any means.

Ford tugs me along and, seeing the bacon needs flipping, stops at the stove to do exactly that. He gestures to a cabinet to his right. "Mugs are in there. Want to pour us some coffee? They must've had to go take care of the babies."

Thankful to have something to do, I fill up two mugs and set one within his reach. I sip mine and look around the room a bit more, my eyes catching on the view out the back door and to the gorgeous expanse rolling hills as far as the eye can see. Luke and Layla's home is positioned at the base of a lush green hill. "Are we still in San Jose, or did we go father out? It was so late last night, I wasn't paying attention."

Ford fishes the bacon out of the skillet to dry on some paper towels. "Yeah. Still San Jose. And there are some hiking trails nearby or we can drive up toward San Francisco or get Luke to take us out on the boat. There's tons to do."

Next time. Next time implies a future. The thought used to terrify me. And not that I'm still not terrified, but not nearly as much as I was.

"Oh, you want me to take my boat out so you can sink it again?"

I pivot at the sound of a deep voice and am greeted by the sight of a man, around six-foot, with dark brown skin and a huge smile. He has two baby carriers strapped to his front, one on each side of his torso, and he's gently bouncing the small bundles that appear to be snoozing.

Ford's grin is wide as he crosses the room to Luke. "That was one time. And it's your fault for buying a piece of shit, anyway. It was a dingy, not a yacht, and I helped you haul it out of the water." The two men embrace as best they can, given Luke's current cargo, and they both laugh.

I make my way over and give our host a warm smile and extend my hand as Ford makes the introductions. "Luke, this is Josie. Don't be fooled by our performance earlier, that was actually her trying to be quiet."

My face flames and I elbow him in the stomach, making

him grunt, before shaking Luke's hand. I narrow my eyes at Ford. "Too bad for you, that might be the last *performance* you get in a while."

Luke cracks up. "Oh, man. Been a while since Ford met his match. I'm glad to see it finally happened. Josie, it's great to meet you. Don't worry, I never believe half of what Ford tells me. I've known him too long and my bullshit detector is finely tuned to his particular brand of shit."

Ford rubs his stomach and pulls me into his side, dropping a kiss on the top of my head. "Don't listen to him, Freckles. Not a word. He'll tell you all lies."

"And which lies would those be? That you used to take Ambien and sleep eat and gained forty pounds during one season and no one could figure out why? Or the time you borrowed a girl's deodorant only to discover it was roll-on Nair? Or, my personal favorite, the time in Florida—."

Ford covers Luke's mouth with his hand, his eyes wide. "We swore never to speak of Florida again. I just convinced this woman to pursue a relationship with me. I don't need her getting cold feet just yet."

I can't help but laugh. Watching the exchange between Ford and Luke reminds me so much of Cole and Silas, it's entirely bittersweet. "No, please, I need to know about Florida."

"Trust me, you don't want to know. You'll never look at seafood the same way," a woman pipes up as she enters the room. Nearly as tall as her husband—seriously, are all the people in Ford's life this tall—Layla is gorgeous, with medium-brown skin, and curly black hair pull up into a mass on top of her head. Layla, equipped with her own baby carrier on her chest, steps forward and, after giving Ford an affectionate kiss on the cheek in greeting, offers me a warm, friendly smile, a dimple popping high on her cheek. "You must be Josie. I've heard so much about you. But Ford definitely downplayed how gorgeous you are. Damn, girl."

I blush. "You're one to talk. Are you sure you just had three babies?"

"Most definitely," she says with a laugh. She loops her arm through mine and starts leading me away. "All these babies are finally in a milk coma." She tosses Ford a smile. "Ford, be a dear and keep an eye on the food. Casserole is in the oven. Fiona and Val will be here soon with the booze and mixers. I'm going to steal Josie away for a little while so you two can hash out last night's game. I'm tired of hearing about it."

She doesn't wait for an answer and walks me to a room down the hall that could almost be considered a library. Floor-to-ceiling bookshelves line three of the walls and a gas fireplace takes up the empty wall, with a large television mounted above it. Three bassinets are lined up beside a large brown leather sofa, where a Yorkshire terrier sits on the far end on top of a round cushion. The dog raises its head, but doesn't move or bark.

"That might be the calmest yorkie I've ever seen," I remark as we sit.

Layla grins as she unlatches the baby from her chest and lays her into one of the bassinets. "Well, she's about a hundred years old, so not much fazes her these days." Once she sits, she turns to me. "So, how did you like your first game?"

"It was something else. It's so violent."

She nods. "Yeah, Luke's got the partial to prove it. I'm shocked Ford only escaped with that nose of his."

"Thank you so much for having us. I know it meant a lot to Ford for us to get to visit."

"We're happy to have you guys. We've miss Ford so much and we were so glad he could come in for the game. Luke's never had to be without him, so him moving across the country has been hard on him. Me being hormonal and as big as a house didn't help, I'm sure."

"I'm sure having three babies at a time isn't a walk in the park. But y'all look to have everything under control. They're beautiful, by the way. What names did y'all pick? I can't remember if Ford ever told me."

Layla sets her hand on the nearest bassinet. "This is Jordan. Luke has Ellis and Olivia."

"How do you tell them apart?"

"Right now, we have strings tied around their ankles in different colors. Thankfully, it's cold outside, so no one looks at us sideways since we keep them covered up. I'm sure once they get a little bigger and start getting more personality, it'll be easier, but for now, it's still a struggle."

"I'm sure. I can't imagine."

"Maybe someday you'll have your own brood. Then I can call Ford in the middle of the night and wake him up when he's just getting some sleep."

I've learned how to dodge this conversation over the years; to deflect. And with everyone but Ada and Silas and now, Ford, that's what I do. But something about Layla makes me want to open up. I've just met this woman, but I feel a sort of kinship with her. Perhaps it's the fact that she's essentially Ford's sister-in-law and these are people who are important to him. But her warm, brown eyes scream, *I'm here for you.*

I shake my head. "No brood for us. Not one that I can produce, anyway."

She blanches. "I'm sorry; that was thoughtless of me. I should learn to keep my mouth shut. Luke and I have always been so open about our infertility journey, I forget other people don't talk about their reproductive health with people they just met. Forgive me. It's none of my business."

I shake my head again, and give her a smile, letting her

know I'm not offended. "No need to apologize. And I probably shouldn't have worded it that way. I'm fertile, as far as I know, but I had my tubes tied." She blinks and opens her mouth and closes it again, as if she's not sure what to say, so I elaborate. "My brother passed away from a genetic heart condition and my grandmother died from breast cancer. I'm a carrier for both genes. I chose to have my tubes tied to prevent the possibility of passing those down."

She nods. "I see. I'm sorry to hear about your brother and grandmother."

"Thank you. Ford has been a great help to me in working through all my issues. Well, him and a therapist. I wanted to be a mother and although I chose my path, sometimes it doesn't really feel like I had much of a choice. I know blood doesn't make a family; I've seen that firsthand. So, I know I have options; it just took me a lot of years to think that I deserved them."

Layla gives me a soft smile. "I understand. Ford's good at putting things in perspective. And nothing wrong with getting professional help, either. I'm of the opinion that everyone would be better off with therapy. And the people who think they don't need it are ones other people probably go to therapy and talk about."

I laugh. "Probably."

Luke steps into the room and over to the bassinets. As he gingerly removes the babies from their carriers and sets them down, he gives his wife a smile. "Fiona and Val are here. I've got the video monitor charged up; let's go eat."

We stand and walk back out toward the kitchen and dining room, which holds a black wooden table that seats ten. Two women, one I recognize from the wedding and the other is a petite Latina with light brown skin, cropped black hair, and big brown eyes. She sports a slim gold nose ring and several diamond studs along the shell of her ears.

They both stand when we come into the room and turn away from Ford, who's filling glasses with bloody marys. Fiona steps forward and she's just as beautiful as she was at the wedding, if not as formal. Everyone wears some form of jeans and casual tee or sweater, save Layla, who wears a pair of leggings and a button-down shirt—presumably to make it easier to nurse or pump. "It's so nice to officially meet you, Josie. I'm sorry about the misunderstanding at Piper's wedding."

I give Fiona a small smile. "My fault. I've been very assume-y where Ford is concerned and it's my own fault. I'm trying to break the habit. It's lovely to meet you." I also shake Val's hand and we all sit.

After taking a moment to pass around platters of breakfast casserole, bacon, fruit, and pastries, Ford clears his throat and we all give him our full attention. "I just want to say that I'm glad my west coast family could see me while I was in town and that I could bring Josie with me to meet all of you. Y'all all know how much I miss you, but having someone to share my life with helps to soften the blow." His eyes connect with mine and he winks, making me blush.

Luke groans. "I told you not to start saying 'y'all'. You're being converted. Come home STAT, bro."

I can't help but laugh. "Uh-oh, Ford, best not tell him about the moonshine."

Luke's mouth falls open. "They've got you drinking moonshine, too? Sweet Jesus. This man needs an intervention."

Everyone laughs, and Ford's grin is wide. "Guess we better also not tell him you're the one who makes it."

The other man's expression morphs into one of interest as he turns his attention to me. "You make moonshine?"

I nod. "Yeah. I'm a forth-generation bootlegger."

He frowns in thoughtful consideration. "You didn't happen to bring any with you, did you?"

"Don't you know that's how they get you? Transporting across state lines is a big no-no. Y'all will have to come to Knoxville. I'll make sure you get the good stuff."

Fiona pipes up. "It's really good. Ford let me try some of that jar of apple pie you gave him when I was in town. You could make a killing off that stuff."

"It's just a hobby. Too much red tape to go legit. Pap, my grandfather, wouldn't stand for commercializing his 'product' as he calls it. He fancies himself the Walter White of moonshine. And honestly, he's pretty good. He's forgotten more than I'll ever learn about the craft."

Layla sips a glass of water. "I'm thinking, once these babies are old enough to leave for a few days, we all make a trip out to Knoxville. Ford can put us up and we can all defile his guest bedrooms and Josie can give us all a tasting lesson on the intricacies of moonshine."

Even though I'm blushing, I smile. "That would be perfect. We'd love to have you."

CHAPTER TWENTY-EIGHT

FORD

"So, you're really not going to tell me what happened in Florida?" Josie prods.

I shake my head as we lie on the bed swing on the balcony of Fiona and Val's Tybee Island house that overlooks the ocean. It's after dark, but the light of the full moon spills onto the porch, giving us just enough light to see each other. "Nope. That story will be strictly relegated to the period after I someday drag you down the aisle."

She pushes off my chest and looks at me. "And what if I never want to get married?"

I give her a playful smile. "Then you'll never learn the Florida story."

Her eyes narrow. "You'd really blackmail me into marriage?"

"That's up to you. Although, is it really blackmail if you want to do it?" She blinks and her mouth opens and closes and I lean down to press a kiss to her lips. "Don't have a freakout, Freckles. It wasn't a proposal."

"I'd hope not. I haven't even officially met your kid yet."

"You will. And she'll love you. Can't promise she won't love Gouda more, but that's just because she wants to be a vet when she's done with her swimming career."

"Well, no one could fault her for loving Gouda more. Gouda is the best."

"I really do want you to meet Emerson," I say seriously. "Soon."

Apprehension flashes in her eyes and she swallows. "Has she ever met any of the women you've dated before?" I shake my head and she blows out a breath. "That's a lot of pressure, Ford."

"What, you don't think I'm nervous about meeting your parents? Do they even know about me?"

"Yes. We have family dinner every week. It's not voluntary attendance. Silas, big mouth that he is, shared the story of me finding out you were a hockey player at that next family dinner. Lucky for you, Bea put in a good word on your behalf."

Laughing, I drop a kiss on the top of her head. "Always knew I liked that kid."

"You could come to the next dinner. I mean, if you want. You've already met Pap and Silas and Ada, so my parents are it for the Campbell crew."

Hearing her invitation to meet her parents is just one more thing that lets me know Josie wants *us*. "I'd love to. And the next time my parents come to town, maybe we can get everyone together."

"Okay. That might be nice. After it starts warming up, maybe?"

"Sure. We can do it at the house. Emerson's dying to open the pool up already, even though it's only February. I swear, she must be half fish."

"And what about this one?" She points to a scar on my knee. We're in bed, naked after we've made love, and Josie is asking about all of my scars.

"ACL tear my junior year of college. I had surgery in the off season so I wouldn't miss any games."

"And this one?"

I narrow my eyes, trying to remember how I got the scar on my left shin. "Skate blade, I think. That one's really old."

I point to a small scar to the right of her belly button. "What's that one from?"

She doesn't even look down. "Tubal ligation." I nod and she points to my right shoulder. "Here?"

"AC joint. Skate caught a rut in the ice during practice. Tried to catch myself and overextended my shoulder."

"But you still have all your own teeth?"

I laugh. "Yes, actually."

"I figured it was a rite of passage for hockey players to lose teeth."

"Back in the day, it was a badge of honor. To some players, it still is. I enjoy having all my teeth, thanks."

"Have you been injured a lot?"

"Yeah."

"Did you play injured?"

I snort. "All the time. Pulled muscles, broken fingers, sprains. I never messed around with concussions because I want to keep my wits into old age, but pretty much everything else, I'd play through it unless it was so bad they made me sit out."

"Do you miss it?"

"That's a loaded question, Freckles."

"So, yes?"

"Yes. And no. It's nice to remember what not having daily pain is like. I miss playing with Luke and I miss the rush of defending the net. I don't miss the celebrity for the most part. I will say, I could walk into almost any bar in San Jose during the season and never had to buy a drink. That saved me so much money in thirteen years. But I'm not sad that I have more time with Emerson. I'm not sad I have you. I like coaching and I'm good at it. I like having the respect of my players."

"Would you ever consider playing again? If Piper and Conrad moved to a city with a team that wanted you?"

I think for a long moment and remember what Silas said about Josie not leaving the farm, and it's a no brainer. "No. Knoxville is home now."

She smiles. "I'm glad. I think Knoxville likes you."

I lean in to kiss her. "I think you like me."

"I do? What makes you think that?" Josie asks playfully.

I slide my hand between her thighs and she sighs when the pad of my middle finger sweeps over her clit. "I think this is a pretty good indication."

"You know, I thought as men got older, their recovery time was longer."

"I'm only thirty-five, not sixty."

She presses a kiss to my chest. "I guess I should be happy about that."

Giving her ass a possessive squeeze, I whisper in her ear, "How about you get on your hands and knees and I'll give you something to be real happy about?"

As all vacations do, ours ends and we return home after five days on Tybee Island. We spend our days seeing the sights in Savannah and eating at great local restaurants. We took morning runs on the beach and evening strolls hand in hand, talking, and fucked on every surface of the house every night. I think we're both a bit punch drunk by the time we toss our bags into the back of my 4Runner when we arrive in Knoxville.

"Do you just want to come back to my house and we can crash, or do you need to get up to the farm?"

"You could stay at the farm with me, if you want, unless you have an early day tomorrow."

I shake my head. "No, I have to put in an appearance at a news station for a PR thing, but it's not until the afternoon. Will Pap be okay with me staying?"

She snorts a laugh. "Please, he practically encouraged us to get it on the day you tracked me down at the farm."

Nodding, I grin. "That's right, he did. You think he'd be opposed if we got it on now?"

"Like, now now? I feel like there are rules about having sex in airport parking lots."

"No, smart ass, I meant at the farm."

"Oh. No, there aren't any rules like that at the farm. We have separate beds, though, and I, for one, can't wait to see you sleep in a twin. You'll look like Buddy the elf at the North Pole. It's going to be hilarious."

An hour later, as we pull in at the farmhouse, Gouda jumps off the porch to greet us, barking wildly and wagging her entire body. Fred steps out of the house and waves as we pet the dog. "Y'all survived, I see. Ford, you staying for supper? I've got a pan of biscuits about to come out of the oven."

"Sounds good to me."

"Ford's going to stay here tonight, Pap. That okay with you?"

"Fine. Just fine," Fred says with a nod. "I'll make sure to take out my hearing aids."

Josie rolls her eyes. "You don't wear hearing aids, Pap."

The old man grins. "You just remember that."

I can't help but laugh and Josie pinches the bridge of her nose. "I swear, Pap, I'm going to put you in a home."

Wrapping my arm around her, I tug her into the house. "Come on, Freckles, let's go eat some supper."

She smiles up at me. "You said supper. It's so cute you're trying to fit in."

"I do fit in. I fit in everywhere."

"You aren't going to fit in that bed later," she says with a laugh.

After a simple supper of biscuits, eggs, and sausage gravy, we sit on the porch. Fred is in his rocker and Josie and I are on the swing with a blanket draped over our laps. "Ford, you play guitar?"

"No, sir."

"Well good, 'cause I only got the one and I don't feel like sharing."

I whisper in Josie's ear as Fred begins to strum his guitar. "I don't like to share, either."

"That's an understatement." She intertwines her fingers with mine as the swing sways gently. "Oh, I got confirmation on the dates of your break next month, and Ada and Silas said they'd love to have us join them at the cabin. Silas said it was actually great you were coming because there's some tree work that needs to be done. Can you swing an ax or use a chainsaw?"

"Sure. We had to bust up a lot of firewood in St. Paul. I'm happy to help. This is the place on the river, with the herons?"

She nods. "Yeah."

"Sounds perfect. Any chance you'd want to come to any home games we've got coming up? I mean, you can come to the away games, too, but I know you have work."

"I can. As long as you promise not to fuss if I still don't understand all the rules yet."

"Freckles, you've been to one game. I don't expect you to know all the rules after an entire season."

She feigns relief. "Oh, thank goodness. I thought I'd lose major girlfriend points if there was stuff I didn't know."

"Nope. Not for you." I lean in and whisper in her ear, "And when we get home, we can pretend you're a puck bunny who's followed me to my hotel room."

She cackles. "Yeah. I don't think so. Not much into role playing. But I will happily play supportive girlfriend who's ready to celebrate or commiserate, depending on the outcome of the game."

"Even better."

A week later, on my one off day this week, Josie is meeting Emerson, and she's a nervous wreck. We're at my house and I'm making fajitas and margaritas. I've only been putting half shots in Josie's drinks because she's so anxious, she's been shotgunning them, and I'm worried she's going to be drunk before Emmy even walks in the door.

"You're going to have to calm down. Technically, you've already met Emerson. This is merely a formality."

"Yeah, but that was at Piper's wedding. I was just the cranberry-brie-puff girl. I wasn't her dad's girlfriend. What if she hates me?"

She goes to take another drink of her margarita, and I take it out of her hand. "You can have more of that with supper. You have no food on your stomach. Drink some water. You have no idea how excited Emmy is to meet you. She's been hounding me to settle down with someone for literal years. You are the answer to her prayers at this point. It had gotten to the point that I think she was ready to set me up on Tinder just so I'd go on dates.

"She remembers you from the wedding. Of course, I didn't tell her how we were before, but I told her how we met and how we'd been seeing each other on and off for a few months." A car door slams outside and Josie nearly jumps out of her skin. "Trust me, you'll be fine. She's going to love you because I love you, remember?"

She blows out a breath and nods, apprehension still clear on her face, even as Emerson walks through the door. She greets me with a big hug, dropping her duffle and backpack on her way to the kitchen. "Hey, Daddy." She looks at the offerings. "Ooh, fajitas. Any chance there are virgin margs?" She sees Josie standing just behind me and offers her a wide grin and a wave. "Josie, right?"

Josie nods. "That's me. It's so nice to finally meet you, Emerson. Your dad talks about you all the time."

My daughter leans in conspiratorially to mock-whisper. "I've gotta say, I kinda miss the tie. I was totally vibing with the gender-fluid look you had going on at Mom's wedding. It worked for you."

Josie laughs. "I'll have to remember that."

We crowd around the kitchen island to eat, opting to skip the dining room. "So, Daddy says you have a dog?"

Josie nods, munching on a tortilla chip. "Yeah, she's at the vet right now. She had to get her teeth cleaned, and she doesn't do well with sedation, so they always have to keep her overnight. Hopefully, you'll get to meet her soon. She's a ball of energy."

"And her name is Gouda? That's so quirky. How'd you come up with that?"

"Well, her previous owner called her Miriam. And no hate

to any Miriams, but that is just not a name for a dog; especially one like her. She's about the color of Swiss cheese and with her curl pattern, she sorta resembles it, but I wasn't wild about that either. Gouda is my favorite kind of cheese, so I figured, why not?"

"Well, I love it. And if you got other animals, you could totally stick with the cheese theme." She counts off different types of cheese on her fingers. "Cheddar, mozzarella—or mozzy, for short—parmesan, feta, the possibilities are endless."

"I think you're right." Josie looks at me. "Looks like we need more dogs."

"Or, cats," Emerson offers.

I shake my head. "I think Gouda is enough for now." I point at Josie. "If you have your way, you'll have this place turned into a foster home for all kinds of animals before I know it."

Josie looks around. "You do have a lot of room and a big yard. Shame to waste all the fenced-in space."

I shake my head again. "Gouda's it."

Emerson pouts. "Oh, come on, Daddy. What's a few more animals?" She gasps in excitement, a thought hitting her. "When you guys get married, you can totally do one of those things where instead of bouquets, the bridesmaids carry puppies. People adopt them. You can have doggie ring bearers. It would be adorable."

I laugh. "Puppy bouquets, huh? Well, Josie would have to agree to marry me first."

Emerson turns to Josie. "You'd marry Daddy to have puppy bouquets, right, Josie?"

Josie's face flames and I'm unable to keep the smile off my own. "Okay, now I'm feeling ganged up on. No one is talking about getting married."

I shrug, considering. "We're not *not* talking about getting married. You'd finally get to hear the Florida story if you married me."

Emerson's eyes go wide. "Oh, God. Not the Florida story. I still haven't recovered."

Josie laughs. "Dear lord, what is this 'Florida story'? Some kind of urban legend?"

Emerson shakes her head. "Totally real. And it's like Bruno. We don't talk about it."

I laugh at the Encanto movie reference. "It's a family story. Only legal—or adopted, I guess—family gets to hear about it. And I'm sure as hell not going to adopt you, Freckles. It would be untoward."

Josie snorts. "*Untoward?* What is this, regency London?"

I shake my head. "No, because if this was regency London, you would've already been forced to marry me since you'd be considered *compromised*," I say and wiggle my eyebrows.

Emerson scoffs. "Stupid patriarchal bullshit."

"Emmy, language," I scold.

"What? It's true. The fact that women couldn't even own property or have a say in any public matters is totally bull. The fact that women were considered damaged goods if they weren't virgins when they got married. All the while, their husbands-to-be were out screwing everything on two legs and probably contracting syphilis to spread to their virgin brides who knew nothing about sex, but were expected to satisfy their husbands. I'll tell you this, I'm not bowing to the will of any man."

I nod. "Yes. You should keep that attitude. For a long, long time."

CHAPTER TWENTY-NINE

JOSIE

"So, there's really no TV at this place? Or Wi-Fi?" Ford asks as we make our way to the cabin several weeks later.

I shake my head and point to the gravel drive up ahead. "Nope. Turn there."

He gives my thigh a squeeze. "Well, whatever will we do with ourselves to pass the time?"

I shrug. "We could always play cards or go for a walk or just sit on the porch."

"What, no sex?"

"Not unless you want Silas and Ada to hear us. The beds are ancient and can be heard from half a mile away."

"You act like that would deter me."

"It should. Would you want Emerson to hear us having sex?"

He shudders. "No."

"Exactly. I know it's different because he's my brother and not my kid, but I could do without having him hear how well you rock my world."

"Well, if at any time we're alone in the cabin, I make no

promises that I won't attempt a quickie. I'm not above dragging you to the floor."

"Noted," I say with a chuckle. A moment later, we're pulling up to the cabin and seeing Silas's Broncho, I know that he and Ada have already made it. "Hopefully, they've already started supper; I'm starving."

We hop out of Ford's SUV and he carries our bags up the steps and allows me to open the door for him. Silas and Ada are nowhere to be found. "Where do you think they are?" Ford asks, glancing around the rustic space. "Wow. This place is great. Luke's uncle has a cabin a lot like this in Duluth."

"Did you ever go ice fishing?"

"Sure. We always froze our asses off and drank more than we ever caught anything."

I snort. "Sounds about right." I look into the bedrooms and see the bedroom on the right is empty of bags, so I gesture to that one. "Looks like this is us." He steps past me to take our bags and I walk over to look out the back door and see Ada and Silas sitting on the swing laughing about something.

Even all this time later, it's still such a bittersweet thing to see them together. I'd never wish for things to be different than they are because they're both so happy. But I also wish everything was different. I paste a smile on my face and step outside. They both hop up off the swing when they hear the door open and greet me with warm hugs and handshakes for Ford.

After a few minutes to catch up, Ada pipes up. "I'm going to go start supper."

"You need any help?" I ask, readying myself to assist in any way I can.

She shakes her head. "No, I've got it." She turns to Ford. "Although there is a bowl on a really high shelf, if you wouldn't mind to get it down for me?"

"Sure. Just point it out."

I start to follow them inside so that I can at least keep Ada company while she prepares dinner, but Silas grabs my arm as I begin to go by. "Sit with me for a minute?"

"Okay." I join him on the swing and he pushes off, letting it sway under us. "Did y'all have a good drive in?"

"Oh, yeah. We always like the drive." He reaches over the side of the swing and opens a cooler I didn't know was there and brings out two bottles of beer and extends one to me.

I thank him and twist off the top and take a long pull. "It's so quiet here."

"Yeah, until you get up near the herons, and then it's so loud. At least until all the fledglings fly away."

Knowing Silas and his nature, I know he didn't bring me out here to talk about herons. "What is it, Si? I know you're not making small talk with me. You don't do small talk. You hate small talk."

He sips his beer and nods. "You're right, I do. I need to tell you something."

My first thought is that he's sick. His HCM test results were somehow wrong, and he has it. Or something is wrong with Bea or Ada or Mom or Dad or Pap. My chest immediately goes tight, but I keep my voice even. "Okay."

He searches my eyes and there's an apprehensive look in his own and it makes bile rise in my throat because I'm now terrified. He takes my hand in his and gives me a smile, but I don't know how to read it. "Ada's pregnant."

A mix of relief and envy and joy floods me, but I smile, even as tears spring to my eyes. "Oh, Si. That's wonderful."

He nods, his own eyes welling with tears. "I know. I just didn't want you to find out in front of everyone else. And I wish there was a way it could be you. And I don't mean that the gross way it just sounded," he says with a watery laugh and I can't help but laugh, too.

I give his hand a squeeze. "Thank you for telling me. I'm okay. Bea is my favorite person on the planet. How could I ever feel anything but overjoyed that you and Ada are going to give me another favorite person?"

Silas examines my face. "It's okay if you have big feelings about this, Jos. It's okay if you're not okay about it. And I'm really sorry to ruin your weekend by springing this on you right at the beginning, but Ada's got some wicked morning sickness and there's no way we can hide it, so I had to tell you."

"Really, I'm all right. I've made peace with everything. It was my choice."

He nods again. "Yeah, but it was a fucked up choice to have to make."

I huff a sad laugh. "You're not wrong." I look out toward the river. "Ford says if I wanted to experience pregnancy, we could do a donor egg. Or, we could become foster parents or adopt. Or, we could do nothing at all and have ten dogs."

"You think you will?"

I shrug. "I'm not sure. If I start entertaining hopes of donor eggs and IVF and all that entails, it's too overwhelming. He's just trying to convince me to get married at this point. I'm not sure which hurdle will be the bigger one to leap."

"Married? Well. And which way are you leaning about that?"

I bite my lip and give my brother my full attention. "I think I would do it. I love him. And there's no one else I'd rather fight with for the rest of my life."

Silas grins. "That's a good philosophy to have. Works for Ada and me."

"Are you happy, Si?"

He thinks for a moment and tears well in his eyes again. "So fucking happy, Jos. More happy than I have any right to be. And even now, it's so hard because I still miss Cole so much."

I nod, my own tears beginning to roll down my cheeks. "I know. If it's a boy, you're going to name him Cole, right?"

Silas nods. "No other name would feel right. He's the whole reason I get to have Ada and these babies to love in the first place."

"Good. That's the way it should be. There should be a Cole Campbell in this world again."

Despite how happy I am for Silas and Ada, I push my supper around on my plate and I'm quieter than normal. I know Ford notices, but we don't have any alone time for me to tell him why I'm so contemplative until we turn in for bed. Lost in my thoughts as I am, I don't even feel him crawl under the covers beside me. Not until he drags a knuckle down my jaw and leans over to kiss the side of my neck. I turn to face him and give him a soft smile and he searches my eyes and tucks my hair behind my ear. "What's got you in your head tonight?"

"Ada's pregnant. Silas told me earlier."

He gives me a sympathetic nod. "And how are you feeling about that news?"

"Mixed feelings," I admit. "I'm not unhappy. I'd never be unhappy. Not when Bea is my favorite person ever. It's just... hard."

"I'm sure. Do we need to go home?"

I shake my head. "No. I'm okay. I'll process it just like I did when they told me about Bea. They were gentle in their delivery of that news, too. Silas and I had a good cry. I'll be all right."

"Would it take your mind off things if I asked you to marry me?"

I roll my eyes and laugh. "Sure."

His expression grows serious, and he takes my face in his hands. "Okay. Josephine Hope Campbell, will you marry me?"

I blink, sobering instantly, and pull back. "What?" He slides his hand under the covers and when it reappears, he holds a small, black velvet box and my mouth falls open. He opens it to reveal a gorgeous bezel-set oval diamond set in white gold. "Ford," I reply, breathless and heart pounding. "What did you do?"

He laughs. "I fell in love, Freckles. You were there; you should know. I've been carrying this ring around since right after you met Emerson. I knew that night—and honestly, I knew before then, too—you are the woman I want to spend the rest of my life with. Whether we have kids of our own through IVF or fostering or adoption or no kids at all, we'll still be a family. I told you I wanted you to be my family, and I meant it. Marry me."

I smirk. "That didn't sound like a question."

Ford shakes his head. "It wasn't."

"So bossy," I say, attempting to keep my happy tears from spilling over.

"For the rest of our lives," he confirms. He takes the ring out of the box and slips it on my finger.

He grabs my face and kisses me deeply and after a beat, I pull back. "I demand puppy bouquets."

He laughs. "Deal."

CHAPTER THIRTY

FORD

Over the next month, Josie adjusts to both the news of Ada'a pregnancy and our engagement. And aside from a momentary freakout when we decided to move in together, she's handled everything perfectly. It's a lot of change for her and I get it, but I honestly couldn't be happier with the direction things are headed.

Tonight, as we sit in bed with our respective laptops, we're going over the final details for our engagement party next weekend. "And just so I remember correctly, Fiona, Val, Luke, and Layla are the only ones staying here, right? Your parents didn't want to stay at the house?"

I shake my head. "No. They've born witness to what an overnighter with Luke and me entails. I think they're still traumatized by the shenanigans we pulled in high school."

She taps her keyboard and nods. "All right. And what about Emerson? Is she staying here or at Piper's?"

"Piper's. She's got a swim practice early the next morning, so she won't stay late. I look for Piper and Conrad to stick around a while longer than she does. What about Jess and Brooklyn?"

Her eyes go wide. "Oh God, I didn't tell you. They broke up. Last month; right around the same time we got engaged. Between work and party planning and your road trips, I guess it slipped my mind. It was messy."

I wince. "Damn. I hate that. I thought they were happy. So, who's he bringing? Or is he coming stag?"

"Probably Ophelia. They've gotten pretty close over the past few weeks."

I lift a brow. "Close how?"

Josie shrugs. "I don't think they're sleeping together, but they spend a lot of time together. Especially since his work schedule changed, and he got put back on days. And honestly, he could do worse. She's a total sweetheart and has really come out of her shell since they became roommates."

"Okay, and what about Pap?"

She shakes her head. "Nah. Not his scene. But he did offer a gallon of apple pie if we wanted it."

"Hell yeah we do. I already told Luke he was going to try some when they came in."

"How're they coping with thinking about having to leave the babies for a weekend?"

"Okay, I think. They're almost six months old, so I think they're both ready to have some time for just the two of them."

"It'll probably be good for them."

I lean over and kiss her bare shoulder. "Alone together time does foster a healthy relationship."

She huffs a laugh. "Yes, I'd say you're correct." Josie seems to consider something. "What was your wedding with Piper like?"

I snort a laugh. "We didn't have one. We went to the courthouse."

"Do you ever feel like you got cheated by not having a big wedding?"

I think for a moment and shake my head. "No. I'm indifferent to weddings. I'm glad Piper got her big fairytale wedding with Conrad, but I don't have strong feelings either way about big or small, flashy or simple, string quartet or DJ. Why?"

"I don't know. When I was a little girl, I never thought about what my dress or cake or any of that would look like. I know some girls kept whole ass binders of ideas about their dream wedding. Even back in the day when I thought about getting married, I didn't. And I guess because I never thought it would happen, I've given it even less thought."

"So, are you saying you don't want a wedding?"

"I think it's a lot of money for one day. I think I'm more interested in being your wife than being your bride."

I can't help but smile. "That's a pretty good line, Freckles. So, what are you saying?"

She shrugs. "I think we're already having a dinner next weekend and a cake and I've bought a dress. I think I'd be okay if next weekend was a reception instead of an engagement party." I blink, shocked by her answer. Not that I'm opposed, because I would have dragged her off the farm and married her that day I went to get her back. When I don't say anything, Josie continues, "We've already signed the prenup, so no one would be able to say I'm rushing you so you wouldn't have time to do that. Not that I give a shit about your money, but it is what it is. If you want a wedding since you didn't get one before, I'm cool with that. But it's not something I need."

"You're serious? You want to elope?"

"I'd prefer forever start sooner rather than later. I know whether we do it now or a year from now, we'll still be married, but I don't need to have a big, fancy dress or party to prove to people that I'm committed to you. I only need you to know that."

A surprised bark of laughter escapes my mouth. "You realize if you agree to this, I'm dragging your fine ass to Vegas. Like, this weekend."

She leans over and gives me a kiss. "You wouldn't even have drag me. I'd go willingly."

I grab her face and pepper her cheeks and lips with kisses as she laughs. "Woman, you better not be joking."

Josie sobers and shakes her head. "No joke. Let's do it." I'm unable to contain my glee and my grin is probably the widest it's ever been. "So, that's a yes?" she asks, her tone hopeful.

"That's a fuck yes, Freckles."

Her eyes go wide and she covers her mouth with her hands as she laughs. "Oh, my God. We're getting married."

I pull my phone off the nightstand. "Okay, we have a lot of planning to do if we're really doing this. Flights, hotel reservations, chapel." I check my calendar. "With my game schedule, we'd only have Saturday. We'd have to fly in Saturday morning —provided we can get a flight—and back out Sunday since I have a game Sunday night. It will definitely be a whirlwind."

"What about witnesses?" Josie asks.

"Silas and Ada?"

She shakes her head. "Ada is still so sick she's barely able to function and Si won't leave her. Luke and Layla?"

"No. Not with them coming in next weekend. Pretty sure he has a game this weekend, too."

"Fiona and Val?"

I sigh and shake my head. "She's got a potential client she's visiting in Canada. It's one of the reasons we scheduled the engagement party for next weekend and not this one. What about Jess? And maybe Ophelia?"

She grabs her phone and taps furiously on the screen. After

a moment of back and forth, she looks up at me, a big smile on her face. "They're in."

"Okay. So, I guess tomorrow, we run around getting everything together and once I secure the reservations, it's go time."

Josie nods. "All right. I also told Jess that I would cover their flight and hotel, so just let me know how much I owe you."

I shake my head. "Are you kidding? By us eloping, we're going to save so much money on wedding costs, I would happily pay for their stuff. So you can pay me in sexual favors for the rest of our lives."

"Well, that was a given. Fine. I'll donate the equivalent to the animal shelter. It's the least I can do since we won't be having puppy bouquets."

"Emmy will be pissed."

"Not if we let her adopt a puppy." I open my mouth to protest and she presses forward. "She might never get any brothers or sisters. The least we can do is get the girl a dog."

"Fine. But nothing too froo-froo."

She rolls her eyes. "Oh, please. I bet, when we go to the shelter to let her pick a dog, you'll leave with the smallest, cutest ball of fluff there is. It'll be all pitiful and scared and you won't be able to help yourself. You like damaged things. You like to coax them back from the brink of despair and make them dream again. I know because you did that for me."

"You weren't at that brink of despair, Josie."

She nods. "I was and didn't even know it. I kept myself so involved in going, going, going that anytime I got still, all I could see was how pointless it all was. Not that I was a danger to myself or anything, but I was like one of those pitiful dogs at the shelter who has no hope."

"Jess said you were a feral cat. Pretty sure that's a more apt analogy for you."

"Probably. Even so, you loving me helped me love my life

again. It helped me see that I could have dreams again. And who knows what will happen, but I'm so thankful you were bossy and possessive and didn't stop fighting for me."

"Josie, I will never stop fighting for you. For the rest of our lives. Which, apparently, is going to start this weekend."

"And then I get to hear the Florida story?" she asks hopefully.

I can't help but laugh. "As a sign of good faith, I'll go ahead and tell you now."

Her eyes widen. "Really?"

I blow out a breath. "Yeah, but you have no one to blame but yourself for asking to hear it." She rubs her hands together maniacally and I roll my eyes. "So, my first season in the league, our first game was in Florida. And I'd been playing for years, but being in the starting lineup of your rookie season is a whole other level of pressure.

"The night before the game, when we came into town, Luke and I went out for supper. We ate at this little hole-in-the-wall seafood place. And back then, Yelp wasn't a thing, so we just stopped at the first place we came to. Big mistake."

Josie frowns. "Food poisoning?"

"Yeah. But I didn't start getting bubble guts until we were getting ready to go out on the ice. And it was my first game, so I wasn't about to let what I thought was nerves ruin my experience."

"How bad was it?" she asks gently.

I shake my head and heave a sigh. "Bad. We were five minutes into the first period and I felt like I had to fart."

She gasps and covers her mouth. "No."

I nod. "Yeah. And I trusted the fart. Huge mistake. Needless to say, I did not finish the period, let alone the game."

"Oh God, that's horrible."

"Yep. But at least I can say I got my most embarrassing

moment out of the way in my first game. I signaled to one of the refs to tell him what happened and I started throwing up. I swear, I've never been so sick in my life. Thankfully, as it was a preseason game and since we weren't at home, I think it saved me from a lot of the press. Of course, it made the news, but all anyone knows about is the throwing up. No one—well, no one outside the family—knows I shit myself."

Josie gives me a sympathetic smile. "Wow. I am totally scarred for life."

I chuckle. "Told you. And now that you know, you're sworn to secrecy and have to marry me."

She grins. "Good thing that's happening this weekend, huh?"

"Thank goodness," I say and pull her to me for a kiss.

EPILOGUE
JOSIE — TWO YEARS LATER

"Okay, now one of just you and your dad," I say, holding up my phone to snap a photo of Ford and Emerson on her graduation day. They stand together and beam out toward the camera. Ford presses a kiss to her cheek and whispers something in her ear and her eyes go wide and she looks at me.

"Really? No joke?"

I nod, and she runs over and throws her arms around me for a big hug. "When?"

"We got the call this morning. The court date is set for thirty days from now."

Emerson's eyes well with tears, and she smiles. "So, he's going to be ours forever?"

I swipe her tears away. "Yep."

She squats down to the little boy, whose hand is still clasped in mine. "You hear that, little bro? It's going to be all legal and everything. You won't have a choice but to claim me as family."

Three-year-old Felix, who came to us as a foster son almost six months to the day Ford and I got married, rolls his blue eyes when Emerson ruffles his strawberry blonde hair. "Emmy, quit," he scolds, attempting to smooth his hair back in place.

She chuckles. "Sorry, kiddo, I'm just so excited."

Ford walks over and scoops Felix up into his arms. "What do you say, pizza to celebrate?"

Our son's eyes go wide. "With extra cheese and extra, extra, extra sausage?"

We all laugh as we make our way to the parking lot. My husband pulls me into his side and whispers in his ear. "Just like his mom. You like extra, extra, extra sausage, too."

I playfully punch him in the ribs, even as heat climbs up my neck. Changing the subject, I ask, "Are Piper and Conrad joining us?"

Ford nods. "Yeah, the whole family will be there. They should all already be headed that way."

When we pull up at our favorite pizza restaurant and make it to the room we've secured for our large party, everyone is already seated with their drinks of choice. I can't help but marvel at this eclectic, blended family we've created, my heart squeezing at the sight of so many people who love us and our kids.

Ford's and my parents, Silas, Ada, Bea, and Cole, Jess and Hensley and their respective spouses, Piper and Conrad, and even Luke, Fiona, and their families came in for the weekend. Pap, all ninety-two years of him, is also present and as ornery as ever.

If you'd told me a spilled drink would lead to the greatest and best adventures of my life, I would have laughed in your face. But now, having seen how everything has been weaved together into the gorgeous tapestry that is my life, I can appreciate every hard-won victory. I can look back at every heartache and see how it was all leading to this moment.

And if I had to relive every terrible thing over again to be exactly where I am right now, I'd do it in a heartbeat. Learning to love and allowing myself to finally be loved has made my shattered heart mend and grow and make room for all these people who make up my family. As he usually is, Ford was right and blood doesn't make a family. I'm not sure I'd be able to love a biological child any more than I love my rambunctious Felix. And although I didn't come into her life until she was nearly grown, Emerson is my daughter. And looking over at my husband and the father of these children I love so much, I'm thankful for his steadfastness and faith that even when I question myself or my ability to be a good wife and mother, he's there to reassure me and be my strength when I don't have any of my own.

ABOUT THE AUTHOR

For as long as she can remember, Rachael has been a voracious reader. At the age of eleven, she discovered her grandmother's stash of clench-cover romance novels and she was forever changed. A lover of many, many fictional men and one very non-fictional one, she strives to write real and emotional characters who always get their happily ever after. Rachael lives in East Tennessee with her husband and two sons on their family farm. When she's not tackling her endless TBR, she can be found drinking all the coffee in existence.

ALSO BY RACHAEL OGLE

Until August (Until Book 1)

Until Forever (Until Book 2)

Fake it Till You Fall (Summer Lovin' Book 1)

Falling into Forever (Summer Lovin' Book 2)

My Ada Mae (Knox County Book 1)